ROMERO'S TUNNEL

ROMERO'S TUNNEL

Karl Vincent

iUniverse, Inc.
New York   Bloomington

Romero's Tunnel

iUniverse books may be ordered through booksellers or by contacting:

iUniverse
1663 Liberty Drive
Bloomington, IN 47403
www.iuniverse.com
1-800-Authors (1-800-288-4677)

ISBN: 978-1-4502-5015-3 (sc)
ISBN: 978-1-4502-5016-0 (ebk)

Printed in the United States of America

iUniverse rev. date: 08/04/2010

ROMERO'S TUNNEL

Ottawa, Canada, 2008 (by Christian calendar)
Moustafa Rajai had entered the Consular section of the
Iranian Embassy to Canada with no appointment or even
prior notification. Lacking any standing or invitation,
he'd nonetheless arrogantly demanded to speak with the
Ambassador. His insistence on this matter appeared even
more absurd given that he was in the wrong building…
the Consular Section. Implacable to these apparent
oversights, he'd audaciously entered the main foyer of
the Consulate and strutted up to the nearest gaggle of
people queued in a somewhat haphazard order. They were
crowding in line before a long counter.

In fact, there were several undisciplined lines formed
in front of the extended counter; but Moustafa had picked
this one only because it happened to be closest to the
entranceway. Standing immediately behind this counter
which stretched halfway across the expanse of the foyer
were several clerks each manning their stations as they
minded a specific service stated on a sign hung above
their heads.

Over the long queue which Mr. Rajai had chosen
to exploit hung a sign marked "Visas" printed first in
English and then below it written in Farsi. He'd walked
up to the head of the line and aggressively muscled aside
a lady about to state her request to the clerk. The woman

serving behind the counter was clearly offended by this interloper's brusque behavior. Her lower lip trembled and her eyes narrowed with consternation as she demanded that he should please go to the end of the line and wait his turn.

Moustafa Rajai ignored her huff. "I must speak with the Ambassador. It is a matter of the utmost importance." He'd expressed this to the clerk in Farsi.

She appeared unaffected by his sense of urgency as she sniped impatiently in English, "This is not the line waiting for appointments with the Ambassador. We take care of visa applications here. Furthermore, this is the Consulate. The Ambassador's office is in the Embassy."

"Don't get smart with me! Go get the Ambassador!" He'd switched to English and purposely modulated his voice to offer a threatening tone as he glowered at her.

The clerk backed up a step in order not to be within his reach and then stared at him silently while her lower lip continued to tremble. She expressed on her face a mixture of anxiety and annoyance. It appeared as if she were having difficulty believing that this man could be so genuinely obtuse.

"The Ambassador!" he again demanded.

"Please wait," she stammered as she took still another step backwards, but then paused as if lingering to see if he would stay or go. She appeared incredulous that the man could be genuinely serious. Moustafa stayed, and intensified his glower which he continued to direct at her.

Finally she jerked away as if a force had held her in its

grasp and in doing so turned her face from this belligerent stranger. She immediately scurried off some distance to a gentleman sitting behind a desk. Moustafa watched as she spoke with frantic gestures. Her back remained to him but he could see the face of the fellow listening to her. The gentleman she addressed rose from his chair and stared in the direction of this disruptive visitor. Moustafa reacted by turning his angry glare directly towards this man now gazing at him. It was a method he employed to hide the apprehension which gripped him.

Moustafa had never done anything in his life quite as bold as what he was now undertaking. He hid his anxiety by feigning a character filled with anger and one perhaps a bit unhinged. The Consular official continued to gape at him. Finally, it appeared that the gentleman was successfully coaxed by the concerned clerk to attend the situation because her hands stopped gesticulating as her arms returned limply to her sides. But she continued to keep her head turned away from this troublemaker at the Visa counter station.

Instead of making any sort of decisive move, the gentleman summoned by the clerk continued to study the mysterious intruder. This passive reaction by the man still abiding at his desk confused Moustafa. He'd expected the fellow to immediately approach him with pomp and rancor.

Moustafa finally averted his eyes from the official, but continued to abide at the Visa counter. He now noticed that the short plump lady he'd pushed aside was leering at him with visible disgust. He had the instant urge to tweak this woman on that prominent Persian nose dominating her face, but instead he turned away from her and gazed back at the female clerk and the gentleman at the desk.

Moustafa did not perceive this fellow who the clerk had enlisted to have the bearing of an Ambassador. In fact, Mr. Rajai didn't really wish to speak with the Ambassador. No, no, not at all! He just needed to get the attention of an official here. He hoped that this person could then shuttle him to the appropriate operative... an Intelligence operative. No doubt, MOIS would have an active representative somewhere in this Embassy.

MOIS (Ministry of Intelligence and Security) was the modern Iranian Republic's secret police and an analog of the despised Shah's SAVAK which was disbanded in 1979 when the Shah was deposed. Ex-pats like himself often still referred to MOIS as SAVAK out of habit. He had little doubt that every Embassy would have at least one if not a contingent of these evil secret police. Yes, it was a MOIS Agent with whom he needed to speak.

But at the time he'd planned this little project, the idea struck him that simply walking into this Consulate and asking to speak with a MOIS Agent seemed extremely awkward or even frivolous. Likely as not they'd chalk him up as a loon before he'd ever been given the chance to speak his piece and would be summarily shown the door. In order to capture their attention, he needed to arouse their wonder. How could these Consuls take serious regard of a stranger coming from the street and then straightaway making such a thickheaded request?

He was an avid viewer of intrigue movies and a reader of spy novels. He imagined that Smiley, "the Needle", or 007 might have executed this plan in more or less the way he now proceeded. However, Mr. Rajai did not offer the appearance one might cast for a Nazi spy or British Intelligence operative; he was a somewhat overweight middle-aged engineer working in the United States with features clearly betraying his Persian birthright; in fact, he was a naturalized American citizen and a dedicated family man.

Moustafa observed the gentleman move away from his desk and from the clerk who'd approached him. However the fellow did not come directly towards the Visa station. Instead he headed in a direction away from the troublemaker, and finally pushed through a low swing-gate at the end of the counter which allowed him passage into the open foyer, and placed him on the same side of the counter now as Moustafa.

This foyer was packed with people who stood in haphazard lines at the long counter, while others milled about chatting mostly in pairs. There were several lonely figures with forlorn looks on their faces. They silently stood in place like statues. Meanwhile the clerk slowly rotated until she faced him and then at a reluctant pace cautiously returned to her station. She stared warily at Moustafa as she approached him and periodically cast brief furtive glances in the direction of the gentleman she'd summoned who now stood in the foyer forward of the swing-gate.

"The Visa Control Officer has agreed to speak with you," she stated in scarcely more than a whisper to him. "Perhaps he can help you arrange an appointment with the Ambassador. Now, could you please step aside? There are people here in line."

Moustafa grunted and complied, taking two steps away without even glancing at her. He ignored the complaining caterwaul of the woman in line who he'd pushed aside. Apparently she was now emboldened by his retreat and by the return of the clerk.

His eyes were on the Visa Control Officer. As soon as he'd caught the gentleman's eye, this Consular guy motioned for the disruptive visitor to approach him. Moustafa immediately reacted, and when he reached the gentleman he thrust a single page at the man. He'd been holding this page in his hand since walking into the Consulate.

The Visa Control Officer appeared distracted by the sheet of paper Moustafa waved in his face. Thus, he swallowed his words before he'd expressed anything more than a salutation. He immediately comprehended that this stranger wanted him to take the page. The bizarre visitor had also reached into the inner pocket of his suit coat and retrieved a second offering. He dangled it between his thumb and index finger. It was a CD captured in a clear plastic jacket.

"This sheet explains what's in the CD," Moustafa

stated in a staccato delivery as he rattled the page close to the nose of the Visa Control Officer. "It's a synopsis. I've written it in Farsi."

Although he had an excellent grasp of English, Moustafa now spoke in Farsi to this man who'd introduced himself as the Visa Control Officer here at the Consulate. Farsi was Moustafa's native tongue; but that hadn't been his reason for employing it. He simply wasn't sure how fluent these Iranians were in the English language, even though they now served the Embassy in English-speaking Canada.

His concern in this matter reflected an overarching lack of esteem on his part for the Revolutionary regime ruling Iran since 1979. Yes, he'd read that they held elections; but there was no democracy as far as he was concerned. The regime was controlled by a bunch of medieval Shia clerics imbued with a religion which denied the core concepts necessary to democracy. How could there be real democracy in Iran? There was no precedent for such a notion in the minds of Persians other than the minority of secular and educated citizens who dared not speak their minds above a whisper.

He'd been a young man when the Shah had still reigned in Iran. Moustafa graduated University not long after the Revolutionary regime had seized power. This was during the early days of the war against Iraq. His father had held great contempt and suspicion for the previously exiled Ayatollah who the people in the street had subsequently hailed as their new spiritual leader. And in the privacy of his family his father had been extremely critical of the arrogance this new regime flaunted by disregarding international law and invading the sovereign space of an Embassy. He warned that Iran would rue this senseless act against the Americans.

Clearly, it had been better for his family in the old days under the Shah; but also worse for certain other people. Now those certain other people had it better; well, at least some of them did. Fortunately, that was no longer any of Moustafa's concern. He'd spent the past two and a half decades living in the United States. His parents and one brother had moved to Australia. The other brother had immigrated to Chile. He'd lost contact with his cousins, although he understood that one of them now lived in New Jersey. He hadn't attempted to contact the cousin, fearing that this fellow might ask for financial assistance.

The Visa Control Officer accepted the visitor's page scrawled in Farsi, but he did not immediately read it. He likewise extended his hand palm up, inviting the stranger to lay his CD on it. Moustafa shook his head in the negative.

"No, first we must agree to the conditions. I have described on that page in general terms what is contained in this CD." He pulled open his suit jacket and pushed the disc into the inside pocket, closed his jacket and gave it a pat from the outside.

"We must first conclude a bargain," Moustafa re-emphasized with a forced smile. "That's why I must talk with the Ambassador."

Moustafa was satisfied with this brief exchange. He felt reasonably sure that this Visa Control officer would not appeal to the Ambassador; rather he would go directly to his Chief who in turn would summon MOIS. However, he continued to reflect a stern unrelenting visage in order to invoke a sense of urgency in this gentleman who at the moment appeared to be in somewhat of a waffle.

"Please wait," the official politely stammered.

Carrying the single page, he turned and strode away, having pushed through the low swing-gate. Moustafa watched him like a hawk until the Visa Control Officer finally disappeared through a door into the bowels of this Consular wing. The visitor was left to linger in the same spot for almost twenty minutes. As he glanced about, Moustafa located two video cameras, there no doubt were more. He felt sure that they were watching him. What if they rebuffed his proposition, he worried? Or worse, what if they abducted him?

The notion left him feeling uncomfortable in the way he might feel if everyone around were clothed but he stood there stark naked. This discomfort caused him to sweat. He pulled out a handkerchief and dabbed his forehead. He would sweat profusely when under stress. There was nothing he could do to stop it.

At last, a different fellow emerged from the same door of the inner sanctum into which the Visa Control Officer had entered. The man immediately fixed his eyes on the visitor and briskly strode towards him. His unrelenting gaze immediately caught the attention of Moustafa, who stood there awkwardly near the low swinging gate.

Moustafa noted that this new player was not accompanied by the Visa Control Officer. The clerk he'd first met had long since gone back to manning her station and still remained there. Anyway, he concluded that this latest fellow did not appear to have the bearing of an Ambassador either, although with the Revolutionary regime, one could not be certain based purely on appearances. He watched the fellow move briskly in his direction.

The man ignored Moustafa's outstretched hand offering a shake. "Say nothing until we're inside," he whispered in Farsi. "Out here it is not secure."

"Have you read my explanation of what the CD contains?" Moustafa inquired with a touch of irritation as the fellow urged him at his elbow to quicken the pace once they'd passed through the swing-gate.

"Shh!" the official responded, and said nothing more.

Once through the door from where this official had originally emerged, he conducted Moustafa down a hallway of offices. Finally the fellow slowed his pace and shuttled the stranger into a very modest conference room. It contained a small table bounded by two chairs on one side and one chair on the other.

"Why have you taken me here?" Moustafa suspiciously inquired.

"This room is secure. We can speak freely here."

"Who are you?"

"Shhh!"

"I thought you said we can speak freely here?"

The official motioned for him to sit in the single chair. Moustafa begrudgingly complied but as he did so, the man departed from the room without any explanation. This official had shut the door behind him, and Moustafa believed he'd heard the click of a lock. He had no idea who this individual might be or if he was MOIS; but Moustafa was quite certain that the fellow wasn't an Ambassador.

The man had not offered him even so much as a cup of tea, he silently groused. Well, he conceded, the Revolutionary regime was not noted for its amenities or sensitivity. On the far wall which the single chair faced was a large mirror. Moustafa had seen enough television shows in America to guess that this mirror represented a one-way see-through glass. He sat there for forty minutes. He'd entertained the notion at one point to make silly faces at the mirror; but he maintained his discretion.

Finally he began to wonder as the duration of his wait continued, whether they might detain him here and then return him to Tehran. But he was a bona fide American citizen! He'd been naturalized eleven years ago. They wouldn't dare, he silently comforted! This comfort was not given, however, with one hundred percent conviction. The regime considered itself exempt from all laws and customs not ordered by the Qu'ran.

Anyway, he further considered, for what reason would they do such a thing to him? But he also understood the insanity which sometimes guided the decisions of this regime. No possibility could be entirely ruled out simply based on reasonability. He silently cursed his wife. He was doing this for her. He was risking his job, the future of his children, and possibly his life all for her petty obsession!

Finally the same gentleman who'd brought him to this little conference room opened the door, entered and shut it again. He did not look like Moustafa's preconceived notion of a MOIS agent. He was short and wirey. His beard was close-cropped by not groomed, and had streaks of gray. After closing the door behind him, he said nothing. He then moved towards the table; however he stopped short, now standing directly behind Moustafa.

It forced the visitor to uncomfortably twist his neck and torso in order to make eye contact. For a moment, Mr. Rajai had the unpleasant notion that he was about to be garroted. But when he turned, he observed that the man's hands were empty.

"How much are you demanding for this information," the official asked unpleasantly as he looked down at the visitor awkwardly gaping at him.

"I'm not interested in money," Moustafa emphasized with a wave of his hand.

The official muttered something under his breath which remained indistinguishable to the visitor. Moustafa watched the man move again, circle the table and then sit down on the opposite side. The chair squealed as he pulled it under him.

"Suppose then, that you tell me what does interest you!"

Moustafa carefully explained that his purpose for

offering the CD was in order to prove the credibility of subsequent submissions. These future findings would occur in the event the Embassy wished to cooperate with him, he further disclosed. For this first contribution---the CD in his jacket pocket--- he requested only an initial concession; but he was unwilling to divulge the nature of this concession until the Iranians affirmed whether or not they were interested in doing business with him.

"I've downloaded and burned this CD myself," he stated as he patted the jacket pocket. "I will hand it over to the Embassy right away if they agree to comply with my first request. Well, are you interested or not?"

The fellow stared back at him with an inscrutable expression on his face. No doubt it was a practiced response to create uneasiness in the opposing party. "Perhaps," he responded at last.

"Have you read the description I wrote of what the CD contains?"

"Yes. I read your sheet of paper. You must be Iranian to have written Farsi so perfectly."

"Thank you," Moustafa muttered. His synopsis explained that the CD covered procedures to be employed for various emergencies which a nuclear generating facility might anticipate.

"For whom do you work?"

"I explained that on my written sheet."

"For whom do you work," the fellow repeated without emotion as if he were a recorded message.

"I'm an engineer working at the PVNGS---uhh, Palo Verde Nuclear Generating Station."

"And where is that?"

"Forty-five miles west of Phoenix, Arizona," and Moustafa then added with a bit of bluster, "Palo Verde is the largest NGS in America. I downloaded the information I describe from their network."

"I'm afraid it's old technology," the fellow sniped.

He was dressed in a solid color tie, white shirt and an ill-fitting suit which appeared to Moustafa like the fellow might have picked it up from a second-hand bazaar. The scrubby beard covering his face did not portend a man of elevated standing here at the Consulate. But his eyes were what dominated Moustafa's attention. They gazed at him with a piercing stare. They were an unusual color for a Persian's eyes… steely blue-gray.

This undistinguished-looking man continued his debasement of Moustafa's offering in a voice filled with scorn. "Palo Verde began construction in 1979. The equipment they installed is much more than twenty years old and has never been updated." And then with particular mockery he added, "Do you wish to contribute to our technology museum in Tehran?"

Moustafa was a bit taken aback, first by this gentleman's familiarity with Palo Verde and secondly by his seeming adversarial comments. He'd thought one of his major stumbling blocks would be to make the Embassy understand the significance of this facility in America where he worked, that he had unencumbered access, and the potential value to Iranian Intelligence which this portended. Yet, here was a gentleman who seemed thoroughly familiar with his facility. Of course, the Embassy could have gotten such information as the fellow had just offered from consulting Google on the Internet.

No doubt the man was a MOIS agent, Moustafa quickly calculated. He'd correctly guessed that every Iranian Embassy had these Ministry of Security Officers. It was pure conjecture on his part, to be sure. But if he was correct in his assessment, then this was the very man with whom he needed to speak. He breathed out a sigh as he engaged the fellow's steely eyes.

Anyway, this fellow had neither properly introduced himself or for that matter had treated Moustafa with any sort of courtesy which one might suppose comprised the amenities expected of a usual Embassy staff member. This man was not usual. Nah, he was MOIS! The fellow appeared to be full of distrust, and reflected all the hard insensitive attributes easily ascribed to a MOIS agent.

However, Moustafa also made an immediate concession on the fellow's behalf. This man's demeanor was to some extent understandable. Moustafa Rajai had come to the Iranian Consulate here in Ottawa uninvited and unannounced. And he'd come from America. Furthermore, he was an ex-pat Iranian. The current regime distrusted his kind most of all.

Moustafa again wondered if he might be forcibly detained by the Embassy and shipped back to an Iranian prison. He'd begun to genuinely regret having listened to his wife. The beads of sweat percolating off his forehead broadcast his nervousness, but he couldn't help it. How do you control sweat?

"Palo Verde is also the last NGS to have been constructed in America," Moustafa parried in response to the trivialization of his offering here by this presumed MOIS Agent who continued to gaze at him with a stone cold expression on his face.

"So?"

"Well, that also makes it the latest American technology then, doesn't it?"

"You should have gone to work for the French or the Japanese. Japan has the largest nuclear generating station in the world. Both nations are orders of magnitude ahead of the Americans in NGS technology. You are probably wasting my time. What do you intend to bring me which you believe will pique my interest? A download of these safety procedures you describe are not even classified documents."

"It proves I have access to the PVNGS network. That was all my specimen was intended to show. What would you like? If it's in the network, I can download it. I have clearance."

"First, tell me what it is that *you* want," the alleged MOIS agent insisted.

"You mean 'how much'? Well, it depends on your request. I have to calculate what your request will cost me in time and then I must consider the risk of course."

"You said that you needed a concession from me. What is this concession?"

"Yes, I am bringing you this CD as an article of good faith, and in return I wish an article of good faith from you. It is not a difficult concession for you to arrange. But first I must know; are you prepared to do business with me? I must have an answer before I can go any further in these matters."

The Embassy man again cast an icy stare that endured several moments before he diverted his eyes and stated, "Yes, yes… I am prepared to do business with you if you have something worthwhile to offer."

Moustafa nervously rubbed his hands together as he slowly inhaled a deep breath. "Alright, I will trust you. My wife is a Jew. Will that affect our bargain?"

The man smirked, "I really don't care if you are married to a baboon. It's your access to information that concerns me. Are you Jew?"

Moustafa disregarded the slight intended by the man's tone of voice, and he decided to disregard the question as well. He was Persian and spoke perfect Farsi, but that much must have been obvious to the official. "She… my wife… has a sister who lives in the north, in Azarbayjon. The husband, a Jew, was arrested and imprisoned and… uhh… died. My sister-in-law is destitute. I want her and the two children issued exit visas." He raised a halting hand. "I will pay for all transportation costs."

"Why was he arrested?"

"He was accused of smuggling and of sedition."

"Accused?"

Moustafa deftly avoided the trap which he saw being laid. "I was not at the trial. I was not in Iran. I can not form an opinion; but if the authorities found him guilty, then no doubt he was guilty. But my poor sister-in-law and her children had nothing to do with his activities."

"And to where will they go?"

Moustafa swallowed hard. "America."

"But they will need permission from the Americans… entry visas."

"I have a lawyer working on that."

"I see. But let's not get ahead of ourselves. Do you understand that we have agents active in America?"

"I would have guessed so."

"Do you have a family in America?"

Warning bells went off in Moustafa Rajai's head. Well, he'd already admitted to a wife. MOIS would easily trace his family's whereabouts with the information he'd already provided them. Clearly, he'd gone one step beyond any tactical retreat.

He'd also realized the risk to his sister-in-law and her children in his coming here and then disclosing his mission which concerned them. Moreover, he'd explained to his wife the risk to himself, to her and to their three children as well. His wife had nonetheless urged him to do so. "My sister's situation can't be worsened," she'd argued. "They are destitute. I must take the risk. She's my sister!"

"Yes," Moustafa answered, concerning the question

whether he had family in America. The Embassy man continued to leer at him.

Suddenly the presumed MOIS agent pointed a rigid index finger straight into the air. "We will hold your family, as well as you, responsible if you betray my trust. Do you fully understand this?"

He gulped. "Yes."

"How do I know you don't work for Mossad. You said your wife is Jew. For all I know you may be a clever Jew as well!"

Moustafa shrugged his shoulders. "What's the difference? It is I who am offering information to you."

"But of what value is information which I can not trust? You may intend to feed us disinformation."

"You will check me out, I'm sure; and you will learn that I'm Persian. I've hidden nothing from you. I am cooperating in order to bring my sister-in-law and her two children to the United States." He leaned to the side, pulled out a handkerchief and patted his forehead.

"Do you pray?" the presumed MOIS Agent inquired in a quiet voice.

"Huh?" Moustafa softly reacted and stopped patting his forehead. He retrieved the fist holding his handkerchief to his lap.

"Are you a Muslim? Do you pray?"

"Yes, I am a Muslim; but I do not pray."

"Then you are not a Muslim, you are a blasphemer! Thus I am free to promise that if you betray me in any way, MOIS will kill your entire family and you as well."

Sonora, Mexico

Ruben dreamed of one day becoming a famous writer and singer of *canciones nortenyas* (songs of the Northern Mexicans). Thus, when he heard the applause at the end of his *corrido, El Tunnel para la Carga Blanca,* (Tunnel for the White Cargo) he felt pride and excitement. The clapping had come with particular enthusiasm form one table where three men sat.

Ruben wrote and sang *corridos*, a brand of *canciones nortenyas* glorifying the *narco-traficantes*. He had a pleasant tenor voice, and knew enough chords to strum his guitar convincingly. He'd intended to work for the narco-traficantes when he migrated from Chihuahua to this border town opposite Arizona. But he'd grown cold feet after getting caught by the Border Patrol on his first attempt as a *burro* for one of the local *narco-traficantes*.

The good luck was that he managed to dislodge his contraband before they took him into custody, and he was simply returned across the border. The bad luck was that the local *narco-traficante* held him responsible for making good the loss of his load. It was 25,000 pesos, or so the man claimed.

He hadn't made that much money in his entire adult years. He was 22 years old. The *narco-traficante* threatened his life if the money was not returned, and Ruben knew very well this man did no bluff. He was a local boss. It wasn't the money that mattered to this man, rather that he must maintain his reputation. But he allowed Ruben to make small payments each week. And the *charro* (musician) had composed several songs that eulogized this *narco-traficante*, which clearly pleased the man. It was a mark of deep respect to be praised by a *charro's* music. He made it a point to sing these songs whenever the local boss was present.

Thus, Ruben had managed to survive. Trying to run away from here was out of the question. Sooner or later he would be found, especially when he became famous *charro*. He believed in his future. And the *narco-traficante* would order them to slit his throat. No, once his talent was recognized and he became famous he would settle his debt and then get on with his life.

He was considering which of his songs to sing next, when the burly fellow with bushy hair stepped up and wordlessly motioned for him to come to the table where two colleagues of this man abided. It was the table from which had come the enthusiastic applause. Unlike the man silently beckoning him, the other two sitting at the table were both well-dressed and their hair glistened with slick. One had a full moustache, whereas the other had a scrubby growth of beard.

The cantina here had a tile floor with perhaps twenty tables arranged somewhat haphazardly over it. Only half the tables were occupied at this point in time. It was still early. Customarily, Ruben would move around from table to table and sing a song, hoping for a few pesos tip or at least a drink from the patrons of that table. The *gomeros* (narco-traffickers) often came here, but usually later in the evening. They could be very generous, but they could also be very drunk.

They were a dangerous bunch with unpredictable moods, especially when they were very drunk. If you offended them for what you perceived as no particular reason, you might be in for a very bad time. But Ruben took his chances. *Gomeros* tipped the best, and this was his sole livelihood. And he was in debt to the local boss. He must dutifully offer his weekly payments. That liability, however, also offered one advantage for him.

These *gomeros* would not break a pot of beans belonging to the *jefe* (chief; boss). Thus, he could intrepidly absorb the insults they sometimes hurled at him, knowing that they dared not do him any serious harm. Otherwise, they would inherit his debt to the *jefe*. That was unwritten *narco-traficante* law.

"What do you want?" Ruben politely asked as he carefully cradled his guitar. He did not suppose this man to be a *gomero*, or his colleagues either. He didn't think the guy was even Mexican.

However he had a clear notion of the reason for this summons. It was not uncommon to invite a *charro* to one's table for a drink if the songs pleased the patron. And, if the musician pandered properly, he could usually wheedle a tip from them as well. But in response to Ruben's question, the man only motioned again without speaking, as if he were mute… or didn't speak Spanish.

Well, Ruben would certainly not refuse the hospitality of a free beer; his throat was dry. Moreover, he didn't have the courage to offend this ox of man who now beckoned him. Was this fellow a foreigner? He and the other two could have passed for Mexican; but something didn't seem quite right with that picture. They certainly didn't look *gringo*; but then the *Norteamericanos* came in many stripes and colors.

Some *gringos* could pass for Mexican. Some of them had Mexican heritage. But when they spoke Spanish, that's when you knew what they were. Even among Mexicans there were distinct regional inflections and words. You could certainly determine if a Mexican was *nortenyo*, or from somewhere in the south.

It became clear to Ruben almost immediately that the fellow with the full moustache was the *jefe*. It was the way in which the bushy-haired man deferentially passed Ruben to him and then withdrew a step, and awaited a nod from the *jefe* before sitting down. So he concluded that he'd been summoned by an important man… a *jefe*.

Importance was measured in *pesos*. This could portend a generous *propina* (tip), he quickly realized. He was overdue on his payment to the local boss, and so he desperately hoped that this mysterious bunch would feather his nest.

The man with the moustache smiled at Ruben and gestured with his hand. "Please take a chair. I wish to speak with you," he stated in Spanish.

Ruben immediately concluded the fellow was not Mexican even though his Spanish appeared quite fluent. He spoke with a foreign accent… but not like a gringo. No matter! The *jefe* did not appear offended, or drunk; in fact, quite the contrary. Ruben girded a mind-set that would play on the pleasures of this important man. Perhaps he would offer to compose a *corrido* for the *jefe*. Well, he would have to see how things transpired.

"Did you write this song?" the *jefe* asked.

"Which one?"

"The last one," he responded civilly.

"*Tunnel para la Carga Blanca*? *Si*! I only sing songs which I have written."

"Is the tunnel in your song one which you actually have seen?"

Ruben paused briefly as he considered his answer. To speak the truth and say "no" would lead to a far less impressive characterization than if he said "yes". The game after all was to entice a munificent recompense out of this foreigner. What could this tourist possibly know? The singer set his mind to the task at hand. He would engross the fellow with outlandish tales, and predictably by the end of it all he will have been rewarded with a couple or three beers and a generous *propina*.

"Yes, of course I have seen the tunnel. I only write songs about things which I have seen for myself!"

"In that case, may I invite you to have tequila with me?"

Tequila! That was a rare invitation. Ruben became excited. There could be a *very* generous *propina* at the end of this if he played the man like a fine guitar.

"I would be honored," he responded and tipped his head.

"Then please sit down!"

Ruben had remained standing out of deference to this patron, although the invitation had been offered earlier. However the forcefulness with which this man issued his words made it seem more like a command than a request. Well, he was a *Jefe*; that much was clear. He would be accustomed to giving commands. And so Ruben did as he was bid.

Jefe turned to the man with a scrubby beard and uttered something completely incomprehensible to Ruben. It was clearly in a foreign tongue. It was not English. He understood some English. The words sounded *very* foreign. Scrubby Beard nodded in the affirmative and stood up as Ruben descended into the last empty chair at this square wooden table while he carefully lowered the guitar to the floor and leaned it against his leg.

"Mi amigo is going to fetch us all tequila," *Jefe* stated to Ruben. "We shall drink together, and you will tell me about your tunnel."

Ruben wanted to ask why this man was so interested in the tunnel; but he knew that such a forthright question might offend. "Which tunnel, senyor? There are many tunnels. But none of them are *my* tunnel."

"I thought you just claimed to have seen it?"

"But it is not *my* tunnel!"

Jefe flashed a brief grimace, breathed out, and then forced a smile as he stated in a gracious tone, "You said in your song that it had shuttle carts riding on tracks, so I would think it is a very large tunnel. How big is it, and how long?"

Ruben felt a sinking feeling. Who were these guys? Could they be the American DEA (Drug Enforcement Agency)? They weren't Mexican constabulary, of that he was quite sure. His strategy of garnering a generous *propina* gave way to caution.

"You are asking me a sensitive question, Senyor. These are matters we do not discuss here in Sonora. You must be careful with whom you ask such questions. I'm just a *charro*; but there are many *narco-traficantes* who come to the cantinas. They might take offense to such questions."

He observed *Jefe* nod in the direction of the bar. Ruben turned and could see that the gesture was received by scrubby beard. Then he heard *Jefe* in that strange foreign language mutter something to the big bushy-haired man. The ox gathered to his feet with an audible breath, and sauntered towards the bar where his colleague stood. *Jefe* cast the singer a reassuring smile.

"He will help my friend to carry back the drinks. I suggested that we get beers to wash down the tequila." He reached over and gave the fellow a pat on the shoulder. "Don't worry. No more questions about tunnels. Suppose you sing me a song?"

In the middle of his *corrido* the two men returned with tequila-filled double-shot glasses and bottles of beer. Scrubby Beard set down a tequila and beer in front of the *charro*. Then the three men raised their tequilas in the gesture of a toast. Ruben, who'd sung the current stanza of his song distractedly, now abated his singing as he laid his guitar over his lap and reached for the double shot-glass of tequila set before him. He raised it on high and they all slugged it down in good *Sonorense* fashion.

The after-taste made Ruben wonder what brand of tequila Scrubby Beard had brought. It wasn't quite right. He quickly washed the bitterness away with a chug-a-lug of beer. *Jefe* gazed at him with a smile but said nothing.

The other two leered at him as if expecting something to jump out of his head. Their stares disoriented him. He decided to finish his *corrido*, but something strange overcame his mind. He couldn't remember the words. His arms began to feel heavy and his fingers went numb.

****

Ruben awoke. His eyes felt extremely dry and his head ached. In his initial instant of awareness, he thought he had awakened in his bed. But slowly he became aware of certain contradictions to this notion. In the first place, he wasn't lying down, nor was he in a bed. It took several moments for him to realize that he was tied to a chair, and another few moments to comprehend that he sat there stark naked.

Memories slowly seeped back into his mind like an expanding puddle of piss as it splattered and ran down the wall. He recollected images of the cantina, of drinking tequila with those foreigners, the *jefe* with the big moustache, and…. He shut his eyes because his vision was blurred. He tried blinking them, but it didn't help.

He allowed them to remain shut because he found it was a strenuous effort which his mind required for him to put forward these thoughts. Oh, yes, and the talk about tunnels, he suddenly remembered.

He opened his eyes and again blinked in an effort to clear his vision. His chair was tipped back, supported by a table. It was reclined at an angle too steep for him to lunge forward and return the chair to its upright position. But even if he could have done so, he wasn't sure that he should dare to do it. Someone had gone to a great deal of effort to secure him here. Their intentions did not appear to him particularly benevolent.

He anxiously looked around the room as best he could. It appeared that he was inside a kitchen. The bushy-haired guy stood leaning against a counter. Ruben immediately recalled this man. He was now eating an orange as he made eye contact with the singer. Bushy Hair immediately turned his head and yelled out in that strange language which *jefe* had employed a few times in the cantina. As Bushy Hair posted his exclamation in that incomprehensible foreign language, Ruben could see juice and orange pulp visibly splatter from his mouth.

Jefe entered the room. He approached Ruben with a condescending smile. "So, you are awake? You shouldn't drink tequila, my friend. It seems to affect you badly."

"Why have you tied me up? Where am I? Where are my clothes and my boots? Where is my guitar?"

"You are tied up because you offended me. You did not answer my questions. And that is why we have brought you here. In this apartment there are no *narco-traficantes*, so we may speak freely."

Ruben gasped. "*Lo siento, patron… lo siento*! I am just a poor *charro*! I meant no offense! How did I offend you? Was it my song?"

Jefe just stared at him as a menacing expression began occluding his face. It soon became obvious to the singer that no immediate answer would be forthcoming.

"Is it about the tunnel?" Ruben desperately probed. "I did not mean to offend you. I was only trying to warn you against such things. I told you this as a friend, so that no harm might come to you. I meant no disrespect. Do you intend to kill me over such an innocent matter?"

"Perhaps."

"Please, I promise to tell you whatever it is you wish to know!"

"First, let me make a promise. In fact, I will make you two promises, *charro*. Are you listening?"

"*Si, patron, si*!"

"My first promise is that I will not kill you. Do you understand?"

"*Si, patron*!"

"My second promise is that if you do not answer questions to my full satisfaction, you will sorely regret my first promise. When I am through with you there will be little left of your body to live for. You will beg me for a merciful death, and I will not give it to you. I never break a promise."

"I will satisfy you , *patron*… as best as I can… to my limit. I can not offer more."

"That's your problem, *charro*. I want answers… good answers… complete answers… and you will be held accountable for what you say!"

"I will tell you all that I know, *patron*! Is it about the tunnel?"

Ruben hoped it was something else, anything else, but he knew it was not. *Tunnel para la Carga Blanca* was a *corrido* he'd made up from hearsay and from events of the past. There had been many tunnels. Some of them were famous, and when the DEA discovered them, you would read about it in the newspaper or see on television or hear it on the radio.

Back in the cantina, *Jefe* had referred to *Ruben's* tunnel. But there was no certain tunnel to which he'd referred in his *corrido*. It was just a *pinche* (fucking) song. He had never actually seen a tunnel.

He wrestled with the dilemma of how to explain his flight of fancy without further offending this foreigner and incurring the almost certain consequences of a disappointing response. He formulated the first sentence of an apology, "*Lo siento, lo siento, patron*, we *charros* must use our imaginations…"

His composition of an apology was interrupted by the voice of *jefe*. "It is important for you to understand that I mean business. It will make a more efficient use of my time if that fact is established at the beginning. My time is very valuable. Do you understand this?"

"*Si, patron, si*, I understand!"

"It is also important for you to understand that we have the stomach for such proceedings."

"Proceedings, patron… to what kind of proceedings do you refer?"

He ignored the singer's question as he continued with his statement which seemed to flow like practiced lines. "I do not want to hear apologies. Just answer my questions!" he erupted.

"*Si, patron*!"

Then suddenly modulating into a much gentler tone of voice the foreigner asked, "Tell me, which finger is least important for your playing the guitar?"

Ruben stared at him with bugging eyes. Tears gathered, causing his vision to blur. He felt a wet tickle stream down his cheek.

Jefe slapped the *charro* on the side of his head. It was not a blow meant to do damage, more like one intended to get a person's full attention. "Tell me which finger, or I shall make the choice myself!"

Peoria, Arizona

Peoria is a west-side chartered suburb of Phoenix. A lot of Palo Verde Nuclear Generating Station employees lived in this town. Moustafa Rajai and his family resided there in a comfortable ranch-style home. Each of his three children had their own bedroom. His neighbors were not unfriendly although reasonably private which suited him just fine. There was a Persian community throughout the greater Phoenix area, and it was from this pool of residents that he and his wife drew most of their social connections.

They'd lived in this same house for the past sixteen years.

The value of their home he smugly calculated had during these years more than quadrupled in value. The problem was that so had all the other homes in the greater Phoenix area. Thus, there was no point in selling and accruing the profit, unless he wished to return to Iran where these proceeds could allow him to live like an Ayatollah. No thanks, he was quite satisfied with his life here in America!

He then cursed under his breath as he self-flagellated over having succumbed to his wife's constant harping that he must help her hapless sister and the two children escape from Iran and come to Arizona. Her sister was the only living member of the wife's immediate family. From the content of Sofia's infrequent letters, there was a real question of how much longer she could survive. They couldn't call her. The poor woman had no telephone. And they dared not visit. That could be extremely dangerous for ex-pats given the current regime.

Iran offered severe hardship for a Jewish widow of a convicted criminal punished by death and stripped of all his possessions. She survived because Moustafa's wife would wire her money. But the full amount of the money she sent never reached Sofia. And lately the "Iranian taxes on foreign income" had become particularly onerous.

Moustafa had sacrificed the bedroom which previously served as his office when the third child came of an age requiring privacy. They needed privacy in order to study and do their homework. The Rajais raised their children to obsess over excellent grades at school, and the children dutifully incorporated this notion.

The master bedroom was large enough for him to install a desk and his computer without disturbing the integrity of he and his wife's sleeping quarters. If he needed to work on his computer at night, his wife never complained. Admittedly, he conceded, there was little over which she had ever complained, except now concerning the situation with her sister, Sofia. Although Moustafa perceived their ability to help the poor woman as somewhere between scant and none, he could not bring himself to be insensitive to his wife's concern or disregard her desperation. He loved and respected his wife. Thus, he had applied his mind in search of a solution to Sofia's dilemma.

His oldest child was a senior in high school. The young man would be entering university next year, and had already applied to Harvard, Chicago, and two California schools. He was a straight-A student, and intended to earn an MBA. Thus Moustafa contemplated being able to reclaim his office-rights to the vacated bedroom. He anticipated the transition with relish.

At this particular moment, the children had finished their homework and were playing their allotted half hour of video games which they hooked up to the television set in the family room. He'd called his wife into their bedroom and closed the door. He motioned for her to sit on the bed, and she did so. But she couldn't hide her anxiety.

"Is this about Sofia?" the wife finally whispered in Farsi as she watched her husband slowly pace with his hands clasped behind his thighs.

"That and much more," he muttered, responding in their native tongue as well. Then he raised his voice. "Do you have any idea what you've gotten me into... and your sister for that matter?"

He didn't wait for an answer. As Moustafa prepared to relate the story to his wife, he relived in his mind today's events. His forehead was already perspiring.

"Yesterday evening I called Manley Smythe at home and informed him that I had an emergency dental appointment, and would be in late for work this morning." He paused, and measured her attention to his words.

His wife had her large dark eyes fixed on him. "I didn't know you had a problem with your teeth. Why didn't you tell me? Did you go to Dr. Felix?" She slowly erected herself off the bed and faced him. "But what does that have to do with my sister, Sofia?"

He gazed at her with unblinking eyes, and as he did so, pulled a handkerchief from his pocket and patted his forehead. "No, I went to a dentist named Dr. Razi. He is from Tehran," he answered in a calm voice, but then suddenly spat, "And, yes, it has everything to do with your sister!"

His energetic delivery immediately caused the woman's face to blanch, and tears began filling into her eyes. "Did he give you news of Sofia?"

"I never spoke to him."

"You didn't go?"

"Yes, I went... but not to see Dr. Razi. I have no tooth problem. No I have a far bigger problem. And not just me, but you and our children, we all have a big problem. And Sofia. I was directed to go to this dentist's office where I met with an agent of SAVAK. Now they call themselves MOIS, but they are the same people."

His wife gasped upon hearing the acronym. All ordinary Iranians were conditioned to this response. No one wanted to be a person of interest for SAVAK, she silently shuddered.

"But we are in the United States," she objected. "What can SAVAK do to us here? What did he say? Was it about Sofia?"

"It's about all of us, don't you understand?" he screamed. He was still holding his handkerchief, and once again patted his forehead. "I'm sorry. I didn't mean to raise my voice."

A tear from each eye coursed down her cheeks. "What is the problem?" she whispered.

"They want information about Palo Verde." He began speaking rapidly. "Of course, it was I who originally volunteered information, but what they are now asking from me is worrisome. It is very disturbing information for which they ask. He says that they've taken Sofia and her children into custody. If I don't cooperate, then they will never be heard from again. And if I go to the authorities here, MOIS will kill our children."

She stared at him with a dumbfounded expression. More tears streamed down her cheek. "Will you give them this information?" she finally murmured.

He reached over and a laid a comforting hand on

her shoulder. "I do not want to do what they ask. But the consequences of disobeying them affect us all. It is a decision we must make together."

"What does he wish to know?"

Moustafa cocked his head to one side as he retrieved his hand from her shoulder. "He's asked for a lot of technical information, but not about the process. It's about the facility. What's clear to me from his questions is that they intend to sabotage Palo Verde. I think they mean to blast it!"

She appeared unperturbed by this revelation. "And if you give them this information?"

"Sofia and her children will be given exit visas."

"How can you be sure?"

"I can't, but they are willing to bring them into Canada as a sign of good faith. I will be allowed to visit them one time in order to verify their identity and that they are there. And after I turn over information which the MOIS seeks, they will release your sister and two children to me. That is what they have promised."

Tohono O'odham Indian Reservation, Arizona

Lewis Reddy was the name he'd called himself in the days before his enlightenment. It was an anachronism that still remained on his driver's license. It was the reference by which his parole papers were filed, and represented his identity on the dishonorable discharge papers from the Marine Corp.

He was a black American. So were his score of

followers. The name, Lewis Reddy, which he'd offered these Indians wasn't a falsehood; nonetheless, it was a device of convenience. To non-believers his Christian name would avoid the immediate suspicion and even revulsion that his true name before God would invoke in them. His parents had given him the infidel name at his christening. But it was not the name he used in Allah's presence or when he gathered with the True Believers.

No, to them he was known as Ali Ul-Faqr. Moreover, he was further bestowed with the office and stature of *Sultan*, Sultan Ali Ul-Faqr… graciously self-anointed. He'd taken the liberty of appointing himself to this station. Well, he granted, the title might presently be considered an over-reach. As matters stood today, his dominion was not impressive, but there was unmistakable potential for growth. His initial group was only the seed-corn. Soon there would be fields of followers. Anyway, he mused, it was good to be the Sultan.

The funds for his project here on this Indian reservation had come from someone whom he'd privately dubbed *Moustache*. The man had never offered his name. The fellow was Iranian. He had a prominent Stalin-like moustache, and more importantly had a source of money… apparently lots of money! Money spoke far louder than names or claims, Ali reflected.

The inspiration for this project had come from Moustache as well. And so he did exactly as Moustache had instructed him to do. The promise was that in return for his cooperation, funds from a Shi'ite Muslim charity would be donated for the completion of the mosque he was constructing in South Tucson. As matters currently stood, the construction of his ambitious project had come to a stand-still caused by a dearth of funds.

Originally, Ali had intended to finance his construction and provide for his followers through the manufacture of amphetamines. But without distribution, these drugs were worthless chemicals. He learned too late that he'd intruded into the domain of a motorcycle gang, and a competing Mexican ring. Both entities joined forces to put him out of business. Four of his followers had to be taken to the Emergency Room at Tucson's Santa Maria Hospital. One of them died. And because of this the police became involved, and now they were watching his activities in Tucson like a hawk. But Allah had not abandoned him. No, the benevolent All-knowing had sent Moustache to Ali and his followers. Allah had directed the attention of the Shi'ite Charities to take notice of Ali Ul-Faqr and his struggle.

So transposing as Lewis Reddy, Ali had negotiated with these Indians to lease a small tract of land abutting the Mexican border. It was located almost midway between Christmas Gate and Papago Farms Gate. Moustache had insisted upon this precise location. The tribal council made an outlandish demand for the lease money, and they were thunderstruck when Ali returned with the money in cash. It was money handed over to him by Moustache, and a repeated promise of the reward to build his mosque in South Tucson. Moustache explained the next phase of his project, but not the underlying purpose. Thus on this tract of Indian land, Ali and his nineteen followers had supervised the construction of a compound using mostly day-laborers from the Mexican side who freely snuck back and forth across the border.

The border here was porous. The Tohono O'odham Indians and the illegal Mexicans crossed almost at will. Apparently the petty drug-smugglers did so, as well. It was the experience of the major *narco-traficante's* that DEA and Border Patrol were much more likely to react when they perceived that a significant shipment of drugs were being crossed than they would to the crossing of illegal migrants. No doubt it was a stark consideration of their limited manpower and resources. They kept a watchful eye on the border, but relied on intelligence gathering as well.

Using these handy migrants as *burros* to cross the drugs was fraught with a different set of dangers for the *narco-traficantes* who shipped their illicit cargos in quantity. You dared not strap very much value onto a migrant or they would certainly abscond with it. Thus the numbers of migrants needed to cross a shipment valued in the millions was entirely unmanageable.

There was a dirt runway on the Mexican side half a mile from the border directly south of the Ul-Faqr compound which accommodated STOL (short takeoff/landing) aircraft. Many such STOL strips were arrayed along the border from Texas to California. However, connecting the two sides of the border at this particular place was a long tunnel. It allowed a large shipment to cross the line undetected. But it was not a public conveyance. And few persons knew that it even existed. It was Romero's tunnel.

Outside the compound he'd assembled a rigorous martial training area. He'd completed the project more than two months ago, but still Moustache had sent him no recruits to train. Lewis Reddy was an ex-Marine… and an ex-convict. The former had qualified him to serve as Drill Instructor. The latter had prepared him for his conversion to Islam.

Having transitioned to Ali Ul-Faqr, Islam had taught him the virtues of patience, wisdom and obedience. He did not question Moustache or his motives. He was convinced that all things moved by the hand of Allah, and so he must not resist that hand.

The Border Patrol had of course become immediately curious concerning the activities of this new group. Moustache had warned him that he and his followers must show no belligerence to the authorities, or to the Tribal Police. "We must be clever to hide our purpose," he insisted.

The ostensible purpose, so far as Ali could immediately discern from the taciturn Moustache, was to train a militia. But slowly the Sultan came to realize that there was a second and perhaps far more overarching purpose… it concerned *the tunnel*. The tunnel had been there before the arrival of Ali Ul-Faqr and his followers. It was operated by Mexican drug-traffickers. Both sides of the tunnel were on traditional Tohono O'odham Indian lands. One hundred and fifty some years ago their lands had all been a part of Mexico.

Prior to the Gadsden Purchase of 1854, the Gila River just south of Phoenix, Arizona had marked the border between the United States and Mexico. The Papago (who officially changed their name to Tohono O'odham in 1980) had lived in Mexico and were largely ignored by the Mexican Federal and State authorities. Their vast lands were worthless desert, other than a few patches of rich copper deposits.

Papago was a name given to this tribe by the Conquistador, Cortez. He'd picked up that name from tribes unfriendly to the Tohono O'odham. It was a name laced with derision… *tapery-bean eaters*. Their true tribal name now officially accepted---Tohono O'odham---meant *people of the desert*.

When Mexico ceded to the United States the territory acquired by the Gadsden Purchase, the tribe and their lands were split by a boundary they considered artificial. However, Moustache had cautioned that these Indians resented the Mexican drug-traffickers as much as they resented the federal authorities. Those narco-brutes had harassed and in a few cases killed members of the tribe who were unlucky enough to cross their paths. The Tribal Police actively engaged smugglers and fully cooperated with the Border Patrol.

"You must appear to be good citizens," he coached, "who abhor the drug smugglers. We will arrange for you to tip off the Tribal Police on a few---how do you say---little *drug busts*? We must assuage the suspicions of these law enforcement agencies. You must seem as a group of devout peace-loving disciples of the Prophet who seek the solace of the desert to practice your religious beliefs."

So far, Moustache had been true to his word on the money and drug bust information. Ali had twice now tipped off the Tribal Police based on information given to him by Moustache. He declared that his sentries had spotted the illicit activity and he'd rushed to inform the Tribe. On the second occasion, he was met by a member of the Border Patrol who waited for him at the gate to his compound and thanked him for his cooperation.

"What exactly are you doing here?" he then inquired.

Ali was prepared for this question. Moustache had instructed him in the answer. "We pray, and we wait for the Twelfth Imam to appear. He is coming soon. Did you know that?"

"No," the patrolman drawled as he rolled his eyes at his colleague. "Do you expect him to come here?"

"Yes," the Sultan responded with an intense earnest. "And when he comes, he will put an end to the world."

"Well," playfully warned the patrolman, "tell him to make sure he has a work visa before he crosses the border."

Ali had to stifle his natural belligerence, especially when he was required to act like a buffoon. He fancied himself a warrior. He wanted to engage in *jihad*. He wanted to train and then lead his minions on a mission that would surpass 9/11. Moustache had assured him that this is exactly what he was doing. But, as yet, the man refused disclosing to him the genuine nature of this mission.

So, he bided his time by honing the martial skills of his followers. They trained at sundown and into the night. The training field was well-worn. And the men rubbed sleepy eyes from constant sentry duty. He needed to keep them from thinking about the heat, the flies, the unavailability of pussy, and the fact that they had no clear concept of their mission.

Now in mid-May, the desert floor was beginning to get uncomfortable in the afternoons. The mornings and evenings were still pleasantly cool; but he'd been warned by the Indians as they clucked incredulously at the dark canvass tents that within a couple weeks the desert heat would make things here inhospitable. He needed to talk to Moustache about this; but he had no way of initiating communications with the man. When this arrogant Iranian was ready, he would be the one to make contact. It was demeaning, he sulked. After all, he was a Sultan!

The construction of the compound had followed the end of Ramadan. The tents went up first. The most ambitions phase of the project was setting the eight foot high cyclone fence that surrounded roughly two acres of land. Equally daunting was building the warehouse. It was constructed by using bales of hay as building blocks. It was roughly six feet high and eight feet wide, but very long… about forty feet. Planks of wood were laid across the top edges of these walls, and then a series of tarpaulins were spread over the planks. Then piled neatly on top of the tarpaulins, they tightly layered a roof of hay bales which served to blanket the interior of their warehouse, protecting it from the heat of the sun and the wind. The hay proved to serve as excellent insulation.

Moustache had left a man behind who was charged with supervising the warehouse project and dispersing funds for Ul-Faqr's provisions. He was a Jordanian, and claimed to be a civil engineer. Ali hadn't liked him from the start. The Sultan resented any competition to his absolute authority over his men; but additionally this Jordanian was arrogant and condescending towards him.

The Jordanian had offered a sneering disparagement of black Muslims to Moustache in earshot of Ali. It was a touchy subject. He and his men had endured scorn from their white brethren as Christians. To again endure it from True Believers of their new faith caused resentment, to put it mildly.

Tehran, Iran

Three armed men had stormed into the hovel and taken Sofia and her two children away. They wouldn't tell her to where or for what reason. Neighbors quietly peered from behind curtains, but no one dared protest.

She wasn't given the chance to pack any clothes or ask any questions. They were MOIS Agents who'd invaded her house and rounded her up with her two children in the late evening. Of course, none of the three men made any such admission concerning whom they represented. They were armed, however even if they hadn't been Sofia certainly would not have dared to resist. But the fact that they were MOIS soon enough became obvious to her. Who else could provide a private airplane in which to transport them?

Her mind was in an utter muddle during the flight. Her children repeatedly cast furtive glances, but had the good sense to keep their mouths shut. She would force herself to offer them a reassuring smile.

"Are we going to visit Father?" the older one asked at one point.

"Perhaps," Sofia responded in a choked voice. The daughter knew her father had been executed. She wondered why the child had asked this question. To presume that the true inquiry of her daughter was to ask whether or not they themselves were being taken for execution would ascribe a maturity beyond this child's years. But hardship has a way of maturing the young, she vouched in afterthought.

She'd lost all sense of how much time had passed. But as the airplane began its descent she glanced out the small window and discerned from the lights of the city that they were in the process of landing at Tehran. Sofia had attended University here in the capitol city many years ago. But this was her first time to see it from the air. It was at university in Tehran where she'd met her future husband. Things had gotten extremely difficult for Jews in those days, and so they'd found solace in each other's company.

Years earlier, Sofia's sister had as well met her future husband at the same university in Tehran. But he had been Persian… Moustafa Rajai. He was not religious, but for his family's sake he endured a Muslim wedding and his Jewish bride agreed to bear the indignity. Sofia's father had refused to attend the sister's wedding or speak to his impious daughter who'd chosen to marry outside their religion. He warned that such a union would be cursed. In fact, it turned out quite the opposite. Moustafa had wisely chosen to pack off with his wife and head for America. He was a graduate engineer and his family had solid means. He was the eldest son and for the most part this decision to go to America had come at his father's urging, her sister had confided during their final goodbyes.

"Right now the Revolutionary regime is busy with the war; but when it is finally over, they may give me trouble," Moustafa's father had said according to her sister.

"Why?" Moustafa had respectfully inquired.

"I supported the Shah. These people now in power will never forgive me for that."

"Then we should all go to America, father!"

"What? And leave all this? I have worked a lifetime to build my businesses. No, I am too old to start a new life. I haven't the energy. But you must go to America, Moustafa. Take your new wife, and give me grandchildren. When I sense that things have normalized here, I will send for you to return." Evidently, Sofia mused, Moustafa's father had never sent that signal. Instead, the old man and his wife had finally emigrated to Australia.

During the Iraq-Iran War, 1980-88, Iran had garnered few supporters among the international community. The two superpowers as well as all of Europe except for Greece had gathered on the side of Saddam Hussein. Granted it was for them a tough choice, a tyrannical dictator versus a fanatic theocracy. Evidently Saddam offered a less repugnant alternative then the Ayatollahs. As Kofi Anan, the U.N. Secretary-General was to remark much later, he was a man with whom they could do business.

On the other hand, Israel, along with the two other pariah nations, South Africa and Libya, as well as Argentina and Taiwan supported Iran. For that reason, during the war years the Iranian regime did not overtly mistreat their population of Jews dwelling inside the country. Israel traded with them, supplying military hardware, and they needed all the help they could get.

Sofia and her future husband had enrolled as university students two years after the Iraq-Iran War ended. The honeymoon between the regime and its Jews was abating. In the early 1990's the regime began a serious campaign against Zionism. Thus, in their second year of studies they were both dismissed from the University because they were Jews.

Her fiancé took her back to Azerbayjon where his family resided, and they were married. Her husband was the only son in his family, and began working in his father's mercantile shop. The father died and so her husband took over the business. In a matter of months, her mother-in-law also died.

After the husband's arrest, Sofia's pride at first created an obstacle to asking her father for help. She knew that he himself was in financial straits. She had no brothers. She only had her one sister. And the sister was in America. Finally she wrote to her father explaining her demise. He did not respond to her appeal. Finally she managed to reach a cousin by telephone and learned that the old man had been on his death bed when the letter arrived, and subsequently had died. They had tried to reach her, but by this time she had no telephone and had lost her house. Clearly, they'd not tried very hard.

Sofia's mother could barely help herself, and Sofia further understood the danger she would bring to the old woman and others in the extended family by asking them to harbor or even give succor to the wife of a criminal convicted of a capital offense. After her husband's arrest, the government had closed his business and taken away the inventory. They'd kicked her out of her house and frozen her bank accounts. She'd become a destitute widow with the responsibility for two children. Her several cousins would have nothing to do with her, fearing the political consequences. They were Jews in a hostile culture. They had their own families to protect.

Sofia was treated as a pariah by her neighbors as well. Only her sister in the United States helped. Without the regular sums of money sent by her sister, Sofia and her two children would have starved and had nothing with which to pay rent.

As they sat in the cramped quarters of this little airplane, she tried comforting her children. The girl was eleven and the boy was nine. They were clearly stricken with fear, as was she. Especially her daughter seemed affected. She'd been old enough three years ago to understand the horror when they'd dragged her screaming father out of the house.

Six months after the incident, Sofia learned of his execution. She did not hide this fact from her children. They had a right to know. Now, the girl appeared convinced that they too were going to be executed. The poor girl just stared out in a visible daze and it was difficult for Sofia to make her respond.

The MOIS Agent pushing her along after they disembarked from the small aircraft announced that Sofia would be taken to a prison. "And what about my children?" she demanded.

"That will depend upon your good sense and cooperation."

"But they are innocent children. They have done nothing to harm you!"

"Blame yourself. You should never have brought these two filthy monkeys into this world! They are a blasphemy to our Islamic Republic."

"Why am I being arrested?"

"Shut up!"

Her husband had been held in the infamous Evin Prison. As they drove through the night, Sofia wondered if they would be taking her to that same prison. The rabbi in her home town, with a genuine concern for her best interest, had strenuously warned her away from ever trying to visit her husband there. At least not until after the trial, he'd counseled. Thus, she'd never seen the place. After learning of her husband's execution, she regretted not having gone.

But, at the moment, Sofia's overarching concern was for her children. Once inside the terminal, they immediately separated the children from her. Thus far, MOIS had given no reasons for her detention. When Sofia had first demanded an explanation as she was briskly ushered out of her home, one of the men slapped her to the floor, right there in front of her children. She had no idea what they intended to do with her poor children.

****

She'd been interred for quite some time now and still wore the same clothes in which she'd first arrived, now drenched with sweat and the smell of mold from the heat inside her prison cell. There was no opportunity to bath. The scant water they'd provided was hardly enough to slack her thirst. The rice she received was dry and tasteless like a second day left-over. But her hunger, thirst and discomfort were minimized by the concern for her children.

The food was delivered once a day by a taciturn guard who ignored her questions. No one had replaced her bucket. They'd not provided her a mattress or even a blanket upon which to sleep. Only the rats visited Sofia. Even they paid scant attention to her. Their attention was fully focused on her rice bowl. She slept in her shoes, fearful that they might gnaw on her toes. One rat had bitten her on the finger while she slept. The bite was becoming infected. She bathed it in her piss as a rudimentary attempt to provide an antiseptic.

There was no way she could count the days other than by her rhythm of sleep. Her cell had no windows to the outside. The only light creeping into her room was from a small observation window. She knew when someone looked in because the light would be blocked.

Nevertheless, she calculated that it was on the fourth day when the isolation was broken. She was gruffly conducted out of her cell by two guards and brought to an interrogation room. It was a small room devoid of any furnishings except the chair. They strapped her into this steel chair which was bolted upon the concrete floor. Then they left the room.

She endured a long period of time in this chair, suffering the discomfort caused by her tight bindings. At last a man entered. He was lean and his face appeared filled with anger. He walked directly up to her, leaned forward and spat a slimy gob directly into her face.

"You are a Jew whore. Who fathered your children?"

She felt the gob slowly disperse down her face. She was numb to the discomfort. This was the end. She accepted it. But she could not accept this for her children. Not for her little boy and little girl! These monsters had no right to harm the two innocents.

"What have you done with my children!" she demanded in a dry voice.

"Who is their father?" he repeated in a threatening tone.

"My husband!"

"So then," he exclaimed as if this was indeed a moment of eureka, "they are little monkey-Jews, as well!"

The interrogator was preparing this Jew whore for her journey out of Iran to Canada. That could prove to be a sticky operation. They had to pass her and the children through Canadian Customs and Immigration authorities. Drugging them to incapacity would not work in this case.

To prevent her from initiating any tricks during transit, the usual technique was applied of immersing the prisoner in gridlock induced by terror and fatigue. In this case the woman must be filled with dread over the well-being of her children. The children themselves would be manageable, but they would travel on a different flight than their mother, and given a promise of seeing her again only if they behaved.

MOIS was responding to a request from their Embassy in Canada. The interrogator now confronting Sofia also knew that this business with the Jew whore and her pair of monkeys had to do with a very hush-hush operation involving Stalin. He was a highly celebrated overseas operative known to most MOIS Agents only by name and exploits. Few had actually ever seen him. Of course, *Stalin* was his code name. It was reputed that this terrorist-agent bore a resemblance to the legendary Soviet leader, especially the way in which he fashioned his moustache.

He'd never met the agent, and he didn't know the details of this current operation. However, he'd heard enough about the daring deeds of Stalin to realize that if this renowned agent were involved, it must portend a major act of terrorism in the works. The project clearly required releasing this whore and her two monkeys to Tehran's Canadian Embassy. His job in this scheme was to break her will so that she could be managed during the journey there.

He withdrew a handkerchief from his pocket. The handkerchief had served to wrap something, and Sofia observed that the white fabric was blood-stained. She watched him as he slowly unfolded the cloth with deliberate care, and then theatrically revealed the contents to her. Craddled in the palm of his extended hand and still nestled in the bloody handkerchief were two small dismembered thumbs. Sofia felt her head swoon, but she fought back to maintain composure.

"These are your children's thumbs," he calmly informed her. "I have questions to ask you. If I am not satisfied with your answers, then on my next visit I will bring you their eyeballs."

Sofia felt the involuntary heave, and tasted the acrid tang of her own watery vomit as it spewed upon her lap, dribbled down her chin and clung to her lips and the sides of her mouth. "No," she feebly uttered.

"Are you familiar with Moustafa Rajai?" He paused, but she did not answer. "Well?" he pressed with menace.

"He is my brother-in-law," she gurgled

"Is he Jew?"

"No."

"What is he?"

"Persian."

"No Persian would marry a Jew. Eyeballs… I will leave immediately and return with them if you do not give me honest answers!"

"Persian," she repeated weakly.

"Why did he marry a Jew?"

"They were at university together."

"Jews don't go to university. They are much too stupid."

Sofia hesitated. It would not serve the welfare of her children for her to take a snipe at his inane proposition. "The government has shown kindness to us," she finally whispered.

"Yes, far too much kindness! Now it is your turn to show gratitude. Listen to me carefully. Are you listening?"

"Yes," she acknowledged.

"MOIS has decided in a moment of extreme benevolence to grant you and your two monkeys exit visas." He paused to let her absorb this news. "But there is a price!" Again he paused, but she only stared at him incredulously.

"Open your mouth! I said open your mouth… wide!"

She obeyed.

He thrust the two dismembered thumbs into her mouth and then covered it with the same hand still holding the bloody handkerchief so that she could not spit them out. "Chew! I said chew!"

He could feel the movement of her jaws. "Swallow them, or I swear I'll make your children orphans right now."

Sofia made muffled sounds of gagging agony, but at last it became clear that she finally had swallowed the contents in her mouth. He smiled and released his hand. "We have many MOIS agents in America. You will cooperate with them. Do you understand? You will work for us. Do you agree?"

She continued to stare at him with utter disbelief.

"The missing thumbs on the left hands of your two children will be a constant reminder that if you betray us---if you do not do exactly as you are told---we will come for them and pluck out their eyeballs. So do not try to be clever. I have done you a favor, after all. This unfortunate event for your little monkeys will convince the Americans that you deserve political asylum. As you can see, we think of everything!"

His deep laugh echoed off the walls of this small room. "Perhaps I should remove your thumb as well; in order to make an even more convincing case for the Americans!"

It crossed her mind to offer him the finger suffering a rat bite. The wound had festered badly, and she believed it was causing her to fever. But he immediately turned away from her and strode out of the room. She continued to occupy her mind with silly thoughts; anything to avoid dwelling upon the indignity of having swallowed the flesh and bone of her children. She could have easily slipped into madness. It was an escape she would welcome. But her concern for the boy and girl compelled her to keep a grip on sanity.

Tohono O'odham Indian Reservation, Arizona

The warehouse was filled with water barrels, food supplies, automatic rifles, small arms and ammunition, gasoline and spare automotive parts. They had four SUV's. Ali was astonished at how cool the air remained inside that "haystack"---as they called it---even now in mid-May as the afternoon heat baked the desert.

The Jordanian had finished the "haystack" project, and provided funds for the provisioning placed inside it. There seemed little purpose left for him at the camp. Ostensibly he was biding his time until Moustache would retrieve him. As far as Ali was concerned, it couldn't happen soon enough.

The man had become a real pain in the ass. He kept giving orders to the Sultan's men which peeved Ali to outright consternation. The Arab muthah-fuckah had absolutely no respect for chain of command. He'd learned early on not to fuck with Ali, so he just kept end-running him. Their competition was causing confusion in the ranks. It became less clear who was the boss. This situation was difficult for the Sultan to abide. If it wasn't that this Jordanian was Moustache's man, he'd have sent the sonovabitch packing with a swift kick from his combat boots.

During the night Ali was awakened by a scream. It was a woman's voice, and sounded as if it came from a distance which would place it outside the compound. The Sultan scrunched barefoot into his boots, and without bothering to tie them he grabbed his sidearm and scurried out of his tent. He wore only a pair of skivvies as he made his way towards the gate.

He heard the scream again, and this time was in a better position to pin-point the origin. There was a craggy elevation outside the compound. Midway up was a cluster of boulders. Ali quickly calculated that the scream came from there. He ran clumsily through the gate and immediately noted with a rush of bad temper that the two sentries on duty had abandoned their posts. As he neared the base of the hill Ali heard muffled noises suggesting that screams of that female had been abated by a hand over her mouth.

A nearly full moon was overhead. It offered sufficient light for Ali to pick his way through the sparse vegetation, and avoid stumbling on the rocks or tripping into the crevices of this precarious desert floor. Even with only starlight, the desert floor which was rich in silicates would reflect radiance to give illumination in the darkness once eyes had adjusted to the scant shine. He felt fatigue in his legs as he began an ascent up the hill.

The noises of the woman were now joined by excited exclamations of men. Then he spotted them, right there behind a boulder. Two men were holding down a writhing body while a third figure with his trousers down around his ankles was clearly fucking her.

As Ali approached, he slowed and took care to make as little noise as possible. The two men disabling the woman were his sentries. The man fucking her was that asshole Jordanian.

He stole to within ten feet of them. "What the hell is going on here?" he suddenly bellowed in his forceful drill instructor's voice.

The two sentries looked up, but continued the grip on their captive as they both cast him shit-eating grins. The Jordanian didn't break stride, but responded in a panting breath, "You can have her next, Sultan. I think she's starting to like it."

As Ali cautiously approached a few more steps he could finally glimpse the unfortunate female. She appeared to be no more than a child in her early teens. "Y'all let her go!" he demanded.

The two sentries quickly drew away from her, but the Jordanian immediately leaned forward and grabbed her with one hand by the throat as he continued to awkwardly pump. Clearly the girl was exhausted. Her resistance was now minimal. Ali leveled his pistol at the man's head.

"I said for y'all to let her go!"

The Jordanian held fast to the female's throat and continued to pump in blatant disregard of the Sultan's command. An explosion echoed in the confines of these boulders, amplifying the sound of Ali's gunshot. The contents inside the target's skull appeared to burst out his forehead, splattering all over the female who began screaming hysterically.

The body above her lurched forward, then to one side and finally sprawled backwards and away from her. Ali side-stepped the lifeless body as it fell near his feet. A second explosion from his pistol resounded among the boulders. In the aftermath was total silence. The woman lay still and she emitted no sounds. Her distorted face pierced by a bullet through the forehead was now splattered with her own blood as well as that of the Jordanian.

Ali had realized that it was a moment in which he would lose the respect and awe of his followers if he hadn't reacted in this way. To have allowed the Jordanian to have his way would have cost him his leadership. He also understood that this hapless girl could not be allowed to remain a witness to the first homicide. He had no idea how Moustache would react to this outcome; but it was done. There was no point in worrying over the matter.

"Who's this girl?" he demanded.

The two sentries remained silent as they looked at each other, not wanting to be the messenger who proverbially gets shot. Finally one of them cleared his throat. "She came to us asking for water, I think. She's one of those Mexicans. She said *agua*. That means water, doesn't it?"

"Yeah, well it sure as shit don't mean 'fuck me'! So, what happened?"

The same sentry replied in a quivering voice, "The Jordanian had come out to pee just as she was approaching us. It was his idea."

"To rape her?"

"Yes."

The other sentry quickly supported this notion. "Yeah, he ordered us to grab her."

"Since when does that muthah-fuckuh give you orders?"

Neither of them volunteered an answer to his question. It was a moot point. Clearly the Arabs tongue would wag no more orders.

Ali contemplated for a moment whether he should shoot his two men as well. No, he would only punish them. They were brothers, and he had a scant enough following as it was. The penalty he would levy is that they must each dig a Pythagorean grave on the hard and rocky desert floor. It would not be an easy task.

"You two muthah-fuckahs are gonna take them bodies back down the hill." He pointed. "There, direkly at the bottom you gonna dig two graves. Now listen up. They gonna be zakly three feet wide, four feet deep and five feet long. The sides of them holes is gonna abut at right angles to the floor. I don' want no sloppy slopes. Do you understand me? And I want the measurements ezack to the inch. When y'all finished, call me. I wish to inspek your work before we bury 'em. If'n your digs are unassepable, I'll shovel out them nex two myself, and throw your dead bodies in 'em. Is that loud and clear?"

He could see his other followers had all been awakened and had gathered at the gate to the compound. This outcome would be an example to them all. Ali was pleased with his reaction. Fuck Moustache!

Mexico City, Mexico

Iran had an Embassy in Mexico City on Paseo de la Reforma. Sneaking in enough C-4 (a very powerful high density explosive sometimes referred to as *plastique*) through diplomatic pouch privileges would have made the ingress an easy matter. From there Stalin could use his *gomero* contacts to convey the C-4 into Sonora and through the tunnel to Ali Ul-Faqr's camp. But now an obstacle faced the Iranian terrorist that made the smuggling of plastique explosives here a settled issue. C-4 wouldn't do. He sat inside their Embassy in Mexico City with a fellow MOIS agent as they discussed the matter.

The MOIS Agent explained to Stalin that regime experts working on the Iranian project to create weapons grade fissionable nuclear material for future bombs had analyzed the information provided to them by Moustafa Rajai. He was an ex-pat engineer employed at the targeted nuclear generating station in America. In the first place, they didn't like the odds of Al-Faqr's soldiers getting into lethal striking range of the radio-active rods that fueled the Palo Verde Nuclear Generating Station, but their real problem lay with the concept of using C-4. Their long analysis in Farsi could be boiled down in English to "a likelihood of success ranging somewhere between scant and none". Therefore, MOIS now had a different plan.

The agent meeting with Stalin explained, "These metal containment enclosures surrounding each of the three generating stations are designed to withstand up to 60 psig of force."

Stalin had no idea what that really meant; but he felt uncomfortable to exhibit his ignorance by asking. So he held his tongue and continued to listen.

"Your little C-4 explosives will be an exercise in futility. Each of these reactors could withstand a jet plane crashing into them. At least that is what they claim, although there is some room for doubt. But it gives an idea of what we're up against. After all, we want to use the approximately 50,000 fuel rods of UO2 (Uranium Oxide-2) in at least one of those three reactors to create an historic explosion that will make 9/11 a mere footnote in the history of jihad against satanic America, Allah willing. It will make the Chernobyl cloud of radiation appear benign by comparison. And it will be a Persian victory, not Arab!"

He paused. It was unclear to Stalin whether the man was merely catching his breath, giving a chance for response, or had finished. Nevertheless, Stalin only nodded to assure this man that he was paying full attention.

The fellow immediately resumed his monolog. "However, there is reason to believe based on the information from Moustafa Rajai that even 55 psig will suffice. It means that you must get through the gates and approach within less than a kilometer of at least one of those metal containment enclosures." Again he paused.

"You said that C-4 would not penetrate the containment walls. So, what is it that we bring within a kilometer of them?

"I said less than a kilometer," the MOIS Agent corrected. "Half a kilometer… just to be sure."

"What are the obstacles?"

"There's only one which really matters. It will be a suicide mission. Can you trust these men you've recruited to drive to their death?"

Stalin extended his jaw to communicate his resolve. "I will do it myself! Only then can I be sure!"

"You shall be blessed by Allah, and be bestowed with the honors of a martyr!"

"What is it I will be driving?"

"A deliver van… it will fit inside a delivery van. That was part of the original C-4 plan, right. You will pose as a contractor just like before, crash through the gate and detonate it when you are within half a kilometer of the containment enclosure."

"It? You still haven't told me the weapon! What will fit inside a delivery van?"

"A nuclear bomb!"

Stalin stared at him with incredulity, "You mean we have already developed one?"

"No. But we have procured one. And it is small enough to fit inside a delivery van."

"Who gave us the bomb? Can they be trusted?"

"That is none of your concern! Do you think that I'm here on a fool's errand?"

Stalin avoided the man's accusing eyes. "How do I detonate it?"

"All this will be explained. The problem is getting the bomb to your tunnel and through your tunnel and then to the Palo Verde site. Clearly, the device must evade Mexican constabulary and their inspection stations on the highways. It's not something we can smuggle in a diplomatic pouch. Then there is the American Border Patrol with which you must contend. I understand you have made arrangements with certain Mexican drug-traffickers?"

Stalin nodded in the affirmative. "Yes but that was for smuggling 40 kilos of C-4, not for a nuclear bomb."

"So, it's a bigger package," the MOIS Agent scoffed. "Are you saying that it can not be done?"

"No, I didn't say that. But it may require a different plan, and I'm sure the new plan will be much more expensive."

The Agent clucked, "Take care concerning expenses. You've already spent a small fortune on your black men's compound, and your charitable impulse to build their mosque. Nonetheless, I await your formulation of a *different* plan. The bomb must be delivered through the gates of Palo Verde to within one half kilometer of a generator. If your plan shows realistic promise, you will get your bomb and your moment to glorify Allah!"

"Where will I receive my bomb? Is it in Iran?"

"No. But it is in a safe place. Anyway, we can not fly it into Mexico. Our best option is to offload from shipboard somewhere along the Yucatan coast. We have consigned a Cuban fishing trawler. From there it will become your responsibility."

"Why so far away? Why not on the Pacific side?"

The MOIS Agent smirked as if he were about to state something clever, "Because Cuba is in the Caribbean."

Stalin sort of got the picture. Nevertheless, he could not imagine successfully smuggling a nuclear bomb across most of Mexico, through the border with America and then on the highways to reach the Palo Verde Nuclear Generating Station which lay approximately three hundred kilometers north of the Ul-Faqr compound. He clucked aloud as he silently considered that detection somewhere along the line was certain. The MOIS organization often astounded him with their amateurish innovations.

Originally, the plan had been to pack off Ali Ul-Faqr and his followers armed with 40 kilos of C-4. They were to sneak into Palo Verde and then penetrate to a containment enclosure where they would blast it with their explosives. The C-4 would be smuggled across the border by a *narco-traficante* of Stalin's choosing, and delivered to the Ul-Faqr compound on the Indian Reservation just north of the border. Stalin had contracted "Gomero" Romero as his "delivery agent". The location of the Ul-Faqr compound resulted from that choice. It needed to lie in easy reach of Romero's tunnel.

Now, MOIS had apparently determined through

their technical staff working from information supplied by the Palo Verde source---Moustafa Rajai---that this C-4 impact would be insufficient to penetrate the containment wall. The plan was breathlessly changed. Stalin liked the part about using a nuclear bomb to disintegrate the steel containment enclosure. But he didn't like how they intended to deliver it.

No, there had to be a more reliable way. Stalin had no intention of engaging himself in a futile martyrdom. He had at the moment no clear notion of what that method could be; but Allah would inspire him with the means necessary to accomplish this undertaking if it was His Will that the mission should succeed. Carrying a nuclear bomb in a van and crashing it through the Palo Verde gates struck Stalin as comedic in its clumsiness.

Culiacan, Sinaloa, Mexico

Many of the successful Mexican *narco-traficantes* maintained an estate in the foothills which overlooked the city of Culiacan and the busy coastline which bounded it to the west. It was still a hub for agricultural produce, and for fishing. Tomatoes, melons, lettuce and such competed with American produce grown in California and Florida for the state-side markets.

In the Sierra Madre Mountains to the east, a second kind of produce competed for American markets... marijuana was flown from dirt STOL airstrips and opium was harvested and refined into heroin from nearby labs scattered throughout the Mexican State of

Sinaloa. Culiacan was the capitol city. There were even labs producing "X" (Ecstasy) and other synthetic drugs in the state. Culiacan was a busy place, and a lot of money passed through a lot of hands in this town just about every day of the year. Because of the means and the routes these smugglers of Culiacan had developed over the decades, they attracted the trafficking of cocaine as well, which they referred to as *blanco*. Heroin was called *negro*.

The *gomeros* got their name from the opium gum which they used to smuggle back in the old days when the Chinese immigrants in Mexico still had a hand in the business. The opium gum was used to produce laudanum, a medicine used to treat coughs and used as a pain-killer or to encourage sleep. It was addictive. And of course opium gum could be smoked as well. Tonics and "snake oils" often contained opium. As recently as World War II and the Korean War, *GI gin* was freely dispensed to military personnel for the treatment of chest congestion. It was a mixture where one of the active ingredients was codeine… an opiate.

The Mexican Revolution began in 1910 and ended in 1920. The new Mexican Constitution included a "loophole" which allowed the government in 1931 to kick out almost all of the Chinese immigrants, especially those in Sonora and Sinoloa. Their opium trade was one of the reasons. No matter, there were plenty of Mexicans eager to become growers, refiners and *narco-traficantes*. The opium business did not suffer. But in those days Culiacan was little more than a sleepy fishing village.

Opiate products as well as cocaine and marijuana actually weren't legally banned in the United States until the Twentieth Century with the advent of Prohibition. *Coca*-cola originally gained popularity by employing a pick-me-up with a mild addictive after-effect. The conniving bottlers added coca leaf extract to their recipe. The FDA (Federal Drug Administration) ended that sleight-of-hand, as well as many, many other questionable remedies such as encapsulating a tape-worm segment and selling it as a one-time effective weight-reducing pill.

However, during World War II, when by this time all the aforementioned drugs had been legally banned, the American government not only had turned a blind eye to the *gomeros*, but made outright purchases from them. The Americans harbored a frantic need for morphine to give comfort to their wounded in battle. Due to the war, sources of opium in Asia had been largely denied them. Domestic growers could not meet the demand. That's when Mexican drug-trafficking took an overarching foothold in Culiacan, and some *gomeros* became quite rich.

In one respect, Stalin was pleased with the demeanor of these Mexican infidels. When they did business, it was relaxed. They would partake of food and beverage, engage in small talk, and exude pleasantness. It reminded him of the way Persians conducted business; and certainly contrasted to the brusque manner of Americans and to a lesser degree even most Europeans.

He was sitting on the veranda inside the walled villa of

"Gomero" Romero. It was this man who had constructed and now controlled the tunnel at the Mexican-American border on the Tohono O'odham Indian Reservation. He was a powerful *narco-traficante*. Initially, he had agreed to smuggle through his channels the C-4 from Mexico City to the tunnel. The deal had been arranged by Stalin. He would enlist Ali Ul-Faqr and his followers to blow up Palo Verde. The Black Muslims were not yet aware of their mission.

'Just as well,' he muttered in his mind's voice. Now the operation had taken on orders of magnitude more complexity. They could have carried their C-4 in backpacks. A nuclear bomb was quite a different matter.

What's more, Stalin could no longer disclose to Romero the true contents of his "package". On the other hand, he needed the channels these *narco-traficantes* employed in order to safely deliver his bomb to the tunnel. However, it would be the height of folly to share with them the fact that they were smuggling a nuclear bomb. They would refuse, or even worse they would sell him out.

Moreover, even if he got the bomb through the tunnel, how would he get it to Palo Verde undetected? It was a dilemma. However, Stalin took solace in his conviction that Allah would provide a way.

Romero set down his glass of beer, wiped his mouth with the back of his hand, and raised his eyes into the fading afternoon sky as he spoke, "You say that you will meet the trawler in Yucatan, and then accompany my men all the way to our tunnel in Sonora where you have your little army encamped? I am curious. Why would you personally take such risks for this… this large Persian carpet? Why must a carpet be smuggled across the border? It is not contraband."

"With all due respect, Sr. Romero, it *is* contraband. Iranian carpets are prohibited by the United States government. As you know, relations between my country and the *gringos* are not friendly."

"Gomero" smiled, and nodded to acknowledge that he understood. He did not know this man by his code-name Stalin. Romero referred to him as "Moustache" It was an appellative he'd conjured on his own when Stalin had responded to Romero's question of how he should address the Iranian by saying, "Call me whatever you wish."

"Moustache, I do not understand. Why do you insist on accompanying my men? Do you not trust them? Do you fear we will steal it? A Persian carpet is not contraband in Mexico. I can buy one even in the *tianges* (open markets). What is so important about this carpet that you feel obliged to put upon yourself such an inconvenience?"

"Well, we haven't paid the duties to legally enter it into Mexico."

"So, why not pay. The sum can't be that enormous."

"It's better not to alert the Mexican officials. They work hand in hand with the Americans."

"Concerning drugs, sometimes; but not when it involves carpets. Get real, Moustache, you can't be worried that the DEA will be bothered over a piece of cloth!"

"It is an extremely important cargo, Sr. Romero. I

would give my life if need be to safe-guard it. This carpet is a gift from the Grand Ayotollah to the Mosque we intend to build in Tucson, Arizona. It is a very large carpet from the Seventh Century according to your Christian calendar, and upon this carpet the Twelfth Imam once sat. We believe that he comes as the Mahdi and shall rule the world. Our Mosque is dedicated to the Twelfth Imam. We further believe that when he returns to this world, he shall seek his carpet upon which to sit, and he will find it in our Mosque."

Romero struggled to maintain a serious demeanor. "I see," he perfunctorily acknowledged. "So tell me, Moustache, when he finally tires of sitting, what will he then do?"

"I told you. He shall be the Mahdi. But before he leaves us, he will destroy the Earth," Stalin responded with a straight face and stern gaze.

Romero scrutinized the Iranian's unyielding composure to affirm that this man was serious about such an insane declaration. Suddenly, Stalin burst into laughter. "Well, it is what the True Believers assert. I respect their piety; but it does not mean that I must share in all their crazy notions, right?"

Romero joined with a belly laugh. It was not humor which had compelled his mirth, but relief. He was reluctant to partner with a madman. Having heard the disclaimer, his confidence in this Iranian slowly reassembled.

"So, Moustache, then you don't believe this religious nonsense?"

"I'm not a religious man, Senyor Romero. But neither do I reject out of hand the teachings of our religious scholars. One can be skeptical without taking sides. These are mysteries for which I leave to those with an inclination to unravel them. I am not so inclined. But I have been commissioned to deliver their precious carpet. That is my professional concern apart from any cosmological consideration."

Romero sighed in a final expression of his relief as he unconditionally accepted the notion that this foreigner was an extremely intelligent man who expressed himself more like a professor than a professional smuggler. So which was he, the Gomero pondered? And what was he really up to? He wouldn't even disclose his name! He'd assembled a gang of *negritos* at the border. For what purpose did he require this entourage? Was it religious, as he claimed; or was he masking their real objective?

All this fuss over a carpet, he scoffed. He found the claim difficult to believe. But if his cargo was not a carpet, then what was it? Was Moustache perhaps a terrorist? The fellow was Iranian after all, and a Muslim. Romero didn't mind. He enjoyed watching on TV when the *gringos* would get a good spanking. It did not affect his business.

"I can make the arrangements for your… uhh, carpet, but it will be extremely expensive, my friend. I'm sorry, but the routes through Quintana Roo and across Mexico are controlled by other cartels. I can trust them, but only if I make it worth their while to be trustworthy. If it were only me, I would do it for you as a favor, you understand? But there are these others."

"How expensive?" Stalin cautiously probed.

"I can only give you an estimate."

"I'm listening."

"I would need one million dollars up front."

Stalin gasped. "That's a lot of money for one carpet."

"It is contraband, Moustache; and it is clearly very precious to your clients."

"But not so risky as drugs. Surely you can recognize the distinction!"

"The procedures are no different for drugs or for carpets, Moustache. You can find cheaper avenues, of course; but do you wish to risk losing your cargo? I can guarantee delivery."

"No, but a million dollars was not anticipated by the True Believers. I do not think that they have this much money. This will come as a complete shock to them!"

"I see. Then I'm afraid that they must do without my participation in smuggling their carpet. But why must this carpet rest in the United States? Perhaps you could build your Mosque here in Mexico, Moustache."

"I cannot dictate such matters! That would be an insult to the Grand Ayotollah. I'm afraid it would leave the True Believers of the American Mosque gravely conflicted. They are my clients. But I must find a less expensive way. Have you any suggestions?"

"Well, there may be an alternative to the million dollars." Romero paused as he leered at the foreigner now staring back at him with an uncomfortable expression.

"I'm listening." Stalin urged.

There may be a way by which you can compensate me for this delivery through a service. I believe it is called a *quid pro quo*."

Stalin straightened his back and placed his hands on his knees as he impatiently repeated, "I'm listening."

"You have your little army on the border near my tunnel, right?"

"Yes?"

"If you could do me a favor, I will return the favor by delivering your carpet through the tunnel. Shall I go on?"

"Please."

"A large consignment by an… uhh… associate is scheduled to move through my tunnel three days from now. It is a consignment which I would like to acquire. The problem is that I do not want to risk a war with this associate. So it becomes a delicate matter, does it not? However, the situation might be resolved with the cooperation of a third party, making it appear that I have been victimized as well as my associate's shipment. It will be dangerous for you in the aftermath. I would not suggest you ever return to Mexico. He has a long reach in this country. Are you following me so far?

Stalin nodded. "You would like my party to intervene on your behalf, acquire the consignment once it's passed through the tunnel and then turn it over to you."

He sighed. "In a very general way, yes, but there are important details. One of those details is that you would deliver it to my *amigos* in Arizona. They will in due course be forced to disclose to the associate your identity. But by that time the consignment will be resold, and my amigos could not be held responsible. After all, at the time they didn't know. But you will be held responsible, Moustache. Is that worth a million dollars to take this risk?"

"Tell me *all* the details. I do understand correctly that in return for my cooperation and the risk, you will deliver the carpet to my camp without charge?"

It was Romero who now nodded in the affirmative. "If you do me this favor, then I will ask for no money." He snatched his glass and took a quick gulp, cleared his throat and then added. "But I will need to hold collateral until you've accomplished your end of the bargain."

Stalin gazed at him for a moment as if trying to fathom the *narco-traficante's* intent. "What do you have in mind?" he finally whispered.

The Mexican set down his glass as he smiled at him, showing several gold teeth. "Your carpet will be my collateral. I will release it once you've delivered the consignment to my *amigos* on the Arizona side. Do we have a deal?"

"Where on the Arizona side must I deliver?"

"It's a small detail which I must coordinate with them."

Stalin paused a moment before again fixing his eyes on "Gomero". There was no way he would turn over control of the bomb to this narco-trafficker. But that was an issue that could be resolved at the border. Getting the bomb there was a first step. His mind was muddled by the complexity of this issue. He needed to break down the process into its component parts and assess his moves step by step.

"But you said your consignment comes in three days? How long will it take for you to deliver my carpet? It must be at least a two day drive down there, and then a two day drive back. I can't be in the Yucatan picking up the carpet and also in my camp directing the acquisition of that consignment at the same time."

"I wouldn't expect you to be, my friend. We will leave Culiacan early tomorrow morning and fly to the border. I'll pick you up at your hotel in the morning and we'll go by my private plane. It's about two hours flying time to the dirt air-strip near my tunnel. You will hand over the command of your troops to one of my men. Then together you and I will fly to Yucatan. Can you make arrangements with your people to deliver tomorrow evening?"

"Tomorrow evening," he muttered out loud in a whisper and stared for a moment into the ether. An airplane, he marveled. He hadn't considered that as a possibility.

Finally he responded, "I will let you know for certain in the morning. That might be rushing them."

"Then we can make it for the following evening."

"How will the carpet be moved? It's almost three meters long. And it is heavy."

"Is it crated?"

"Yes, a wooden crate."

"Don't worry, we'll manage. We'll take my DC-3."

"DC-3?" He had no idea what sort of airplane this might be, but that was an issue he side-stepped. He was unfamiliar with aircraft.

"Will the carpet fit?"

Romero guffawed. "Yes, it will fit. It is designed to haul cargo."

"The carpet is heavy. How will we load it?" These were perfunctory questions which Stalin now asked. He was buying time to consider "Gomero's" offer, and the more he pondered it, the better he liked it. But it was an instinctive enthusiasm. He hadn't yet gathered together the pieces which would formulate a plan. But the idea of air transportation immediately captured Stalin's fancy. It was, in fact, the answer! Allah was revealing His way.

"Trust me, amigo. We were building pyramids throughout Mexico long before Spaniards even knew that the world was round. I think these associates in Quintana Roo can figure out how to load a carpet onto my cargo plane."

"And how do we carry it from the dirt strip to the tunnel?"

Romero clucked a subdued chuckle that imparted irony. "You worry about details that I am responsible to resolve. We have moved material far more cumbersome than a carpet. It is your end of the bargain which I want you to be concerned. You secure that consignment I want and turn it over to my *amigos*. Then I will bring your carpet to the American side of the tunnel. Do we have a deal?"

"But I must accompany you to Quintana Roo. You understand that? They will never turn over the carpet to you if I am not present."

"Of course!" Romero assured as he extended his hand across the table for a shake.

Stalin slowly raised his arm. He still needed to get approval before he could consummate the pact. However, he understood the time constraints. He had no plan yet; but he could feel the Hand of Allah impatiently pushing him. He thrust his arm forward and grasped Romero in a firm handshake. If the project was to proceed, then clearly it must do so with the help of this man, "Gomero" Romero, Stalin concluded. And if in the end he decided against it; well then he would never see this narco-trafficker again, so the handshake wouldn't matter.

Tonopah, Arizona…
Palo Verde Nuclear Generating Station

Moustafa Rajai was bedeviled with confliction. Since his second visit to Ottawa, he'd increasingly suffered headaches, insomnia, and a burning indigestion. He'd become offensive to his wife and children, suddenly erupting in anger over trivial matters. His boss had noticed a change in the employee's behavior as well and called Moustafa into his office.

After inviting him to sit, the boss plunged into his chair behind the desk, and issued a sigh. "What's wrong, Moose?"

Moustafa gazed at his boss several moments before responding. "What do you mean?"

"Are you having problems at home?"

"Why do you ask?"

"C'mon, Moose. It's not just me. Everybody you work with has noticed how... uhh, jumpy you've become the last several weeks. They're starting to avoid you. We're a team. You can't bring your problems from home to work with you. It's not fair to the others. I want to help. But you've got to level with me, okay?"

Moustafa felt tears well into his eyes. He'd been wrestling with a particular notion ever since the return from his second trip to Ottawa when he'd met briefly with Sofia and the two children. He'd observed the tiny stumps where the left thumbs of her children had been severed. Sofia was thin and drawn, her eyes had dark rings. He dared not relate this to his wife. He felt panic for them. But there was an even darker force which haunted his sleep and every waking moment. Guilt occluded his mind and followed him like a shadow. He had comprised his integrity.

He was not a religious man; but Moustafa nevertheless was a man who cherished his self-ordained principles. He'd realized from the beginning that this project to rescue his wife's sister and the children would place him on an extremely slippery slope. Once he'd begun the slide, there seemed to be no stopping it. And now he'd hit bottom.

The notion he entertained still remained in the

shadows of his mind. The cost of purging himself would be immense. But the demon he harbored was slowly consuming him. He could only exorcise it by bringing this creature into the light of day, like destroying a vampire for which truth would serve as the wooden stake.

However terribly bad he felt for poor Sofia and for the shame it would bring to his family, the guilt he felt stemmed largely from his conviction that MOIS was planning a destructive assault on PVNGS, and he had aided and abetted them. His co-workers were being betrayed by him. But there was even a more abhorrent theme. It was what his children would think of him when they had learned about this travesty which he'd committed.

They would discover that he was a traitor who had endangered the lives of hundreds of thousands of Arizonans; and frankly, no one could calculate how far the collateral damage might reach beyond the initial blast. He felt ashamed and dirty. It was mostly because of his children that he could not bring himself to confess; but not doing so was slowly driving him mad.

He would go through bouts of blaming his wife, and twice had even struck her down. Moustafa simply couldn't go on this way, but there was only one logical egress. He'd conceived an exit strategy, but garnering the will to execute it did not come easily.

He couldn't hold back the catharsis induced by the questions coming from his boss. His shoulders began to heave. He bowed his head as tears began to stream down his face and he gurgled trying to stifle his sobs.

The boss patiently abided, although he'd not anticipated such a dramatic reaction to his appeal. Finally he ventured in a low soothing voice. "Want to tell me about it, Moose?"

Moustafa finally raised his head and stared at him through teary eyes. "Will you promise to keep this confidential?"

The boss was slow to respond. "I can't make any promises until I know what it is you wish to tell me. But I'm here to help. I'm not just your boss, Moose. I'm your friend. Trust me."

Again there passed an interval before Moustafa replied. "I want immunity… in writing. Can you arrange that?"

The boss looked at him with a flabbergasted expression. "Immunity…immunity from whom… from what?"

"The FBI. I have things to tell them. Some very important things, but I will only tell them if they give me written immunity."

The boss stared at him silently, exhibiting no more animation than a statue.

"Can you do that for me?" Moustafa pressed.

"You want me to call in the FBI?"

Mostafa nodded in the affirmative, then leaned to one side, pulled out a handkerchief from his pocket and dabbed away the wet streaks on both cheeks and then the beads of sweat on his forehead.

"Can you tell me in a very general way what this is all about?"

"I will say nothing until I've been given immunity.

Then I will tell everything, I promise. And they must provide me and my family with a new identity as well. What I have to say will put my family in mortal danger."

Moustafa had thought about his poor son who was prepared to enter university, and now would have to abort those plans. He'd thought about the consequences for Sofia and her two children. He'd thought about having to start all over in a new career that would be low profile and probably no more remunerative than clerking at a convenience store or driving a taxi. But no matter, he simply could not abide the possible tragedy which he'd unconscionably abetted.

He needed a release from this demon. Anyway, if his premonition of what MOIS had in mind was correct, soon there would be no more jobs at Palo Verde, and if he remained here to the end, there would be no more life for himself or for his colleagues. To purge his soul was the only practical solution to this dilemma.

FBI Field Office, Phoenix, Arizona

Agent Leslie Nellis was sitting with her supervisor. The meeting had been hastily improvised at her insistence. The expression on the supervisor's face clearly reflected that he was not pleased with this sudden intrusion. He motioned for her to sit. She had a briefcase in one hand and a voice recorder in the other. She set the voice recorder on his desk.

"I just cancelled a 5:10 tee-time, Agent Nellis. It was

with two of my superiors visiting me from headquarters. They were not particularly thrilled by my sudden dedication to duty. I hope your emergency has redeeming value which will duly impress them."

She was the junior Agent here. Phoenix was her first permanent assignment. The supervisor did not cotton to female agents in general, and this one in particular chaffed at his sensibilities. She seemed to almost prance with puppy eagerness; and she talked like his teenage daughter. He'd been uneasy from the moment this surfer-tanned, sun-bleached blond had uttered her first hello to him. He recalled at their introduction that in answer to his question concerning how she liked Phoenix, the neophyte Agent had answered, "Like, I'm kind-a gonna miss the beach".

There was a serious thrust by FBI Human Resources Department to saturate the Bureau minions with a reasonable number of females. Well, it wasn't just the FBI; it was a common goal throughout constabulary organizations not only at the Federal level, but even at State and local. The office here in Phoenix now had three females, but Agent Leslie Nellis was the only "recruit" of that gender. The other two had previous experience before reporting here. He also understood that to some degree his reaction to her was the same "old breed/new breed" generational gap that dogged every profession since time immemorial.

The other two females were competent Agents he had to admit; but he had grave reservations about this newest one. Well, she'd graduated from UCLA law school, so she couldn't be entirely bereft of gray matter, he granted. Moreover, she'd passed the California bar. Anyway, he cautioned himself, one must be extremely tactful with these ladies. And not just in the arena of physical contact. More than one supervisor had landed in hot water by appearing to psychologically harass a female Agent.

She let out a sigh as she stood in front of the desk behind which he was sitting. "Frankly, sir, I think I'm operating way over my pay grade on this one."

He again motioned for her to sit down, and this time she did so. "Which one?" he asked a bit more caustically than he'd intended to sound. He needed to take care, he again silently cautioned to himself. The last thing he needed was some fragile female ego to screw up his career.

"Which pay grade?" she asked with incredulity and unblinking eyes.

"No, Agent Nellis, to which *case* do you refer?"

"Oh," she muttered in a sigh, and then took in a deep breath. "It's an engineer at PVNGS. He claims to be cooperating in a conspiracy with the Iranian Embassy in Ottawa to blow up the place.

"Ottawa or Palo Verde?"

Leslie stared at him with clear annoyance. "Palo Verde, sir! Would you like to hear it?" She pointed to the voice recorder.

"Give me an overview first."

His name is Moustafa Rajai. He's Iranian, but claims to be a naturalized citizen. He lives in Peoria with his wife and three children… first marriage. He's worked at

Palo Verde for nearly twenty years. His boss was the one who called our office. The boss was present during the interrogation and confirms all the personal information concerning Mr. Rajai."

The supervisor interrupted impatiently, "What's the conspiracy?"

"To blow up Palo Verde, sir."

"So why's he telling you this?"

"Remorse, as best as I can tell. Like, it wasn't easy getting this out of him, sir. You'll understand when you listen." She pointed to the recorder again.

He motioned with his hands for her to continue. "Go on."

"Uhh… I had to insinuate certain concessions on our behalf… I mean, I didn't make any promises, understand. I just assured him I'd do everything possible to get him what he demanded. Well, I sort of promised him, but it was the only way I could get him to talk… and…"

The supervisor threw up both hands for her to desist. His face frothed with consternation. "Settle down, Agent Nellis! Now tell me in as few words as possible what this engineer's demands were and what you promised him."

"Well, like I don't think what I said constituted an outright promise, sir! I mean…"

Again he threw up a hand to halt her. "I'll make that determination when I review the transcript. Just answer my questions, okay?"

"He asked for written immunity and a new identity and relocation for him and his family, sir."

"In return for what?"

"All that he knows concerning this conspiracy."

"How much did he tell you?"

"Only that he's involved in a conspiracy with the Iranian Embassy in Ottawa to blow up Palo Verde. He refuses to give any details until we satisfy his demands."

The supervisor let out a low sigh. "Leave the recorder here. I'll have a listen. I want you to do a background on him and a thorough credit check. My guess, the guy is up to his ears in debt and has come up with a scheme to duck his creditors. Did he indicate to you what his motives were for entering this conspiracy?"

"No sir. It was difficult---well you'll hear it---I mean the guy didn't want to say anything until he had a written immunity from us."

"You didn't give him that did you?"

"Of course not sir, I mean not in writing, I sort of suggested I would make arrangements and bring him down here. I mean there was nothing binding in my statement. Like I said, sir, I think this assignment is above my pay grade. Uhh, his boss wants to know if he should suspend Mr. Rajai?"

"Not now. Tell him to keep the guy working, but keep a close eye on the bastard, and immediately report anything he does out of the ordinary."

He discerned that she had reacted with a startled expression to his use of the word *bastard*. He quickly retreated. "Sorry, that one just sort of slipped out. Excuse my blunt phraseology. Anyway, let's gather up a case file, and then we'll take it from there. Has their Security Office been notified?"

"I don't know, sir."

He slammed a fist on his desktop. "Well, find out! They need to be involved." Dammit, he silently cursed himself. Be nice! "On second thought, never mind! I'll do it myself. I personally know their Chief."

She cast a sullen glare at him. "You seem angry at me, sir. I wasn't given a whole lot to work with. I had no idea what I was walking into. The guy at Palo Verde called our office and said there was an issue we needed to investigate, and that they'd go over the details down there. So the office sent me. You were in a meeting with those big-shots from headquarters. I mean, I had no idea how to prepare, sir."

After a long pause, the Supervisor gathered a pained smile into his face. "I understand," he stated in a tone of voice meant to assure her. He was well practiced in this method having used it many times on his teen-age daughter. He also understood that the Senior Agent who'd sent her to Palo Verde harbored "old breed" resentment for this "valley-girl" recruit. He clearly had not been helpful in preparing her. Moreover, she was right. This case probably was above her pay-grade.

Romero's Air-strip,
Tohono O'odham Indian region, Sonora

It seemed risky to Stalin that they intended to pass through the tunnel in broad daylight; but Romero had pointed to a prominent hill about half a kilometer due south of the dirt runway. "The border is just on the other side of that hill. They can sweep the entire area from up there," he assured. "When they give us the signal, we'll proceed."

"They?"

"I have an amigo there. He cooperates in my business." He cocked his head and offered a sheepish smile. "Well, actually he works for me. He is in radio communication with the shack." Romero swung his finger from pointing out the hill to indicating a small structure near a the wind-sock. It had a prominent antenna extending from the roof.

Romero was in two-way communication with his small group who tended the air-strip from the ramshackle building. There was no tarmac or tie-downs. They'd parked their plane some distance from the shack, and had been met by the SUV in which they now sat. It was air-conditioned.

Romero explained that his men were in communication with someone on the hill, and would signal once they'd determined that the border was clear of *Migras* (U.S. Border Patrol). Lately there were also the *pinche* Minutemen who roosted near the border with binoculars in one hand and a beer in the other; at least that was the assessment of Romero and his ilk.

Four men sat in the SUV alongside the aircraft, a driver and Romero in front; Stalin and Felipe Gomez in the back. The SUV engine was idling and the air-conditioner continued to cool the interior. It was almost noon, and the desert was already very hot. Stalin looked around. Parts of Iran resembled this landscape.

"Anyway," Romero added, "this time we carry no contraband. Felipe has an American driver's license. I will wait in the SUV while you two go across."

He twisted so as to face the back seats and gazed inquisitively at the Iranian. "You have some American papers, don't you? If you're stopped, just say you got lost. What can they do to you?"

"No, I don't have papers," Moustache sheepishly admitted. "Well I have a visitor's visa, but it's expired."

"No papers, no license, no nothing?" Romero fulminated. "Well, fuck... that's *your* problem. I ain't your baby-sitter. How do you expect to operate?"

"What I'm doing does not require legal paperwork," Stalin snapped back, clearly agitated by this man's sudden disparagement; but he quickly gathered his wits and cooled his head. "Look, you can send Felipe to the camp. He can fetch my man, Ali. Bring him back to the SUV and we can discuss the arrangements together."

"Does this guy Ali have papers?"

"He's American."

Romero sighed. "Then there's no reason for you to go tthrough the tunnel. You can wait with me." He nudged Felipe Gomez. "Drive to the tunnel. The camp is only a few hundred meters on the other side."

"You'll see the compound," Stalin added.

"I'm aware of your camp," Felipe remarked.

Earlier, the Iranian had been energized by his experience flying here. Romero piloted what he referred to as his DC-3, although he later disclosed that it was actually a BT-67. Anyway, he'd invited Moustache into the cockpit and allowed him to sit in the right seat. Once they'd leveled off, he'd urged his guest to take control. Although reluctant at first, this man who'd never piloted a plane before in his life put his hands on the controls.

Romero pointed to the compass and explained the heading this new student needed to maintain; and explained the elevation indicator. They were flying at 9,000 feet. He clarified the attitude indicator for Moustache. By the time they'd crossed into Sonora, the Iranian felt like a pro at handling the aircraft. It was as if Allah had inculcated him with the faculty to fly, he silently gasped. Of course, he did realize that flying an airplane straight and level was a far cry from being able to take off and land it. He sensed that Allah had not taken him across that bridge.

"You're a natural," Romero had complimented at one point.

"How old is this bird?" Stalin asked, now flushed with enthusiasm. "Weren't they flying these planes in World War II?"

Romero shook his head in agreement. "They were flying DC-3's in World War II. In fact, the first one was made in 1935. But they had piston engines. The plane you are now flying technically is not a DC-3; it's a BT-67. This one was manufactured in 1996. Originally it was bought by the Guatemalans, but then I ... uhh... bought it from them."

"Then why do you call it a DC-3?"

"Habit… we actually used them in the old days. The BT-67 is a DC-3 conversion, only they go faster and can carry more payload. But they can still land on the short *pinche* dirt strips. They are a perfect vehicle for my business."

"What does BT mean?"

"Basler Turbo… those two engines are turbo-props made by Pratt-Whitney."

"So then," Stalin mused, "I am a turbo pilot!"

Felipe Gomez was the designated guy for representing Romero's interests in the plot to overcome and seize the consignment this *narco-traficante* coveted. Stalin knew that Ali Ul-Faqr would chafe at the proposed intervention of this outsider; but the man would need to come to terms with the notion. Stalin had intended to take him aside and explain matters as soon as they arrived at camp. But he still had not formulated a plan. But that fact he dared not share with Ali.

It was good that he would meet with Ali on the Mexican side. He would have "the Sultan" away from the others in his group. It would be easier for the black man to swallow his ego being away from his followers. They would probably proceed with Ali back to the dirt strip, Stalin calculated. No doubt he would be struck with admiration to see the BT-67 sitting there and realize the impressive conveyance by which the Iranian had arrived. And Stalin would brag that he'd flown it. He liked this arrangement much better.

He turned to Felipe Gomez. "Tell Lewis Reddy I want the Jordanian to also come here."

"The Jordanian," Felipe affirmed.

He nodded to endorse that the Mexican had it right. However there was something hanging in this project which caused Stalin a bit of anxiety. When he'd left this morning from Culiacan, he'd still not heard back from his counterparts at the Embassy in Mexico City about the rendezvous in Quintana Roo. There was no means of cell phone reception out here in the middle of the Sonoran Desert, he chafed. He'd nevertheless assured Romero this morning that the rendezvous was a go; but only the specific time was still in question.

"No problem," the Mexican soothed. "I know a place in Quintana Roo where we'll stay. It's full of little round faced Mayan girls with big tits and tight pussies. We'll have a good time!"

"I hope they have cell phone reception there too," Stalin groused. "I need to talk with my people."

"So, who's stopping you?" Romero countered in a smart-alecky voice. He had his telephone holstered to his belt. He leaned to the side and pulled it out. "Here, you wanna talk with somebody?" He waved the cell phone directly in front of the Iranian's nose. "Here, talk!"

"How can it work out here?" Stalin protested.

"With the *pinche* satellite, amigo!" he responded, staring with incredulity at the man for having asked such a silly question. "Don't you have them in camel country?"

Of course he was aware of satellite telephony! Buy MOIS avoided using them. It was believed that the American NSA had a SigInt network that monitored overseas satellite telephone traffic. Under the circumstances, Stalin decided nevertheless to take that risk. He needed to arrange the rendezvous.

FBI Field Office, Phoenix, Arizona

"Good morning, sir," Leslie Nellis chirped as she entered the Supervisor's office and boldly approached his desk where she laid out her findings.

This morning, at his sudden and seemingly urgent request, Leslie had brought to him the Mustafa Rajai file which she'd thus far assembled during all of yesterday in lieu of his instructions given the previous afternoon. He seemed agitated, she immediately noted. However, he didn't immediately reach for the bulky folder when she laid it on his desk-top.

She'd offered to put all the information on a disk for him. It would have been faster. All the information she'd gathered was digitally stored. But he insisted on print-outs… a file. So she wasted nearly thirty minutes printing and collating. In some ways, she mused, he was a dinosaur. Having delivered the goods, she was about to turn and leave, but he held up his hand and then motioned for her to sit. No one else was in his office.

"Give me an overview," he requested in a soft voice that appeared almost overcautious in its civility. "I'll go through his file later. Does he have financial problems?"

She shook her head in the negative. "None that I can uncover, sir." Leslie knew that in saying this she was blowing her boss's pet theory of what had motivated

Moustafa Rajai in the first place to make this sudden confession of complicity to destroy Palo Verde.

He didn't hide his dissatisfaction with that answer. "So, what have you uncovered, Agent Nellis?"

"Like, he did make two trips to Ottawa, Canada, sir; and one of them was less than two weeks ago."

"Alone? With his family? Any connections or relatives there?"

"Alone, sir."

"Both times?"

She affirmed with a nod.

"How long ago was the first trip?"

"A few months ago… uhh… the exact dates are in the file, sir."

The supervisor acknowledged that he understood the file would contain such details, and held his tongue which ached to lash her with sarcasm. She shifted uncomfortably as he continued to gaze at her. "Well?" he finally urged.

"Like, maybe I should start at the beginning sir. Mr. Rajai graduated engineering in Tehran. After the Iranian Revolution occurred, and y'know, they took the American hostages… and…"

"Yes, Agent Nellis, I know." He stated through clenched teeth. "Were you even born then?"

"No sir." She paused, but he made no further comment. "Like, uhh, shall I continue?"

"Please!"

"Anyway, he came to the United States on a student

visa and took an advanced course in nuclear engineering at BYU."

"Is he Mormon?"

"Who?"

"Moustafa Rajai!"

"No sir, he is Muslim. Oh, like you mean because he went to BYU?"

"Not where you'd expect a Muslim to enroll. I'm surprised they accepted him."

"Maybe they have a cultural diversity program, sir."

"They might now; but I doubt if they had one in the early 80's."

"By the way, sir, his wife is Jewish. And here's what's interesting. The sister of his wife has applied for political asylum to the U.S., and Rajai is filing as her sponsor."

"Does she live in Ottawa?"

"As far as I know, she's still in Iran, sir."

"So no connection between Ottawa and the sister?"

"Not that I know of. But like maybe he's applying to Canada for her asylum as well."

"Tell me, Agent Nellis, do you know where he is as we speak?"

"Mr. Rajai?"

"Yes, Mr. Rajai."

"No, sir." She glanced at her watch. "I would suppose at work."

"Wrong. He never showed up for work. I received a call from PVNGS Security this morning informing me of his absence."

"Maybe he's sick."

"Well, his wife is in serious condition. She was received by the Emergency Room at approximately 11:30 last night. According to one of the children, Moustafa had beaten her and than ran out of the house, jumped into his car and drove off."

"Has he been apprehended?"

"Not yet. The police are looking for him."

"Where does that leave our investigation, sir?"

"I'm sure the police will find him. In the mean time I want you to go to the hospital where they have Mrs. Rajai. Wave your badge and see if the doctors will let you have a few words with her. Do you know what to ask?"

"Like, why did he beat her up?"

"Well, that would be interesting, I'm sure. I'd also like you to ask if this incident has anything to do with her sister. And what does she know about the Palo Verde scheme. Is there anyone in particular she suspects might be tied up in this scheme with him? Do you have his bank accounts and credit cards?"

"They're in the file, sir."

"Confirm with the wife if he had a large sum of cash or traveler's checks."

"Yes, sir."

"Personally, I still think blowing up the NGS is a hoax he's perpetrating. PVNGS Security agrees with me on that. The bastard has something else up his sleeve! Whoops, I did it again, didn't I? I apologize for using profanity in your presence, Agent Nellis. It just sort of slipped out."

She looked at him quizzically for a moment, and then a mischievous smile slowly turned her lips. "Like, sir, with all due respect, I appreciate your sensitivity, but frankly I don't give a fuck!"

Guane, Cuba

Guane is situated on the eastern tip of the main island in a protected bay out of which fisherman sail into the Yucatan Channel to cast their nets. The town is situated more than one hundred miles from Havana. Stalin's cargo had been flown into Havana on a chartered flight. From there it was trucked to Guane.

MOIS had chartered a fishing trawler not unlike many others which skimmed these waters for the fruits of the sea. It would carry the bomb across the Yucatan Channel to El Paraiso in the Mexican state of Quintana Roo. El Paraiso has an airport. It serves as hub for visitors wishing to visit the archeological sites surrounding Tulum a few miles to the east of El Paraiso.

Stalin had gotten clearance from Mexico City. They informed him that the "carpet" was on its way. They agreed on El Paraiso, which Romero had suggested as the rendezvous point. He'd used this connection many times before to pick up "white cargo" from Columbia and Peru. Romero was well-connected with the *narco-traficante* boss there, Senyor Guillermo Ray. This man had the state and local authorities in his pocket. He "owned" Quintana Roo.

The MOIS Agent on board the trawler looked after

the wooden box now wrapped in canvass. It remained above deck. The Agent was wary of this delicate cargo which had the potential to combust him and everything else in a five kilometer radius. He wanted to keep handling of the wooden box to a minimum, and so he refused the Captain's suggestion to stow it below deck. The Captain announced that they were prepared to embark. He assured the MOIS Agent that the weather was good and that they would arrive in El Paraiso early tomorrow morning.

Nevertheless, the MOIS Agent accompanying this shipment felt uneasy. At Havana, as anticipated, the clearance had been routine. However, the only assurance he had that the disembarkation of his cargo in El Paraiso would avoid inspection by the Mexican authorities was from Stalin, whose only further assurance came from a sleazy *narco-traficante* named "Gomero" Romero.

His superiors had signaled him to proceed. Technically, they were responsible; but in reality he too would be held accountable if things went wrong. That's simply how things worked. He would share in the consequences of failure. They wouldn't be pretty.

He turned to the Ukrainian standing beside him at the ship's railing. English was their only common language. It made their exchanges laborious. The Ukrainian spoke English with a heavy accent. He would have to communicate technicalities of arming the bomb to Stalin. That also worried the Agent. He'd never actually met Stalin, and therefore had no grasp of how fluent his MOIS counterpart was in the English language.

The Ukrainian had met him in Guane just last evening. But they had avoided any substantive conversation at the hotel. Now on board the trawler he felt that their exchanges were secure. He nudged at the arm of this man who wore a goatee under gaunt pock-marked cheeks. The Ukrainian bore a cauliflower nose, but the most prominent facial feature was heavy eyebrows flecked with gray hairs which touched his thick wire-rimmed spectacles giving his eyes a sinister cast.

"Where did you learn your… uhh… trade?" the Iranian asked.

"What do you mean, *my trade?*"

"Nuclear devices… how did you gain expertise in such matters?"

"Did you ever hear of Chernobyl?"

"You mean the reactor accident?"

"Yes."

"Of course I did."

"I was one of the engineers held responsible. I helped design Unit 4."

"That was the reactor which failed?"

"Yes."

The MOIS Agent offered a shrug of his shoulders. "Apparently you lived to tell about it," he finally remarked.

"Yes, I managed to escape to Yugoslavia. From there I made my way to Spain. It was 1986. Escape was no longer so difficult; especially if you had friends and some *blat*.

"Blat?"

"*Mordida*… uhh, bribe money."

The MOIS Agent had been staring into the harbor. He now turned to the man. "So, you will arm the bomb after we offload it in El Paraiso? How safe will it then be to move the bloody thing around? Can something go wrong?"

"Don't worry," the Ukrainian admonished without looking directly at the Agent.

He resented the smirk which had accompanied the man's response. "It's my job to worry. I don't want another Chernobyl."

"Your job is to worry? Then you will have a painful life. I would not want your job."

"Why have you avoided answering my question?"

"Because it is a silly question. We have a nuclear device. It will be armed. How can anything so volatile be perfectly safe? On the other hand, I do not lead a painful life, so I seek to preserve it. In my own interest I shall not take a perceived risk outside of what I have agreed to take. As long as my instructions are properly followed, there will be no premature ignition. How do you propose to deliver the bomb?"

"What does that question have to do with mine?"

"It affects the way in which we must achieve ignition. There is more than one approach, but I need to know the situation in order to meet your specific needs."

The Agent paused as he mulled over his answer. The Ukrainian continued staring into the waters of the bay without gazing at him. Finally the Agent answered, "It will be loaded aboard an aircraft and flown to the border.

From there it will be taken by van to the target. It's roughly a two hour drive. The roads this van will use may be very bumpy. That was my concern."

"Then you will need a delayed ignition. The van must be given time to get away… at least thirty or forty kilometers. How much time will that require?"

"There is no need for delay."

"But that will be a suicide mission for the driver."

"No, it will be an act of martyrdom for the sake of Allah. You must arm it for immediate ignition. How will it be triggered?"

"I can construct it as easily as a button or toggle switch. I can also rig a remote ignition, but that is more complicated. I also would need to procure a pair of cell phones. I can create whatever ignition system serves your purpose. Do you have a workshop for me in El Praiso?"

"Not in El Paraiso. You must accompany your bomb to a compound we have on the other side of the border with America. Our martyr will meet us in El Paraiso." He avoided using the code-name Stalin. *Martyr* would obfuscate any clue to the identity of his MOIS colleague. The less this Ukrainian knew the better.

The Agent then added, "He is bringing an airplane. It will fly us to the border. There we have a secure means of crossing."

"Nobody said anything about me crossing the border. That is out of the question."

"Well, there is no safe place that we have in El Paraiso. The camp is where we can do such things safely."

The Ukrainian turned to the Agent and sternly responded, "I refuse!"

"Then you won't be paid!"

"I've already been paid. Do you think I am such a fool? The agreement was that I would arm the bomb in El Paraiso and instruct your...uhh... martyr, and then the trawler will return me to Guane. That is the bargain, and the terms can not be changed."

The Agent had no way of immediately confirming this. On the other hand, he didn't feel that it would be prudent to attempt strong-arming this technician. The success of their operation rested in part upon this man's expertise.

"Is it more money that you want?"

"I will go to El Paraiso and no further."

"But smuggling a live bomb across the border is taking an unnecessary risk. We can not anticipate what might be encountered. It makes much more sense to arm it on the other side."

"That is your decision, but I intend to return with you to Cuba on this trawler. I will go no further into Mexico than El Paraiso! If you want me to arm it, then that is where it must be done. It's possible also to do so aboard this boat. A rather crude facility, but I'll manage."

The Agent stared menacingly at the Ukrainian, but this recalcitrant fellow averted his eyes back to the bay and let that taunting smirk slip once again across his lips. The Iranian finally sighed, "When we go ashore tomorrow morning, I will discuss with my colleague what arrangements we can make for you to do your work. But working on it here aboard the trawler will be a rather public venture, don't you think? This crew has no idea what we have on board, and I don't think it would be wise to let them in on out little secret."

"As you wish, but I'm glad we've arrived at a civil resolution. You must understand something. I am not a part of the organization from whom you purchased your bomb. I contracted with them to do this little piece of technical work. It is they who have paid me, and I am following the agreement stipulated by them. It is better if there does not come hard feelings between us. After all, we are working together, correct?"

"I just follow my orders," the Agent sighed.

"Yes, and you worry," the Ukrainian chuckled.

Merced Hospital, Phoenix, Arizona

Leslie Nellis hit some nerve-wracking traffic snarls traveling to the west side of Phoenix. There wasn't any particular reason for her to be in such a hurry; nonetheless, a sense of urgency gripped the young lady. The details in this Moustafa Rajai case had left her mind in a muddle. She wanted to penetrate the mystery. Perhaps his wife could shed some light. Anyway, being in a hurry was second nature to Leslie, especially when she sat behind the wheel of an automobile.

It was the early stages of afternoon rush hour which within another thirty minutes would finally paralyze to a crawl the freeways and other major arteries of the city.

Unfortunately she had no choice but to plunge into this mounting morass of motor vehicles in order to get to the hospital where they'd reported taking Mrs. Rajai. All the opportunities for egress from downtown Phoenix to the west-side would be clogged. Actually, there weren't really that many options available to her going in that direction.

At least there was one redeeming element which rewarded her endurance of the chaotic traffic. She was an XM subscriber, and took this downtime inside her car to listen on her favorite channel, the *Sixties Decade*, especially when "Motor-mouth" Young was hosting it. She loved the "sixties", at least as they were portrayed in the movies which were set in that period. She dug the purported life-style and she adored the music.

Now, having just parked in one of the visitor's spaces allocated by the Merced Hospital, she'd reluctantly switched off the ignition to her car, which extinguished her radio sounds as well. *Herman and the Hermits* had just started playing. "Like, work can be a real bitch!" she quietly sighed with disappointment at having to tune out the music.

To her pleasant surprise, inside the hospital there were no doctors obstructing her way to a visit with the patient, Mrs. Moustafa Rajai. She'd confirmed what her Supervisor had stated. Just like he said, the lady had been taken here after having suffered a beating at the hands of her husband. One of her children had called 911. That's what the police report confirmed.

According to the police, Mrs. Rajai's condition was reported to be serious, which is what encouraged the Agent to suppose there might be resistance to her visit by the attending physician. However her initial impression upon observing the lady was that Mrs. Rajai did not appear in what Leslie would have imagined to be *serious condition*.

When Leslie had arrived at the hospital, she depended upon the signs for directions having never visited this hospital before. There were several wings, and it was unclear to her where the main entrance lay. She knew to follow the signs because she'd been to hospitals before, thanks mostly to her mother. Anyway, experience in this matter had taught her that going to the "Admittance Office" proved a superior source for information than going to the "Information Booth".

Leslie avoided approaching one of the clerks there and instead headed straight for the nurse in attendance at Admittance. She immediately stated who she wished to visit, using a brusque official tone of voice. The lady had taken one look at the FBI Agent credentials which Leslie flipped at her and immediately took a sideways step and placed her hands on the keyboard. She typed something into her computer, and after a moment she glanced up at the Agent and stated the room number.

"I need to visit her." Leslie informed matter-of-factly.

The nurse offered a curt nod for her to proceed. "The main elevators are over there," she pointed. "But if you take that corridor to my right, and go half way down, you'll see a single elevator. Take it to the third floor. Room 331 is just around the corner, maybe four doors down.

"There's a map by the elevator," she'd then called out, apparently an afterthought. Leslie had already turned and begun her clickity-clack of heels against the floor as she hurried towards the corridor.

She'd taken the single elevator and ascended to the third floor. As promised, Room 331 was around the corner and four doors down the hall. The door was closed. Her first impulse was to knock. Leslie resisted the impulse, took in a breath and opened the door. She paused momentarily before crossing the threshold in order to survey the situation.

There were two beds in the room, but only one of them was occupied. In it there was a woman, and Leslie imagined that the lady could be of Middle-Eastern origins judging by her hair and olive skin. However, her facial features could have been anybody's guess. They showed definite signs of trauma.

Leslie was expecting Mrs. Rajai to look Middle-Eastern; nonetheless she found it unsettling to discern nationalities by scrutinizing a person's physical features. Somehow, it seemed to her presumptuous and judgmental. It was a habit that easily led someone to begin profiling, and she personally believed that profiling was a dangerous practice for law enforcement to embrace. She'd argued this point countless times with her peers.

"Once the "perps" are onto your profile; like, they're gonna avoid showing that appearance and you're gonna get blind-sided! Besides, it's unconstitutional according to the ACLU."

Anyway, the lady had a prominent nose that one might associate with Middle-Easterners. The size was exaggerated by some swelling and discoloration near the top of the bridge. Moreover the face certainly showed an aftermath of battery, especially one lip which was puffed. It offered a color that reminded Leslie of raw beef liver. There was some coloring around one eye and below the eye there showed a swollen break in the skin which prize-fighters sometimes refer to as a "mouse".

Apparently there were no broken limbs, nor a bandage wrapping her head which might have provided evidence of a concussion. The lady was awake, propped with a pillow at her back as she sat in bed reading a magazine. She had no visitors.

Although this woman looked nothing like Leslie's Mom who was a blonde petite over-the-hill housewife and who'd once dreamt of a career in the movies, but now lived as a divorcee existing on 'Mamma's little helpers'; for some reason this hospital scene brought Mom to Leslie's mind. No doubt it was due to the fact that the last two hospital visits made by Leslie were on Mom's account. The woman had clumsily executed two cry-for-attention suicide attempts resulting in her daughter Leslie dutifully having to visit Mom in the hospital. Nobody liked hospitals; but thanks to her Mom, Agent Nellis had a particularly negative recall of these institutions even when she only passed by them on the street.

She wrenched the recollection of Mom from her mind. It was "show-time"! Leslie needed to keep her wits about her. Interrogations were a tricky business. She was a bit confused however; because this woman did not appear to be in serious condition. Well, she was unsure of the metric, *serious condition*, when used in a police report.

Leslie stepped forward, approached the bed and introduced herself, having produced her FBI identification. The woman glanced over at her for a moment and then resumed her perusal of the magazine. She turned a page and then another as the visitor stood there not quite sure how to interpret this woman's unresponsive behavior.

"You are Mrs. Rajai, are you not?" Leslie finally asked.

The woman turned another page of the magazine without looking up or in anyway indicating that she'd heard the question.

Leslie again dangled her FBI credentials in front of the woman. "I need to ask you a few questions about your husband, Mrs. Rajai. My name is Ms. Nellis… Leslie Nellis… I'm an FBI Agent. Hello? Mrs. Rajai, can you hear me?"

Finally, she gave the woman a tentative nudge on the shoulder with her stiffened index finger. Mrs. Rajai briefly looked up at her and spat, "I've got nothing to say. The doctor says I'm in serious condition, so leave me alone."

"It's your husband who put you into this condition, Mrs. Rajai. Doesn't that concern you?"

"It was an accident," she countered and turned another page.

"Not according to your children," Leslie challenged.

The woman still didn't look up, but her knuckles turned white as she clenched the magazine. "Leave my children out of this! I have nothing to say. Now, let me alone! I'm in serious condition. I mustn't be disturbed! The doctors say so. Leave me in peace!"

Leslie stood there several moments in gridlock. She stared down at her, hoping for a sudden reprieve in this woman's attitude, but Mrs. Rajai continued to ignore her presence as she slowly turned the pages of her magazine. The Agent finally jerked away and headed for the door, retreated to the elevator and then clickity-clacked at a fast pace back to the nurse's station. The same nurse who'd helped her earlier was still there, and cast a perfunctory smile as Leslie clearly in a dither approached her.

"What exactly is wrong with Mrs. Rajai? She's got a fat lip and a shiner, but other than that she doesn't appear in *serious condition* to me."

"You mean the lady in 331?" the nurse slowly articulated in a soothing voice which a teacher might employ to calm an overwrought first-grader.

"Yes, Mrs. Rajai!"

"Well, I believe the doctor did so at the request of the police."

"Did what?"

"Ascribe her condition as serious. That way she can not be released from the hospital until her husband is apprehended. They feel she might be endangered if she returned home, and she has no where else to go."

"Hmm, like what about her children?"

The nurse shrugged. "No idea."

"Is anyone from the Police Department here?"

She shrugged again. "I haven't seen anybody in uniform here since I came on shift."

Leslie left the hospital feeling like a puppy who'd just wet the carpet, gotten its nose rubbed in the mess and then had its butt kicked out of the house. She was reaching for the door handle of her car when she heard her cell phone sound off. Rather then sit inside and endure the oven temperature, she remained standing beside her car, grabbed the phone out of her purse and connected.

"Agent Nellis," she announced.

It was her supervisor. She immediately recognized his East Texas twang. "Where are you?"

"At Merced Hospital, sir."

"Have you spoken to her yet?"

"Well, let's say that I tried; but Mrs. Rajai wasn't at all cooperative. And frankly, I don't think she's in a serious condition. The nurse on station admitted that much to me."

"Does she know?"

"Uhh... know what, sir?"

"That her husband is dead, Agent Nellis."

"Dead?" she mumbled in a thunderstruck whisper. "How?"

"No formal determination, yet; but it was either reckless driving or intentional suicide. He went through a railing on I-17 near Wild Horse Canyon and down a roughly one hundred and fifty foot embankment. From what I understand, no seat belt, and there was no evidence of skid marks from braking."

"What about the crash bag?"

"It intiated, but he was found lying on the floor boards. Evidently the vehicle had flipped and rolled."

"Foul play?"

"Naw," he stated emphatically. "Nothing to suggest that… yet. I'm waiting for the police report. Does she--- his wife---know?"

"I don't think so. Who would have told her? Uhh… sir…"

"What?"

"How about if *I* tell her? Like, maybe she'll feel in a more talkative mood after hearing this news."

He paused for a moment before responding. "Yeah, go ahead. And take careful note as to whether her immediate reaction is to regard it as bad news or good news. If she unravels, press her for names that are connected to his story of a terror attempt on PVNGS. As things now stand, she's the only link we have."

"Do I advise Mrs. Rajai of her rights?"

Again he paused. "Naw, keep it informal. Treat it as a fishing expedition."

"I'm on it, sir!" She heard the click of disconnect.

Tohono O'odham Indian Reservation

Felipe Gomez had passed through the tunnel without incident while the SUV driver gunned his vehicle away. Romero had decided that he and Moustache would go to the shack and wait. It was the prospect of a beer which beckoned him; but he also calculated that Felipe returning with both the Black Muslim and the Jordanian, things would get uncomfortably crowded in the SUV he and Moustache remained. There was plenty of time for the driver take them to the shack and then to get back here and wait for them.

The tunnel was sheltered in the shadow of a hill less than one hundred yards on the Mexican side of the border. The SUV had returned and was now parked not far from the tunnel entrance dug at the bottom of the hill. The driver had dropped off Romero and the man he called Moustache at the shack by the dirt strip.

The opening to the tunnel on the other side of the border lay behind a large outcrop of rock and boulders obscuring it from easy detection. A steel chain and padlock secured a wrought iron gate which barred the way at both entrances. Felipe had the key which worked both padlocks.

After emerging from the tunnel on the American side, he'd immediately spotted the spacious compound. It was surrounded by an eight foot high cyclone fence. The entryway was highlighted by two sentries standing there. They did not appear armed. They were both *negritos*. Felipe audaciously approached them as they eyed him with suspicion and concern.

"I've been sent here to collect your leader, Lewis Reddy" he stated in English. Felipe had lived in the States off and on since childhood. He'd attended several years of grade school in California. His English was good, but the sing-song delivery betrayed his Mexican origins as did his appearance.

One of the sentries stepped forward to confront this stranger. "Our leader is Sultan Ali Ul-Faqr. I think you got the wrong address, amigo."

"Sultan? Yeah, whatever. Look, I just walked through that tunnel back there." He extracted a key from his pocket and dangled it in front of the sentry. "Does this tell you all you need to know, *amigo*?"

The sentry glanced at his colleague and nodded. He then turned back to the stranger, "Wait here! Yo'all got a name?"

"I'm an *amigo* of Moustache."

"Moustache?" the sentry chortled. The Iranian had been called Moustache by the Sultan he then recalled. Nevertheless, he decided to toy with this stranger before acceding to his demand.

"I think yo'all been walking under that desert sun a tad too long, man."

"Tell your… uhh… Sultan I come from the man with the big moustache."

"I'll take that pistol first," the sentry demanded.

"Not as long as I'm breathing," the Mexican spat as he clenched his fists and took a step backwards away from the man. "Just go get your Sultan. He's expecting me."

The *negrito* looked over at his companion. As if a silent communication had transpired between them, the fellow finally sighed and turned away. Felipe abided cautious optimism as he watched the sentry retreat into the compound. The other sentry continued to gaze at him attentively.

There were a large group of guys inside the compound doing calisthenics. They were led by a big fellow with a booming voice. The entire group including the guy in front was *negrito*.

He quickly counted them. Including the one out in front, there were eighteen. Add in the two sentries and that made twenty. He was satisfied with the numbers, but he didn't see any weapons. They wouldn't prevail against whatever armed contingent accompanied the coveted consignment if they had only bare hands, no matter how many calisthenics they performed.

"Don't you guys have any weapons?" he asked to the remaining sentry.

The fellow cocked his head and reflected a mocking grin. "Y'aks a lot of questions for a guy with nothing but a key and a straw hat."

"Well, I also have a pistol," Felipe retorted sarcastically.

"Yo'all wants answers, amigo, you gotta aks the Sultan. I jest work here."

Felipe observed the dispatched sentry approach the fellow leading the work-out, and watched as he exchanged words and then pointed towards the gate. The big *negrito* halted and stared in that direction. Felipe raised his hand and waved it one time at him. He watched as the group dispersed and formed an unregimented crowd which followed behind their leader as he aggressively paced towards the gate. The sentry who'd summoned him had blended into that crowd.

"Is that the Sultan?" Felipe asked with a touch of irreverence.

"Sultan Ali Ul-Faqr," the remaining sentry emphasized.

The Sultan continued to boldly approach the gate and then walked through it as the remaining sentry stepped aside to give him berth. "He's got a pistol," the man warned in a whisper as the Sultan passed him.

The crowd stopped just short of the gate. Felipe could hear their heavy breathing from the workout they'd been performing. The Sultan was drenched in sweat. Felipe could smell his perspiration as the man confronted him.

"I'm told you sez that Moustache's sent you."

"Yes. He's waiting for you on the other side. I have an SUV parked at the bottom of the hill. He wants you to bring the Jordanian along. But I have a question. However, first let me introduce myself. I am Felipe Gomez. I work for a partner of Moustache. You and I, we too shall be partners." He offered a handshake.

The big fellow just stared at him.

The remaining sentry shifted his stance, and then exclaimed, "We do'an touch the hands of the Infidel, amigo."

Felipe lowered his hand as his face flushed. He

mumbled something in Spanish under his breath. Ali chose to ignore it, but did not abate the glower he'd fixed on Felipe. Finally the Mexican gathered his poise.

"We have a job to do, but you will need weapons. I was told you have weapons, but I do not see any."

"What job?"

"Moustache will explain it all to you. You must follow me… and bring the Jordanian with you. But I am very curious. Do you have weapons? You will need them for our job."

"The Jordanian cain't come, and I do'an intend on coming either. I ain't crossing that border. If'n Moustache wants to talk, you tell him to cross over here!"

"He's your *Jefe*!," Felipe fulminated. "He orders you and the Jordanian to come with me!"

Ali glanced back at his minions. He couldn't acquiesce to the notion of a higher authority than his own. It would corrupt his image to the followers gathered here. Furthermore, he could not predict what reaction Moustache would exhibit to the news of his Jordanian's demise. There was no way in hell he was gonna confront that man outside his own turf. 'Nope,' Ali silently mused, 'I might be dumb, but I ain't stupid!'

He placed clenched fists upon his hips. "Only Allah and his Prophet are my *Jefe*! I am the Sultan. If Moustache wants to talk, he'll come to me, y'all hear? And just for the record, amigo, we gots weapons!"

"What kind of weapons?" Felipe probed. "How many?"

"'Nuff to arm every man here, amigo. And with a whole lot more fire-power than thet toy pistol y'all gots strapped on."

Merced Hospital, Phoenix

Mrs. Rajai's face clearly expressed her disdain without uttering a word as she watched Leslie Nellis again enter her room. The FBI Agent nonetheless offered her a warm smile in an otherwise serious demeanor. She approached the bedside as the woman turned her head away.

"Please leave," she sourly demanded. "I'm in serious condition. The doctor says I should not be disturbed. Leave now, or I will push the button for the nurse!"

"Like, I have some very distressing news, Mrs. Rajai. Look at me. You need to listen! Your husband is dead."

The woman turned her head back to Leslie. Her lips pursed soundlessly, and then she reached for the button, but she didn't depress it. "Liar!" she finally exclaimed. "Get out of here!"

"I'm not a liar, I'm an FBI Agent, and I am here on official business. Look, this isn't easy for me, Mrs. Rajai. I'm not your enemy. Your husband was killed in… well, sort of like a car accident. He crashed through a railing and went down a ravine. The preliminary conclusion is that his car went out of control; but it also appears that it might have been suicide. Like, was there any reason for your husband to commit suicide?"

Mrs. Rajai's thumb was on the button, but she still didn't press. Finally, the woman retracted her hand as she continued to stare at the Agent. At last she muttered, "SAVAK!"

Leslie cocked her head to imply she hadn't understood. "I'm sorry, what?"

"SAVAK did it!"

"Who is SAVAK?" Leslie asked weakly.

"They are Iranian. They are killers."

"An Iranian gang?"

"No, they work for the government!"

Suddenly it clicked in her head to what this woman referred. She knew the term SAVAK had sounded familiar. "You mean the Iranian Secret Police?"

Mrs. Rajai affirmed with a nod. "Where are my children? They will come after my children!"

"Do you need protection?"

"My children, my children! They need protection!"

Leslie perceived her opening. "We can arrange to give you protection, Mrs. Rajai… for you and your children. But you must give me details of why SAVAK wishes to harm all of you. I need this information in order to process the request. You must cooperate with me. Like, we mustn't waste any time!"

The woman exhaled an audible sigh and pulled herself into a more upright position. "What must you know?"

"Like, I need to know why. Why does SAVAK wish to harm your family?"

She faced away from Leslie, staring out into the ether, and began to mechanically speak. "SAVAK has my sister. They made threats and forced my husband to do things against his will." She began to choke up and tears gathered into her eyes. "I forced him to do it. I insisted!" She began to sob as tears rolled down her cheeks.

Leslie patiently abided. Finally she intervened. "What exactly did they force your husband to do?"

The Agent listened as Mrs. Rajai offered a disjointed account of what had transpired between her husband and the MOIS Agent in Ottawa whom she continued to refer to as SAVAK. It was a common transposition for Iranian ex-pats. Leslie hesitated to interfere with the flow gushing from this distraught woman. She knew she ought to be taking notes or pull a recorder out of her purse. Instead, she concentrated on committing to memory the salient facts Mrs. Rajai was divulging. She could not risk disrupting the woman's confession. After fifteen minutes, it appeared that Mrs. Rajai had concluded. Leslie's head was swimming with information which she desperately attempted to organize in her mind.

"I'll need to prepare a report which you must sign in order to get the process rolling, Mrs. Rajai. Okay?"

"Please hurry!" the woman pleaded. "You must hurry. My children! Where are my children now?"

"Don't worry! We'll take care of the children. But first you must sign the report, okay? Like, I'll come back with it as soon as I can, okay?"

"You must hurry!"

Romero's Airstrip (Sonora, Mexico)

"They are bunch of *pinche negritos*, Sr. Romero, and their *Jefe* calls himself *Sultan*." Felipe Gomez turned to Moustache. "And he refuses to come. He says that you must go to him!"

They were sitting inside the shack by the dirt airstrip at a rickety table on two folding chairs drinking warm beer. Felipe had just entered and stood beside them with a flushed face. He did not hide his agitation. Another guy sat at table in the corner mounted with a radio communication apparatus. He had an earphone headset slung over his head and one ear. He wore a holstered pistol.

Felipe then added in a quiet voice which nonetheless imparted conviction, "These *negritos* do not appear to me reliable. I can not work with them, Senyor. I do not trust them."

Romero cast his attention to Moustache with an inquiring glance. "So, what are we to make of this?"

Stalin looked up at Felipe and spoke with suspicion clearly etched in his tone of voice. "Why don't you trust them? Was it because they are black?"

Felipe paused several moments before responding. "Because he refused to follow your order, that's why I don't trust him. He refused to come with me, and those were your orders, no?"

"And the Jordanian... he too refused to come?"

I only saw the *pinche negritos*. There were twenty of them. Is the Jordanian a *negrito*?"

"No, he is an Arab." Moustache shifted his gaze to Romero. "It was a mistake to send your man alone to them. I take the blame. Lewis is a cautious man. Why should he trust some stranger who wanders out of the desert and comes to him? It appears I have no choice. I must go back with Felipe and make the proper introductions."

"May I ask you a question?" Romero hissed. The expression on his face confirmed the tone of derision suggested by his voice.

"Of course," the MOIS Agent warily replied.

"Exactly what is the purpose of these twenty men you have camped near my tunnel?"

"I have already explained that to you once before."

"Then maybe I'm just a stupid Mexican," Romero stated in a quiet reply, contrived to convey sarcasm. "Please explain it to me again."

"They are there to ensure security for our precious carpet when we deliver it through your tunnel. And then we will load it on a van and convoy to Tucson… to the Mosque."

"A van?" He turned his eyes up to Felipe. "Did you see a van in their compound?"

Felipe shook his head in the negative. "No, senyor."

Romero chuckled as he once more attended the Iranian. "So, where have you hidden your van?"

"The Jordanian is consigning it. I thought by now he would have it there. But evidently he hasn't yet returned with it."

"So, first you lease some land from the Indians. Then

you build a compound and pay twenty men to bake in the desert sun. Then you buy a van. And you hire me to fly it and to bring it through the tunnel. That's a lot of expense for one carpet, no?"

"The carpet has little value to a man like you. But to a Muslim, it is priceless."

"Yes, you told me. The Twelfth Imam sat on it. That is what you say. Nevertheless, it is a bit curious, don't you agree? Look, I am taking risks to transport your so-called carpet. I have a right to know what I am conveying. I want to know what is really in that wooden crate!"

Moustache clenched his fists as his face flushed. He burst to his feet almost knocking over the folding chair. "It is a carpet! That is as much as you need to know. We made a deal! I will keep my end of the bargain. I do not ask what is in this consignment you wish my men to take. Clearly the mission is dangerous or you would do it yourself. And clearly it has a great deal of value to you. But that is none of my business. We must keep our relationship professional, right?"

Romero raised a hand to signal calm. "Please sit down, Moustache. Please… sit down."

The Iranian sighed, reached for the chair and sat.

Romero continued, "You say professional. But Felipe is of the opinion that your little army is not very professional."

"Felipe is in no position to make that judgment," Stalin spat as he cast the man still standing a scowl. He then returned his eyes to Romero. "Would you care to come along and observe for yourself?"

Romero shook his head and chuckled again. "No. You must convince Felipe. If you can convince him, I will be satisfied."

"And what if he chooses to remain unconvinced?"

"Then we must return to my original offer. I want one million dollars, cash!"

In his peripheral vision, Moustache observed Felipe break into a sinister grin. "I will try to keep an open mind," the Mexican stated to his *jefe* in tones that made it clear he was disposed to quite an opposite attitude.

Stalin recognized that a clear obstacle had suddenly been foisted upon his path. But he remained unshaken in his conviction that Allah would show him the way. He rose from the chair and leered at Felipe.

"Let's go," he finally exclaimed.

Tohono O'odham Indian Reservation, Ul-Faqr's Camp

As the two of them approached the camp on foot, having traversed through Romero's tunnel, Moustache stated to Felipe Gomez in an apologetic voice, "I'm afraid I can not offer you beer at the camp. These men are True Believers. And if you need to smoke, please step outside the compound. However, I can arrange for them to bring you some tea or water. No offense, but I need to discuss a few thinks privately with Lewis before the three of us meet. Please forgive the inconvenience."

"I want to see their weapons, and let these *pinche negritos* show me they can use them. That is why I came here, not for hospitality. And there is one more thing!"

Felipe had paused, leaving his stipulation unstated. "Go on, I'm listening," the Iranian urged.

"I must be in charge of those men during our operation. I know how that *chingaso* operates. He may send a donkey through the tunnel first before he sends the horse. I must make the decisions. Your Sultan will only get in my way."

"Donkey…horse… what are you talking about?"

"See, you have no idea about these things. It is a matter of speech. The donkey is a decoy… the horse is the real thing. You think that *chingaso* trusts us? Nobody trusts anybody in this business. If they do, they don't last very long."

"Who is this *chingaso*?" Moustache probed.

Felipe wasn't about to bite, "A *narco-traficante*."

"So, it is a shipment of drugs we are stealing, eh?"

"No," he snarled sardastically, "it's a shipment of women's lingerie from one of the *gringo maquilas*. We like to cross-dress when we go into town. It's how we avoid the DEA." He offered Moustache a sneer to enforce the notion that these transparent interrogations by the MOIS Agent should abate.

"You don't trust me, do you?"

"It is not important what I think. I follow the orders of my *jefe*."

"Do you believe Senyor Romero trusts me?" Moustache asked.

"He don't trust nobody. That's why he's still here."

"So then he doesn't trust you either?"

"More than he trusts you! I have served him for seventeen years. And I am *Sonorense*. You are a foreigner." He pointed in the direction of the compound as he spat, "And they are a bunch of *pinche negritos*!"

Sultan Ali Ul-Faqr was moving in long strides towards the gate as the two men passed through it. Heads were peering out of tents at them, and a few of the men had come out into the open. The hottest part of the day had long since past. The sun would only be visible for another hour at most before it passed behind the low mountains to the west. Once the sun disappeared, the desert would cool rapidly.

Here under these clear night skies, stars would dazzle like polished alloy buttons, and one could actually read the pages of a book from light given by a full moon overhead. The desert was rarely obscured by total darkness. Even when clouds covered the night sky, it usually was accompanied by lightening as bright as strobe lights that would give surreal glimpses every few seconds of the landscape. There were few events on this planet more exciting than standing in the middle of a Sonoran Desert thunderstorm.

Felipe had learned his lesson from his first meeting with "the Sultan", and did not extend his hand for a shake when they came face to face. At the request of Moustache, Ul-Faqr called over one of his men and instructed him to take the Mexican to a tent and serve him tea. Felipe cast the Iranian a disgruntled look, and then followed the man.

The Sultan then gently handled Moustache at the elbow and turned him back towards the gate. "Come with me, there is something I need to show you."

As they passed through the gate, Moustache asked, "Where is the Jordanian? Why hasn't he brought the delivery van?"

"I'm fetching you to the Jordanian," he quietly replied.

"Where? I don't see him! Is there something wrong?"

"*Wrong* is he who resists the hand of Allah," Ali stated in a detached tone of voice.

The MOIS Agent detected that something was terribly off beam. "Where is the Jordanian?" he repeated.

"Not far. Over there, by them boulders near the bottom of the hill."

"Is he behind the boulders? What is he doing behind the boulders? From whom is he hiding?"

"He ain't hiding. He's resting."

"What?"

"I will 'splain when we gets there."

"Has something happened to him?"

"We's almost there, and then I'll 'splain."

Moustache had already begun to intuit the direction which this explanation would take; and therefore why Lewis wished to be out of earshot from the compound in case the two men's voices might be raised during the discussion. He noted before that the Sultan was always concerned about his image reflected to the men who followed him. He demanded tight discipline and blind obedience. It was a good leadership attribute, the Iranian conceded, for the most part.

He listened as Lewis pointed to the gravesite and explained the circumstances which had laid the Jordanian to rest. They actually stood just below the boulders where the ground was more penetrable to a shovel. There was a second gravesite as well. Moustache presumed it was the girl.

"He was given a proper Muslim burial," Ul-Faqr assured.

The MOIS Agent quickly realized that this was a *fait accompli*. It could not be undone. They had no delivery van. For a moment, his immediate prospects looked hopeless, and these were exacerbated by the adversarial attitude of Felipe Gomez and the suspicious nature of "Gomero" Romero.

However, an alternative plan had been brewing in his mind ever since he realized that he could fly that BT-67. It was a plan that had one major impediment. He was very unsure about how to get the airplane off the ground. Once in the air, he was confident of his skills. And, of course, there would be no reason to worry about how to land. His martyrdom was all wrapped up in that final act of crashing Romero's airplane into the nuclear station and creating a holocaust.

He decided that now was the time to divulge to Lewis

the nature of this mission. He must tell him about the bomb, and the target... Palo Verde Nuclear Generating Station near Phoenix. And then he would explain the role which Lewis and his followers would play in this mission. Yes, suddenly it had all come together in his mind. He paused several times, as the schemes occurred to him like bursts of inspiration. He felt the hand of Allah caressing his mind.

And the Sultan listened, embraced in an almost religious rapture. At the end of Stalin's dissertation, he slowly hunched to his knees, placed both hands on the stony ground as he bent forward and kissed the boots of this future martyr. Ali Ul-Faqr had sensed since his conversion to Islam that Allah had a special purpose for him. He'd yearned and prayed to be given that special purpose. And now Allah had delivered to him the opportunity. But Moustache's plan had certain weak points, and Ali's mind began churning to unravel the remedies. The two men continued their discussion at the gravesites until nearly sunset.

The Minuteman Civil Defense Corp

Mission: *To secure United States borders and coastal boundaries against unlawful and unauthorized entry of all individuals, contraband, and foreign military. We will employ all means of civil protest, demonstration, and political lobbying to accomplish this goal.*

Of course, these volunteers unlike their namesakes of the American Revolutionary War are not armed with muskets, nor do they dare bear modern weaponry. They carry to the front lines their binoculars, water bottles and cell phones. The front line is the U.S. border, and they volunteer to watch it. If they spot what they perceive to be an illegal border crossing, they immediately communicate the incident through channels to the officially vested U. S. Border Patrol.

They are men and women who experienced the frustration of unanswered emails and faxes to their elected officials; or of some effete and condescending voice on the other end of a telephone call to their government representatives. They were offended by an Executive Branch unwilling to execute the laws of the land; of a judiciary offering an arrogant abrogation of these laws; and of a constabulary whose hand were tied by the lawyers and the secular-progressive NGO's. They were American citizens who became mad as hell, and decided to do something about it!

The MCDC is mostly made up of persons from the seasoned generations, some are the real-deal ex-military, and some are quixotic "wannabees". They all have their reasons concerning why they volunteered for duty... no matter, they're there and they selflessly serve. They don't get paid to bake in the desert sun; but they are there.

And two of them had posted themselves on a hill overlooking the Tohono O'odham Indian reservation in a proximity allowing the pair to observe a recently built compound by a group of men which they had learned were a purported sect of Black Muslims. In their opinion it warranted a look-see, and so Bob and Charley took it upon themselves to do just that. What they would observe was a far greater eye-opener than they'd anticipated.

The hill where they had posted sloped down just over the border, but the crest was still on the American side. By late afternoon a shadow cast by the hill over the east side obscured a clear determination of what they suspected. That suspicion was aroused the first time they saw a Mexican come out of nowhere, and then hike to the compound. They presumed he was a Mexican because he wore a "ranchero hat", typical headgear for *Mexicanos del Norte*. Later he returned from the compound and disappeared below them like a prairie dog down a hole. Now out of the shadows there suddenly appeared two men, and like the man they had seen the first time they hiked to the compound.

"That one with the ranchero hat is the same hombre we saw before," Bob whispered with certainty to his colleague while he continued to hold the binoculars to his eyes.

"Bob," Charly replied in a low voice filled with dramatic delivery, "We just found us a goddam tunnel!"

"Shall we go have look-see?"

"Call it in! There's twenty of them folks in that compound down yonder and just the two of us. What'cha gonna do, hit 'em with your water bottle? Those hombres don't look none to friendly. They're up to a whole lot of no-good, if'n you ask me."

"Look, it's that same SUV on the Mexican side which

came 'n parked there the first time. Now, jes' what'cha wanna bet that's where our tunnel surfaces?"

"Yeah, and they'll drive back to that airstrip where that airplane is parked. Something very fishy 'bout this exercise if'n you ask me. Hey, you're ex-Air Force. What kind-a plane is that? Looks like a cargo hauler to me."

"It's a DC-3. Damn thing belongs in a museum. Go on, Charley. Call it in."

While Charley connected, Bob watched through binoculars as the two hikers reached the gate of the compound. They were met by one of the Black Muslims. After lingering there, the two hikers separated. One of them followed a Black Muslim towards the hill directly north of the compound. That other hiker wearing the ranchero hat and who'd come here alone the first time then followed another Black Muslim to a tent in the compound. It was approximately fifteen hundred yards to the gate of the compound from the hill top upon which Bob and Charley perched. With binoculars to his eyes it all came through as clear as if you were standing there.

Bob glanced over and observed that Charley no longer had his ear to the phone. "What'd they say?"

"He sez for us to get our sorry asses back to base. He sez *now*! We're into something way over our heads, he sez. He'll make a report to the Border Patrol. We can show them on the map exactly where we think our tunnel is."

"I want to be in on the bust!" Bob complained. "I ain't telling them nothing 'less we can go with them as observers."

"Well, I seriously doubt we'll get an invite! Anyways, we gotta tell 'em, otherwise we become accessories to the crime."

"You ain't no damned lawyer," Bob groused, "so stop talking like one!"

"Well, you do whatever your conscience warrants, Bob, but I'm gonna follow mine."

"I think that plane is loaded with drugs! My guess is that tonight they're gonna bring it across."

"Well, we're gonna have to convince the Border Patrol of your theory. And maybe we can convince them that our presence could be of use. It'll be jest a bit tricky to follow a topo map at night with lights-out. We can give it a shot by pointing that out to them.

"Man, I love this work!" Charley bubbled as he slapped the air near his ear. "'Cept for these damned flies!"

"C'mon, let's get going. It's only a couple hours 'til nightfall. If'n we're gonna get us a drug-bust tonight, we ain't got a whole lot of time!"

"You figure they'll take it into that compound tonight? That's how I got it figured."

"We ain't got time to sit here and figure, Charley. Like the man said, let's get our sorry asses moving!"

Merced Hospital

Agent Leslie Nellis punched the button of the elevator in a mindless motion. She sensed that she was screwing up her opportunity with Mrs. Rajai. She should go back and simply record the woman's testimony. Like, she had a disk recorder in her purse.

Leslie felt a bit foolish, however, having already promised Mrs. Rajai that she would type up a statement for the woman's signature. Well, a signed statement was more credible evidence in a court of law than a tape-recording. She suddenly shuddered as the thought occurred to her that maybe this foreign woman couldn't read English. Shit! But she'd seen Mrs. Rajai reading a magazine, she then recalled. Well, maybe she'd only been looking at the pictures, Leslie reluctantly revised.

The Agent was jolted out of her silent turmoil by the elevator dinging an arrival. She paused before entering while two men exited. One was in the garb of an orderly and the other was a uniformed police officer. She gave them berth and then got into the elevator. She punched a button, the one which would take her to the ground floor. During the ride her thoughts continued to chaotically percolate.

"A police officer,' she pondered. 'Where was he going?' The elevator arrived and the door opened. She exited and took several steps down the hall before she abruptly stopped. The speculation in her mind mounted. That cop getting out of the elevator had piqued her curiosity. 'Maybe they'd decided to put security on Mrs. Rajai…but why now? Could it be because of her husband's demise', she silently wondered.

'This is totally stupid,' she suddenly self-flagellated. She had to get her shit together! Fuck the signed statement!

She would use the recorder in her purse. Moreover, she wanted to go talk to the cop and find out why he'd been assigned to Mrs. Rajai... if indeed that was the case.

She turned around and marched herself back to the elevator. Leslie opened her purse and fingered through the contents to assure that she'd also brought along the little microphone which could be clipped onto a collar or a hem. It offered better pick up than the microphone in the body of her compact machine. She squinted into the purse as her fingers signaled contact with the fine vinyl coated wires. Yes, she confirmed more by feel than by sight, there was the recorder, and under it was the microphone attachment. She was good to go! She jabbed the "up" button on the wall to summon the elevator.

'I have a witness willing to testify,' she rationalized to herself. 'Like, you gotta strike while the iron is hot! The woman is in a hurry to get protective services going for her children. Something can intervene to change her mind. Shit happens! As things now stand, Mrs. Rajai will welcome the opportunity to tell her story into the microphone and short-cut the process. There's no point in dilly-dallying around! Like, make hay while the sun shines!' Impatiently, Leslie again pushed the button to summon the elevator although she realized the futility of that repitition.

The Agent began tapping her foot with annoyance at the tardiness of this lift as she waited for it to arrive. 'Whenever you're in a hurry, machines have a way of conspiring to thwart you,' she griped.

The information which Mrs Rajai had communicated to her earlier made the hypothesis less credible that her husband had driven recklessly or intentionally put an end to his life. Mrs. Rajai had been absolutely convinced that it was the dirty work of these Iranians she called SAVAK. Leslie understood that the acronym stood for Secret Police. And Mrs. Rajai was also convinced that they would probably come for her and her children as well. And the FBI Agent recalled how tears had welled into the woman's eyes as she mentioned the probable fate of her poor sister and the two children being held hostage at the Iranian Embassy in Ottawa, Canada.

A lady walked up to the elevator door and stopped besideLeslie. The lady glanced at her momentarily and then reached forward and pushed the "up" button even though it was clearly lighted, indicating that it had already been pressed. After several moments, she again turned to Leslie.

"Have you been waiting long?"

"About a minute," Leslie responded.

"Maybe it doesn't work. This isn't the only elevator servicing the hospital, but the information desk told me this way would be faster."

"Where are you going?"

"Oh, I'm with Child Protection Services. There's someone here with whom I need to speak."

Leslie raised an eyebrow, and asked in a timid voice, "Would it be Mrs. Rajai by any chance?"

The lady stared at her for a moment before gathering

her composure. "Yes, I'm here to advise her of the situation regarding her children."

"What is their situation?"

"Who are you?" the lady stiffly asked as she took a small step away from Leslie. "Are you a member of the family?"

The Agent offered her credentials and patiently abided as the woman adjusted her head so that the bifocals brought the picture and small print into focus. "I'm with the Bureau." Leslie clarified.

"A Fed," the lady muttered. She resumed a normal posture and returned her eyes to look straight into Leslie's gaze. "What are the Feds doing here? I presume you're here to visit Mrs. Rajai, as well?"

"Yes, I am. And I need to be alone with her. It shouldn't take more than fifteen or twenty minutes. You don't mind waiting, do you?"

"What's going on? Why have they put the Feds on this case?"

Leslie was---so to speak---saved by the bell. The ding of the elevator announced its arrival. The door opened and those two men she'd met on the third floor exited… the hospital orderly and the cop. Well, she noted, clearly the cop wasn't there to provide security for Mrs. Rajai which had been her earlier speculation, else he wouldn't be coming down again. She concluded that their visit probably had nothing at all to do with Mrs. Rajai.

As the two men passed by, the lady asked Leslie, "Should I go up? I mean, I can wait outside the room until you're finished… or what?"

"Like, suit yourself," Leslie muttered, most of her mind now occupied with exactly how she would propose her new plan to Mrs. Rajai.

"Fifteen minutes, you say?"

"Maybe twenty."

"I think I'll wait down here. There's a cafeteria not far. I'll get a cup of coffee. You say twenty minutes?"

"Yeah, more or less."

"Okay, then I'll come up in twenty minutes."

"Whatever."

The elevator door closed, and Leslie felt herself being gently lifted to the third floor. She exited, and clacked her heels down the hallway as she rehearsed in her mind the overture she would make to Mrs. Rajai. The door to Room 331 was closed. She opened it and crossed over the threshold. The woman was lying in bed with her back to Leslie and a blanket covering up to her ears. Only the crown of her head was visible.

The Agent groaned, for it appeared the woman had gone to sleep. She cautiously approached her bedside, reached over and nudged the woman's shoulder. There was something which struck Leslie as very unnatural about the entire feel of this lady, and then she saw some blood on the blanket.

She yanked on the woman's shoulder bringing the body around ninety degrees. The head turned as well. The blanket shifted. Staring up at Agent Nellis were lifeless eyes and a slightly open mouth imparting a hideous expression. Her chest area was soaked in blood. Clearly,

Mrs. Rajai's throat had been sliced. Leslie felt nausea. She eyed the bathroom, and desperately fought back the impulse to run over there and talk with Ralph on the big white phone.

Sultan Ali Ul-Faqr's Compound, Tohono O'odham Indian Reservation

Moustache had been filled with misgiving as he related to Lewis Reddy, this self-ordained Black Muslim Sultan, the true substance and objective of his project. In a twisted way, the fact that Ali straightforwardly admitted his killing of the Jordanian and his simplistic motive---because the man had disrespected him---had actually encouraged the Iranian to confide in Lewis. Moreover, at this particular moment the MOIS Agent presaged a dissonance sounding between his aspirations and those of his Mexican partners. He needed to cement the allegiance of this black man.

"I'd appreciate if'n yo'all called me Ali in front of my men, Moustache," he'd interjected during their conversation at the gravesites. "Lewis was my Christain name. These men---like me---are now True Believers. We all've taken a Muslim name, and we's taken it seriously."

Moustache appreciated simple honesty in his colleagues. It bred his confidence in their character. Moreover, the MOIS Agent simply could not grasp any other direction to follow. There was only one reasonable option left for him and it required this man's trust and cooperation. He felt comfortable with his decision and took this feeling of assurance as a sign from Allah.

Clearly Allah's hand had guided him to his decision in the first place. It had come to him almost like a vision. Moments before he'd been confused and directionless. Then he suddenly was overcome with a clear focus and means. Not only had the "Sultan" embraced this project with commitment, and regarded Moustache with a newly acquired reverence, but he offered a bold plan for solving the Iranian's immediate problem… Felipe Gomez.

"Yes," Stalin had muttered as he slowly nodded affirmatively. Ali's suggestion led him down a new avenue… it was the way!

As he and Ali returned from the gravesites, Moustache could see Felipe standing just outside the gate smoking a cigarette. Two sentries were beside him at their posts. The Sultan had of course observed the Mexican as well, and flashed the Iranian a sly grin.

"Show time," he whispered just loud enough for the MOIS Agent to hear.

As they approached within easy earshot of the Mexican, Felipe flipped his half-finished cigarette in a practiced art sending it some fifteen feet in their direction. His face occluded with impatience. He flashed Ali an expression of disdain, and then turned his gaze back to the Iranian.

"You've been gone almost an hour! Sr. Romero says we gotta get back… now! We're gonna lose daylight pretty soon. Anyway, he's hungry! And we still need an hour to get to Hermosilla. We'll gas up and spend the night there. They got good Mexican steaks in Hermosilla… *a la parilla*. C'mon we gotta get going. He gets really mean when he's hungry!"

"You are in contact with your boss?" Moustache asked in calm response. It was a rhetorical question. He knew of course that Felipe carried a radio phone which communicated with the radio in the shack at the dirt airstrip. It was a bulky affair holstered on his right side, but was counterbalanced by the pistol holstered on his left. It caused him to walk with his arms swinging wide like a body-builder whose "lats" get in the way of graceful ambulation.

Felipe ignored the question as he directed his gaze at Ali. "I ain't seen nothing here to convince me we can use your so-called army. Nobody carries weapons. Look at your two sentries here." He pointed to the pair of Black Muslims minding the gate. "They're standing like a couple of day-workers waiting for the truck. This is a very poor joke."

The Sultan intervened. "You wanna see weapons? Yo'all come with me. I'll show you weapons." He then directed a slight nod at each of the two guards.

Suddenly Felipe was seized by them and found himself on the ground, his face mashed into the stony terrain. They did a search, and dislodged both the pistol and the knife he'd been carrying. Then the Iranian bent down and extracted his radio.

"Now, you doan have no weapons neither," quipped the Sultan. "Okay, let'm up."

Feeling his release, the Mexican gathered to his feet

and perfunctorily dusted himself off. *"Pinche negritos,"* he muttered.

Ali Ul-Faqr took a half-step towards him and then suddenly raised himself on one leg and crashed his elevated boot squarely into Felipe's solar plexus. Moustache was impressed. The delivery clearly demonstrated a practiced discipline of martial arts.

The two guards each grabbed Felipe by an arm as the man collapsed, preventing him from falling to the ground. His mouth was open, but soundless. His eyes bugged with a look of desperation. He appeared like a fish out of water urgently seeking oxygen.

"We'uns requires civility here, and you will address me as Sultan Ali Ul-Faqr. *Comprende?"* He didn't expect a response. The Mexican was gagging for air. "Take him to the haystack!"

The two guards dragged Felipe Gomez through the gate as Ali and the Iranian followed. The Sultan offered Moustache a wink. The MOIS Agent returned it with a brief smile of satisfaction.

By the time they entered the haystack, Felipe had regained his breath and his legs, but certainly not his composure. "Release him," Ali commanded, and then looked directly at one of the guards. "Get me one of the AK's."

"What's going on here?" the Mexican demanded. "You can't treat me like this and get away with it."

"You wants to see weapons, right? Y'all kept on insisting like some rent-lady bitching cuz we waz a day late with your money. Okay, Jose, now we's gonna show you a weapon. And this's the last time I'se gonna warn you. In this compound we conduct our affairs wif civility. Othuhwise, I'se gonna use y'all for target practice." Ali purposely laid on the accent to irritate his captive. He had a pretty good idea of how *pinche negrito* translated, and he had taken extreme umbrage to being called that.

The guard returned with an AK-47 and respectfully handed it to the Sultan, who accepted the weapon and immediately chambered it. He then pointed the muzzle directly at Felipe. "Would yo'all like me to demonstrate that I knows how to shoot?"

The Mexican stared at him in utter disbelief mixed with visible apprehension. Suddenly Ali lowered the bead of his weapon to Felipe's boots, and the sounds of discharge from the weapon filled the place. The bales of hay used to construct this make-shift warehouse served as a sound dampener, but the volley still made an impressive racket. There was a bullet hole at the tip of each of the Mexican's two cowboy-style boots. Felipe gawked at his feet for several moments before finally raising his head to gaze accusingly at the Sultan.

"You've shot me! You *pinche negrito*, you've shot me!"

"Jest the tip of yo boots. Doan be such a cry-baby. Worst I done was give your big toenails a manicure. Now shut yo mouf or I'll raise this weapon to about here!" He lifted the muzzle of the Ak-47 just above the Mexican's belt buckle and gave it a shove, forcing the man to stumble a step backwards.

Moustache gestured for Ali to back off and then offered the captive his radio telephone. "Call your boss."

"Why have you done this?"

"Listen to what Moustache has to say," the Sultan intervened. "He undahstands Spanish, so no tricks. Else my next target area is gonna be yo head! Now take thet damn phone!"

Felipe did not hesitate. He grabbed the phone from the Iranian's outstretched hand. But Moustache did not release his grip on it, so the two of them stood there both clutching the same object.

The MOIS Agent stated in scarcely more than a whisper, "Now listen carefully, Felipe. You tell your boss that you are satisfied with Sultan Ali Ul-Fuqr's capabilities to do the job, and that you will remain here long enough get him started on the preparations. You tell him you really like the guy, and you think Romero ought to meet him. Then you say that you and I will return to the airstrip after you've discussed some details with the Sultan. That's it. That's all you say. Do you understand? And don't forget, *yo hablo espanyol*. If I think you're trying to be clever, we'll put a bullet through your *pinche* brain." He released his grip on the phone.

To emphasize the point, Ali raised the muzzle of his AK-47, and pressed it against Felipe's head. The man's eyes darted wildly between Moustache and the Sultan. Finally he nodded his understanding.

The Iranian pointed a stiff unwavering index finger at the Mexican, as he further directed, "Call your boss, but give the message to your radio operator. Give it immediately to the radio operator, and exactly as I stated it! You tell him to deliver it to Romero. I don't want you talking directly to your *jefe*... you give it to the radio operator! Is that clear?"

Again, Felipe nodded his understanding. With trembling hands and a shaky voice, he connected and then gave the radio operator the message. As he disconnected, the Iranian glanced over at Ul-Faqr who responded with a knowing nod.

"Take off your hat," Moustache stated to the Mexican.

Ali didn't wait for Felipe to respond. He used the AK-47 barrel to knock the ranchero hat off of Felipe's head. He quickly swung the muzzle back and pressed it squarely against the Mexican's head. Another racket chattered inside the haystack as bullets exploded through the cranium of Felipe Gomez.

"Take off his clothes before they soak up the blood," Ali dictated to his two guards. "Figure out who fits into them... maybe Ahmed. He is the right height and he has light skin. We need to dress one of us up to look like that Mexican. And doan forget his hat."

FBI Offices, Phoenix, Arizona

Agent Leslie Nellis felt an irrational guilt as she conveyed to her boss what had transpired during her visit to the now deceased Mrs. Rajai at Merced Hospital. The woman was dead. And the demise occurred while Leslie was there. It had happened right under her nose. She'd bungled the job.

Her boss quietly paid attention, but it was the expressions which transitioned over his face as he listened that made her feel as if from his point of view she'd handled the affair incompetently. She felt like lashing out at him, but didn't have the courage. Even though Leslie blamed herself, nonetheless she felt it was unfair for him to blame her.

However, when he finally responded, she was surprised at the lack of any accusatory tones in his delivery. "I guess I may have to reject my hypothesis that Mr. Rajai committed suicide over personal problems," he sighed with an almost mea culpa contrition.

He then continued, "It's certainly unlikely that his wife slit her own throat. These two deaths have linkage. And you say that she was convinced these Secret Police would come after her? What did she call them?"

"SAVAK, sir."

"He called them MOIS."

"Mr. Rajai?"

He nodded. "Mrs. Rajai's murder appears to affirm what her husband said, doesn't it! So, now we have to go back to square one. Rajai claimed there's a plot by MOIS to blow up Palo Verde. Given these new circumstances, I think we need to take that warning seriously. You have any ideas?"

She shrugged her shoulders. "Like… our two witnesses are dead. I doubt if the children know anything. We could talk to them. They might know who he hangs with. There must have been someone in contact with him. I don't think he was MOIS's designated perp, do you?"

"That's worth a try, but I doubt if his contact was visible to the kids. He says that he coordinated with MOIS at the Iranian Embassy in Ottawa, right?"

"Yes, sir."

"He also said that it was in Canada where they were holding his sister-in-law and her children, right?"

"Yes, sir." She gazed at her Supervisor as a clever smirk took hold of his lips, but he continued to silently fix his eyes on her. She shifted uncomfortably and finaly blurted out, "Like… are you suggesting we go to their Embassy in Ottawa?"

"We?"

"You want me to call the Canadians, sir?"

"I think we need to *coordinate* with the Canadians, Agent Nellis. I hear Ottawa is a beautiful place this time year. I'll make a couple phone calls. You go home and pack your bags. Keep your cell phone on. I'll get back with you."

"Sir, what about the PVNGS Security? Do they have any ideas? And, like shouldn't they be warned? What if anything should I tell them?"

"I'll handle things with Palo Verde. You're going to Ottawa and see what you can dig up from the Canadians."

He watched as she gathered to her feet and headed for the door. As she opened it, Leslie glanced back at him. He offered her a reassuring smile and then suddenly animated, raising a halting hand.

"Before you go home, I'll need a written report of that whole Merced Hospital incident. Crank it out and leave it in my in-box, okay?"

"Yes, sir. Anything else?"

"I think you've got enough on your plate for the moment, Agent Nellis." He offered a dismissive nod.

She exited and closed the door behind her. He leaned back in his chair and folded his hands behind his head as he exhaled a groan. He seriously doubted that Agent Nellis would uncover any substantive information in Ottawa. It was a shot in the dark. But there was little else in the way of leads to follow. PVNGS Security had nothing substantive to offer him either.

He didn't make the call to PVNGS. Partly because of the late hour, but mostly because he'd already gone over with Security at Palo Verde what they had, and it was something between negligible and nothing. But they did harbor a dutiful distress which extended even beyond the facility itself. Their concern it turned out was further compounded by a second danger not so well perceived by the public. In addition to the UO2 rods in the generator was the nuclear waste by-product called TRU (Trans-Uranic Waste). It was stored in fifty five gallon drums, and awaited pick-up to be shipped to New Mexico.

The planned retrieval from the NGS of TRU was way behind schedule. Typical government enterprise, he silently groused. They had a mass of drums in storage there. According to the head of Security at Palo Verde, if that stuff every got blown into the atmosphere, it could make Chernobyl a mere footnote in the history of nuclear disasters. So even if the steel retaining walls withheld the blast, there was a secondary source of nuclear contamination that could be released into the atmosphere. As the Security Chief had put it, "This could become the mother of all dirty bombs."

It occurred to him that maybe he ought to be the one going to Ottawa instead of sending Agent Nellis. Of course, he was indulging in frivolous speculation. But it underscored his feeling of helplessness in how to counter the perceived threat.

He revised his thinking. Yup, it was time to get those PVNGS boys excited. It was called CYA (Cover Your Ass). If he didn't advise them, and something very bad went down tonight, he'd be hung out to dry… and goodbye pension.

He chuckled to himself as he anticipated Palo Verde's reaction. They'll raise the alert level to cover their collective butts, and request additional funding to implement elevated security. By the time all the red tape gets rolled out, the threat will either have been realized or will have evaporated. Oh well… he picked up the phone. This call had more to do with him than with them. It wasn't so much about national security as it was about his own personal security.

Bob and Charley's Hill,
Tohono O'odham Indian Reservation

Bob and Charley were filled with excitement. The Border Patrolman accompanying them appeared less aroused.

They counseled the fellow that it might be risky driving the Patrol SUV directly to the site where they suspected a tunnel surfaced. It would put them in a direct line of sight to the compound. It was unlikely that their presence would go unnoticed, they further warned.

"Are those fellows armed?" he'd asked.

Charley looked at Bob inquisitively. Bob finally responded. "Well, thet feller in the ranchero hat was packing a pistol."

"And you say there's twenty of them?"

"Yeah."

"Plus two more visitors," Charley quickly added.

The sun was now behind the low mountains which defined the western horizon, but there was still plenty of dusky light. It was only color which had become more difficult to distinguish. The entire landscape was shadowed.

The Patrolman had accepted their advice, so he parked the SUV behind the hill and they climbed from the back side, retracing the trail which Bob and Charley had traversed earlier. The Patrolman carried a map, binoculars, and a phone. He had a holstered handgun.

While they climbed the hill, Bob and Charley were animated with chatter; but as they approached the crest, the Patrolman hushed them. Occasional voices could be heard in the distance. They hunched down and awkwardly approached the same position which the two Minutemen had earlier occupied as the compound came into view. They all saw it. A large group of men were crossing the desert floor from the compound and headed smack-dab in their direction.

The Patrolman whispered in an excited voice, "Jeezuz, they're all armed with… looks like AK-47s. Those are a mob of serious hombres down there. Keep your heads low. Those ain't the kind of neighbors you want waving hello at you."

"It's them Black Muslims," Bob whispered.

"Not all of them," the Patrolman hissed. "There's some still there in the compound.

"I count twelve of them in that posse," Charley offered.

"And see that guy with the ranchero hat," Bob pointed out, "that's the same one we was telling you about!"

The Patrolman grimaced and held up a halting hand to hush them once again. He drew the binoculars to his eyes and followed the progress of this band. Sure enough, they reached a clump of rock and boulders in the penumbra at the base of this hill, and disappeared… the whole fucking group of them.

"Yup, it a tunnel alright," the Patrolman muttered.

He signaled with his hand at Bob and Charley to draw back from their positions near him. They silently complied. However, the Patrolman remained on his knees not moving from his spot and began unfolding his map. Bob and Charley looked at each other from time to time as they watched the Patrolman work out his coordinates. Finally, he withdrew back to their place. From there, the crest of the hill blocked their view of the compound.

"What'cha gonna do?" Bob asked in a whisper to the Patrolman.

He grimaced at Bob, and once more hushed him with a gesture of his hand. He withdrew his phone and after an interval made contact with someone on the other end. Following a brief exchange he offered the coordinates he'd calculated. Then he listened, occasionally responding with affirmative grunts. Finally he disconnected.

Bob couldn't rein in his curiosity. "What's going down? Are we gonna bust 'em?"

The Patrolman paused several moments before responding. "I want the two of you to go back to the vehicle. And try to keep down the chatter, understand?"

"You're gonna stay up here?" Charley whined with a clear note of protest in his tone of voice.

"I want to see where they surface."

"We done told you. They'll come up near that SUV parked across the border."

"I'd like to see it for myself, if you don't mind. Whoops, you're right. There they are. They're approaching that SUV. But I can't tell from exactly where it was they surfaced. Damn, somehow I missed it."

"Well, what's the next move," Bob injected. "Are you guys gonna bust 'em? Did'ja see that plane at the airstrip. It's gotta be a load of drugs. They're going over there to move 'em across! You're gonna bust 'em, aren't you?"

"That's a call for HQ in Tucson to make. Now please go on down to the vehicle!"

They stood up and exchanged glances that reflected

disappointment and consternation. Bob led the way as they slowly disengaged from their perch. Suddenly the Patrolman caught their attention, "Pssst!"

They turned. The Patrolman stood up and fished into his pocket. He extracted the ignition key to his vehicle. You guys keep an eye out for me. If I give you a signal, I want you to take the vehicle and get back to base. You got that?"

He tossed the key with an electronic lock switch in a high arc to Charley. The fellow reached for it, but fumbled the catch. The key made a clunk but stuck on the ground. Charley quickly retrieved it and cast Bob a sheepish look.

"If I give the signal," the Patrolman repeated, "you two high-tail it back to base, understood?"

They nodded with a touch of disappointment, turned and began trudging down the hill.

Romero's Dirt Airstrip Near the Tunnel

It was dusk on the desert floor. Nevertheless, Romero's observer on the hill above the airstrip was able to make out the group of men hiking towards him from the border. He counted twelve. One of them looked like Felipe Gomez. He recognized the hat. And he spotted the Iranian. The remaining ten were those *gringo negritos*. He could also observe that they were carrying weapons. He got on his phone and excitedly communicated his surveillance findings to the radio operator in the shack at the airstrip, emphasizing that they were armed.

Romero received the news from his radio operator with calm. "So, Felipe is bringing his new *amigos* for a visit. It appears we're going to do business together."

Besides the radio operator, he had two other men here at the airstrip. They took shifts on the hill and on the radio. Additionally, they provided security here at the airstrip. The two men stood at the ready, anticipating Romero's instructions after hearing the radio operator excitedly relay the message to their *jefe* from the observer on the hill. Thus, they were somewhat puzzled by his unruffled reaction. He appeared unusually composed having just learned that ten armed black men from across the border were approaching his airstrip.

"What about Paco?" the radio operator hesitantly forwarded. Paco was the driver who had delivered Felipe and the Iranian to the tunnel. "Why didn't Felipe drive back with Paco? Why is he bringing all those *pinche negritos* here?"

"Relax. Felipe has a reason to bring them here. He needs me to give final approval. That is how it should be, no?"

"They are armed, Sr. Romero," the radio operator cautiously stressed.

"So are we. Would you travel in these parts unarmed? Besides, I think they want to show off their competence. Relax! The Iranian needs our cooperation much more than we need his assistance. If they had evil intentions in mind, they would have waited until the night to creep up on us. There is nothing here to steal."

"Maybe the airplane," one of his men guardedly offered.

"Of what value is an airplane if you can't fly it?"

"Maybe one of those *pinche negritos* is a pilot, jefe."

"You are just spoiling for a fight. Felipe would not bring them here if he didn't trust them. But if it makes you feel better, go meet them at the strip. You two drive the pick-up truck there and intercept them. Instruct them to disarm and lay their weapons in the bed of the pick-up."

The two men scampered for their AK-47s. But Romero held up a halting hand. "No weapons. *Que simple!* Two of you against those ten *pinche negritos*? You are not thinking clearly. No, you ask them in a very civil manner to please leave their weapons in the bed of the pick-up. Those are my wishes. Felipe will insist that they obey. The Iranian will understand. Now go! And remember, act with civility. When you have brought them here, let them wait outside. Only Felipe and the Iranian may enter. Is that clear? We are all *amigos*. They are going to do me a favor in return for my services. So, relax!"

The two men slinked through the door moving like a couple of hounds who'd just gotten kicked by their master. They could see the group of men way off in the distance traveling towards them. They hopped in the pick-up truck, drove towards where the BT-67 was parked but stopped well short of it. Judging by the heading in which the group moved, the driver stopped where he anticipated the *gringos* would converge onto the dirt airstrip.

They both got out of the pick-up and moved to the front of it. The fellow who'd been riding on the passenger side placed a foot on the bumper and then hoisted up, swiveled and planted his bum on the hood. The man who'd driven the truck extracted a pack of cigarettes and flipped open the lid. He offered one to his partner. They lit up and had a leisurely smoke as they watched the group approach. It wasn't total night yet, but there was increasingly scant light. The group was now only twenty five yards from them. Suddenly the guy sitting on the hood straightened up and pointed.

"That guy ain't Felipe Gomez."

The other man squinted. "You sure?"

"That ain't Felipe. It's a *pinche negrito* wearing a ranchero hat."

The driver tossed his cigarette to the ground, and made a dash around the headlight clearly advancing for the driver side door. As he reached it, there was a chorus of chatter from several AK-47s. Both of Romero's men were dropped.

Romero heard the gunfire. His first impulse was to curse his two men; but then he remembered they hadn't taken any weapons… *his orders*! The radio guy's eyes were bugging. He'd kept one ear free from the head-set.

"What's that?" he gasped.

Romero bounced to his feet, and then turned to the operator. "Talk to the hill. Ask him what he sees!"

As he waited for the radio to make contact, Romero rushed over to where the weapons lay. He picked up an automatic rifle and then just as quickly set it down again. He grabbed a pistol, checked the safety and released the clip. It was full. He then carefully checked the chamber. It was loaded. He reinserted the clip and pushed it through the belt line at his back. He once more retrieved the automatic rifle.

They're coming towards us," the operator screamed, having just listened to the panicked communication from the hill. "Ernesto says that they shot Adolfo and Kiki!"

"What in the fuck has gotten into those *putos*!" Romero muttered, more to himself than to the operator.

By this time the operator had scrambled out of his chair and made a beeline for the weapons. He grabbed an automatic rifle and then looked at Romero with sheer panic in his eyes. "What're we gonna do?"

His *jefe* did not immediately answer. "Get on the floor!" He pointed to the spot where he wanted him positioned. "Let them make the first move. Let's see what they're after. Don't fire unless they open the door and start shooting. You understand?"

"Why do they want to kill us?" the operator bleated.

"Shut up! Make no sound!"

"But they have us outnumbered, Senyor Romero. Has Felipe betrayed us?"

"They are holding him hostage, *pendejo*! Perhaps there is something they wish to negotiate. They need me to get their *pinche carpet* across the border. I think they are coming to negotiate."

"How can you be sure, Senyor? They've killed Adolfo

and Kiki! They've done it all for a carpet, Senyor? How can this be?"

"Don't lose your head! Perhaps they don't like the terms of my service. So, they are trying to give me a scare. It's a very good negotiating tactic. He's an Iranian. That's probably how they do things. Don't worry. I will talk to him."

"But how can you be sure?"

"If I'm wrong, then we can meet in Hell and discuss it."

Bob and Charley's Hill

The Border Patrolman had continued to see if he could determine where the tunnel surfaced on the other side. He kept his eyes glued on the group who now was approaching the Mexican SUV. He'd also noted that there still were men in the compound. He didn't count them. He couldn't afford the distraction. He needed to determine exactly where this tunnel surfaced, hoping that maybe some of these men might return to it. He guessed that the tunnel had to be several hundred feet in length. Most tunnels these narcos dug offered only crawl space, which explained the duration of time it had taken for that group to reappear.

The Minutemen were probably right, he conceded. All this activity was no doubt tied to the airplane parked on the dirt airstrip. It was a twin engine. It was an uneducated guess, but nonetheless he speculated that the plane could probably haul at least a ton of cargo. He didn't know much about aircraft. By rights, the DEA ought to be brought into this rodeo, he speculated. But that was a call for Tucson to make.

Then it happened. The group circled behind the SUV instead of approaching it directly. The man in the lead was that guy wearing a ranchero hat. The driver got out of the SUV. The sound which immediately followed was unmistakable. It was the chatter of an automatic rifle. He watched through his binoculars as the driver went down.

"What in the hell?" he muttered to himself.

The group gathered and then began heading in the direction of the dirt strip. Nobody got inside the SUV. They just left it there. He wondered why they had chosen to walk. Maybe because there were too many of them to all fit in that single vehicle? He blew it off. There were far more pressing curiosities to resolve here.

He felt the impulse to radio back what he'd just witnessed; but when he attempted to formulate the message, he realized that a shooting on the other side of the border would not require an emergency response from the U.S. Border Patrol. Certainly he was in no danger of being assaulted or involved in crossfire. At best it was an item of information to be included in ones written or oral report.

Still, there were all those weapons these Black Muslims carried. No doubt they had more stashed in their compound. It was something he presumed would be of more than passing interest to ATF (Alcohol, Tobacco,

Firearms) enforcement. But like just about any call, he wasn't the guy authorized to make it. HQ in Tucson with their infinite wisdom would come to those decisions.

And so, binoculars in hand, he continued to patiently watch the drama unfold. He hoped to gather in some visual evidence that would support Bob and Charley's notion about a drug crossing going down. He now shared that concept. But hunches, no matter how strong, would not arouse official support for an intervention. He needed to provide overt sightings that would lead any reasonable Patrolman to conclude that a drug crossing was in progress. Nobody in the chain of command wanted to call over the DEA only to end up with egg on their face.

What he witnessed left him utterly confused. After shooting the SUV driver, the group which had crossed through the tunnel walked to the dirt strip where they killed two Mexicans who'd come in a pick-up truck to meet them. He continued to linger even though it was getting dark, and he still had Bob and Charley waiting at his vehicle.

It was now becoming difficult to distinguish the activity of this group even with binoculars, given their distance and the lack of light. But he'd seen nothing that could warrant eliciting action from the DEA or from the Patrol. He knew he had something here, but he couldn't provide proof.

Then he'd heard the next shooting episode. He hadn't been able to witness much. But what he discerned was bizarre. The group had gunned down two Mexicans at their pick-up truck. Still, it did not offer compelling evidence of a drug crossing about to go down.

He began to revise his notion of what motivated this group. Maybe they were a bunch of vigilantes who had become frustrated with the passive roles practiced by the Minutemen. They were taking matters into their own hands.

This notion was given legs when twenty minutes later he barely discerned three men board the twin-engine airplane and take off. Meanwhile, the group of armed Black Muslims was apparently conducting maneuvers towards a hill east of the windsock on the dirt strip. Nothing appeared to have been unloaded from the plane before it took off.

Yup, it appeared that this group of Black Muslims was taking action against these Mexicans. Was it rival gangs? He didn't know. He'd make his report to higher authority and let them wrestle with this enigma.

Of course, the left lobe of his brain argued, maybe drugs had been unloaded earlier. Maybe there was booty stored in that shack. Fuck it! He decided that it was time to go back to base and make his report. He would radio to base for clearance to return. He hoped to hell those two yo-yo Minutemen hadn't driven off with his wheels!

Benjamin Hill, Sonora, Mexico

Stalin stood on the tarmac after Romero had landed the aircraft here at Benjamin Hill. This settlement was located south of Nogales on the main highway to Hermosillo. He quietly thanked Allah as he watched the two Mexicans prepare to gas up the plane. They were hooking up the grounding wires. His confidence in the scheme had consolidated. He now believed that he was acting through the will of Allah. The way in which matters were unfolding seemed to be controlled by forces outside his grasp and ken. He was absolutely convinced that he would deliver the bomb to that American nuclear generating station in Arizona. The realization filled him with a giddy euphoria.

He was also bemused by the fact that aloft there had still been light, but here on the ground it was nightfall. While still in the air, the captive pilot complained that they must get gas. Stalin was suspicious. Romero must have sensed his confliction.

He suggested to the Iranian, "We can get gas at a private field… no government officials there."

"Where?"

"Benjamin Hill."

Thus Stalin had finally agreed for Romero to radio ahead his intentions to gas up there. "I must confirm that there is still someone on station," the Mexican explained. "It is late. Maybe they've all gone home."

Stalin paid close attention to what Romero was saying. It was a short communication, and then the Mexican nodded at him in the affirmative. "Benjamin Hill has confirmed."

Benjamin Hill was just a transit strip, not an official airport. Fortunately, Stalin realized, they had a gas crew which was still available at this late hour. Otherwise they might have had to land at an official airfield, and then oit would require filing a flight plan. He did not want the risk of putting Romero in a situation where he could escape.

There had been no landing lights for this strip, but Romero managed a safe landing in spite of this impediment. As they had approached the ground, dusk occluded into darkness. Stalin had sat in the right seat mumbling appeals to his Almighty. At last, safely on the ground he had to concede that this Mexican was a very accomplished flier and that surely Allah had been their co-pilot.

Ali took custody of Romero. The pair remained inside the aircraft. Having exited the BT-67, the first thing Stalin did was to inquire whether or not these gas-up guys accepted credit cards, and was relieved to discover that they did so. This airplane had a lot of miles to cover between here and the Yucatan Peninsula… and then back again.

He had no idea how to replenish his cash. It wasn't like he could just walk up to an ATM. Hopefully he could get some fresh Mexican folding money in El Paraiso from his MOIS counterpart there. He had dollars in his pocket, but no pesos.

"Is there something close by where I can get something to eat," he asked the fellow who'd assured him that the Mastercard he carried would be acceptable. There were only three persons in the crew. This guy appeared to be in charge. The other two guys were busy preparing to gas up the airplane.

"At the highway, they got a good place. It's called *Trocadero*. You like steaks, or you want good Sonoran *tamales*? They got it, man."

"Do you suppose one of you here might want to earn an extra fifty pesos?"

The Mexican gazed at him for several moments, as if trying to size him up. "You're not gringo, and you're not Mexican. I do not mean to offend you, Senyor. I am only curious. What are you?"

"I'm a stranger," Stalin stated and let it go at that.

The fellow did not press the issue further. Rather, he shrugged his shoulders apologetically. "In what may I serve you to earn an extra fifty pesos?"

"Go fetch me three dinners at the Tocadero. "I'll give you four hundred pesos, and you keep what's left, fair enough?"

"Whaddya want to eat?"

"Something good; but no pork, y'understand? Chicken or beef, but no pork."

"Yeah, I got that… okay. I'll get your dinners. You like steak?"

"Yes, but have them cook it well done."

"I will need more than four hundred pesos, Senyor."

Stalin leered at him aggressively. "Then get me something else. But no pork!"

The fellow acceded with a nod and then asked in scarcely more than a whisper, "Are you the pilot?"

Stalin ignored his question as he reached into his pocket and pulled out a wad of American bills. He carefully extracted two twenties and handed it to the Mexican. "That's about the same as four hundred pesos, right?"

The fellow snatched it without responding to his question. Instead he pressed his own inquiry. "You got a very nice airplane, Senyor. You must be very rich. Does it belong to you?"

"Yes, of course… what do you think? You think that I stole it?"

"No, no, Senyor, I only meant to compliment you on your airplane." That was not true. The man was very aware who owned this unique BT-67. And his suspicion was further confirmed by the tail-number.

Stalin continued holding his wad of dollars in hand. "Are you in charge here?"

"More or less."

"You expecting anybody else here tonight?"

"I'm gonna go get your dinners and then I'm shutting down. Why?"

The Iranian extracted two more twenty dollar bills. "Consider this rent, amigo. We're gonna stay parked here until day break if you don't mind."

Again the Mexican snatched the bills and nodded his accord.

Stalin regarded with awe the way events were unfolding. Ali Ul-Faqr continued to remain inside the airplane with Romero. Romero had no doubt lost his appetite and had clearly lost his arrogance, he mused. That's because he'd lost a finger back at the shack. Stalin chuckled out loud. It worked every time! The fellow was now as obedient as a woman! Nonetheless, he'd ordered a dinner for the Mexican. It seemed to him like the right thing to do.

Back at Romero's strip, the *narco-traficante* had acquiesced to lay down his arms and negotiate. The first lesson he learned is when Ali immediately shot the radio operator. "You will take off and land the airplane for me," Romero then directed.

"And if I refuse?" Romero haughtily responded.

The Mexican slowly discerned that he had offered an unwise rejoinder. It elicited from the Iranian a smirk and a pause. Finally he spoke to the man in soft tones.

"I will let you answer your own question by asking you a second question. The question offers multiple choices for a valid response. There is precisely any one of ten correct answers from which to pick."

Romero stared at him somewhat bemused. "I'm listening," he finally replied.

"Which finger is the least useful for you in order to take-off and land the airplane?"

The Mexican stared at him as the implications of that question began to dawn on him. "Huh?" he grunted.

"If you do not choose one, then I will let Ali make the pick. You may not agree with his choice, but then it will be too late. So tell me now which finger!"

Stalin's recollections continued as he stood there on the tarmac. Ali was the wild card which Allah had slyly dealt him. Without the assistance of this Black Muslim, none of what now was unfolding would have been possible. Stalin understood this as he quietly muttered his prayer to Allah of submission and gratitude.

After all, it had not been the MOIS Agent's intention to enlist Ali for this mission. Rather, it was Ali himself who insisted upon coming along. "There must be at least two of us, Moustache," he resolutely argued. "One of us can sleep while the other keeps watch over that piece of shit. I cannot let you take this on all by yourself. Your mission is too important! You must accept my help."

And Stalin found the proposition sound. It would be a long trip to the Yucatan Peninsula and an even longer trip back. He already felt fatigue from the stress of what had transpired today.

His attitude towards Ali had been totally transformed since their meeting at the boulders when he had in fact contemplated killing this self-proclaimed Sultan over the demise of the Jordanian. Now it no longer grated upon him that this Black Muslim called him Moustache, or even that the man was black. Yes, Allah had ordained this True Believer to be at his side.

Anyway, the revelation that the Sultan must accompany him on his flight to El Paraiso had unfolded as Ali prepared to dispatch his men. He instructed them to surround the hill on top of which Romero's observer sat. "Flush him out and kill him," he'd ordered. He then had turned to Stalin. "What about that consignment you said was coming through the tunnel?"

"Let it go on through. It's none of our business. We

are no longer in debt to this Mexican. I have control of him and that is all that I need!"

"Then there's no reason fer my followers to remain in this here desert, is there? Now thet you no longer plan to use the tunnel to smuggle thet"---he glanced sidewise at Romero who stood near him---"uhh… *carpet* through it? There's no point for them to continue manning thet compound, now is there? After what we done here, I reckon it might be best if they haul their asses on back to Tucson, don'tcha think?"

"Yes, that is true. The plans have been changed. Your men may return to your Mosque in Tucson. But have them clear the compound first… tents, weapons, everything except the fence and those bales of hay."

"We only gots four vehicles, Moustache. How can we possibly haul all thet stuff back?"

Stalin heard him, but did not respond. Clearly he was considering the man's words.

Ali pressed his argument. "Trucking down the highway to Tucson with all that shit is gonna be fuckin' dangerous. The Border Patrol always has them inspection traps set up on the highway."

Finally Stalin replied. "You're concerned about the weapons and ammo, is that it?"

"They'll get searched and busted for sure!"

"You can't leave the weapons and ammo. If the Americans find that cache, they'll go to Tucson and arrest your entire following. Here's what I suggest. Pack six of your followers in each of three vehicles. One guy drives the last vehicle. He will carry all the weapons and ammo. Have him take the back roads. Allah's hand will protect him."

"What about them Tribal Police. They're liable to complain to the Feds thet we left all sorts o' litter, and then we'll get a visit from the FBI."

"Our compound was leased for a year, Ali. Anyway, you're going to get a visit from the FBI one way or another. All these dead Mexicans here isn't going to remain unnoticed. I'm sure the Mexican government will complain to the Americans. We just don't want the police finding any weapons or ammo at the compound."

"They's killing each other all the time, Moustache! I doubt if'n them Mexican *Federales* give a nevermind."

"You think so? Then, on second thought, leave that guy on the hill. Call your men back. No point in wasting the time and energy on him. Get them back to the compound. Tell them to put a chain and lock on the gate when they depart. It must be tonight! And tell them to leave a note by the chain saying you'll be back in the middle of October."

Ali nodded his accord. He sent his remaining man to run forward and instruct the rest of his men to abort the assault up the hill to kill Romero's observer. Instead, they should return to the compound, pack up nothing but the weapons and ammo, and go back to Tucson in the manner which the Iranian had suggested.

"I want'cha all outta there before midnight!" he instructed his follower. "Go in ten minute intervals. I don't want'cha caravanning, unnerstand? In a few days, when Moustache and I have finished our business, I'll meet y'all at our Mosque."

Stalin was moved by Ali's obedience. And he more fully realized that it would be extremely helpful to have him along. Did Ali intend to accompany him on the suicide leg of the mission, he wondered? Well, now was not the time to ask. But it nonetheless occurred to him that he should solidify this True Believer's enthusiasm with a reward.

"I will instruct my contact in El Paraiso that I have promised to fund the completion of your Mosque in return for your group's cooperation. He will make certain that my organization carries out this promise."

"It's a place for us to pray, even now. But any… uhh… financial assistance would be a blessing, Moustache. Thanks. But it's only the Jihad which is important now. Allah will hear our prayers even if the Mosque ain't finished."

Stalin gave his head a shake and blinked his eyes to banish these recollections. He was tired, and it caused his mind to wander. This was something he must guard against. He must remain alert!

As Stalin watched the two men fueling the BT-67, he calculated his next move. They had to keep their gas stops at transit strips, because he did not know how to file a flight plan and he didn't trust Romero to be placed in earshot of a Mexican official. He'd listened enough now to Romero's radio communication to grasp how to call ahead for a gas-up, but he still needed to rely upon the Mexican for where these transit strips were located, and on what frequency they could be contacted.

It was a touchy proposition; but he sensed that keeping fear instilled in the man was the sole bromide for this problem. Maybe he should cut of a second finger. He believed that if need be he could pilot a take off in this airplane, but his grasp of how to land it was still a far reach. And, again, he had no idea of where the transit landing strips were located or how to contact them by radio.

"Allah will provide," he muttered in order to comfort his creeping disconsolation.

Bob and Charley's Secret Mission

The two Minutemen had rolled off their canvass fold-out cots at four in the morning. They'd agreed between themselves to make an unofficial survey of that Black Muslim compound and have a look-see at what might have transpired. *Unofficial* meant without anybody's knowledge or permission. That's why they crept out at the early morning hour under the cover of darkness. The Border Patrolman with them yesterday had specifically forbidden Bob and Charley to return to their hill. Thus, they now noiselessly embarked upon this secret mission.

Last night they had quietly discussed the proposition. Bob and Charley mutually concluded that this was too big and juicy a bone to abandon. Fuck the Patrol! Furthermore, they dared not say anything to other Minutemen about their plans. They didn't want an entourage trailing them and making a commotion.

And they didn't want the Border Patrol getting wind of their intentions either. This was their gig, damn it all! They would not be denied. They didn't need those uniformed nannies minding their affairs. It was the sort of adventure which had prompted them to volunteer in the first place. There was no way they were gonna abandon this project.

Bob and Charley intended to first get incontrovertible visual evidence of drug-trafficking at the border by them Black Muslims, and then call it in for the bust. And so early this morning, with a quarter moon setting in the western night sky, they slipped out of their cots and quietly put on their boots.

They crept away from base in their vehicle at about five miles an hour until they reckoned that they had ranged sufficiently far enough for engine noise not to disturb the sleep of their comrades. Bob was driving. He opened up the throttle.

Charley cranked his torso around and looked out the back so as to assure himself that no one had awakened. He spotted no movement. He broke out in a grin as he clenched his fist and stuck a thumb up. Their secret mission was underway.

By a quarter past five in the morning they were perched on their hill overlooking the Black Muslim compound. The sun was teasing at the eastern horizon but hadn't yet broken over it. Nevertheless there was sufficient light by which to distinguish some details of the shadowy landscape below. What they saw wasn't encouraging.

"Reckon they're all still sleeping," Bob offered with a touch of disappointment.

"Where's their vehicles?" Charley complained. "I don't see a one of them. You don't suppose they've run off, do you?"

Bob surveyed the area with his binoculars for several moments before responding. "Damn, do you reckon maybe they brought them drugs across yesterday evening? Looks to me like we've done missed 'em! I tried tellin' thet fat-ass B.P. it would be goin' down last night!"

"The Patrolman said their plane took off without unloading nothing, Bob!"

"That man don't know shit! No wonder this border security's such a mess. Lookie here, they cud've unloaded the plane when it first landed."

"Yeah, I know! We both told him that. Seems to me he didn't want to consider that notion."

"We had a bust, and thet damned Border Patrol's done blown it again. Them niggers are gone!"

"Yeah'n here we are sitting like a couple of jerks in the crapper who took a dump and can't find no paper."

Bob nudged Charley.

"What?" Charley complained.

Bob cast him a sly grin. "Supposin' we drive over to that compound and nose around a bit."

"Maybe some of them are still there sleeping. We could find ourselves in some deep doo-doo if they take unkindly to our intrusion! Anyways, what would be the point of it?"

"They ain't there, Charley! But if'n they are, we'll just tell'em we saw the compound and it raised our curiosity. Or maybe we could say we're lost and need directions. Fact is that I really don't think nobody's down there. Their vehicles are gone."

"Then what's the purpose of going over there?"

"Cuz I want to get to the bottom of this. Don't you?"

He shrugged his shoulders to reflect acquiescence to the notion. "Whaddya suggest, Bob? We ought to walk down there from here?"

"Naw, let's get back to our vehicle and drive over. It'll look less suspicious then if'n we're on foot."

Roughly fifteen minutes later they stopped at the gate of the compound. The first rays of direct sunlight now teased the desert floor casting long clumsy shadows behind the hills. Bob was the driver. After silently pausing at the gate for more than a minute, Bob suddenly thrust his hand upon the horn and pierced the silence with a long blare. Charley almost jumped out of his skin.

"What in the name of Jeezuz are you doing?" he caterwauled.

"I'm playin' them boys a little reveille. I don't see no heads poppin' out of them tents. Those niggers are done gone, Charley. It went down last night, just like we figgered."

Charley rubbed his chin thoughtfully. "Then I reckon

there's no danger in us taking a gander around the place, eh?"

"Even breathing air has some danger what with all this ozone and poisonous particulates. But that aside, how do you propose gettin' in there? My bones are too creaky to climb that fence, and I ain't no locksmith. So unless you got a key or a set of chain cutters, I don't see much prospect of us taking a gander."

Just then they saw an SUV kicking up dust as it came rocketing around the hill on the barely navigable dirt road which lead to the compound. The two men were frozen in place. Bob caught sight of the emblem painted on the passenger-side door.

"Oh, shit, it's them tribal police."

"We ain't s'posed to be here," Charley lamented. "Let's get our asses outta this place!"

Bob clucked, "Well, making a run for it will only get us in a whole lot more doo-doo! We ain't breaking no law, at least none what them damn injuns would be aware of. Jest stay cool, Charley. I'll do the talkin'."

Benjamin Hill, Sonora, Mexico

It was early morning. Last night they'd tied Romero up. Ali had then used a long piece of bare wire which he twisted twice around the Mexican's neck and then tethered it to his own wrist. The pair slept on the deck of the BT-67. Stalin had snoozed uncomfortably in the right seat of the pilot compartment with a pistol cradled in his lap. He was now roused by the rustling movement of Ali unbinding himself from Romero. The Iranian glanced behind and observed his colleague stretch out his arms as he vocally yawned. Stalin stood up, but hunched over in order to avoid banging his head. He then thrust himself free of the chair.

Ali also needed to hunch in order to mind his head. He was several inches taller than the Iranian. "Good morning, Moustache," he broadcasted cheerily. "Did'ja get some 'Z's'?"

"What's that?" the man responded devoid of humor.

"Sleep!"

"Yes… some, and you?"

"Like a 'ho' on holiday. 'Ceptin that the sack o' shit down there snores like a freight train."

Stalin could see that the Mexican's eyes were open, but they were directed at no particular object. "I have to piss," Romero finally complained.

"Go ahead and piss," Ali chortled.

"Are you gonna leave me tied up? I can't fly the *pinche* airplane lying on the deck! C'mon, I need to piss!"

Stalin yawned and then pushed the pistol into his trousers to the left of his navel. "So, Senyor Romero, I am happy to hear that you had a restful night. We have a long day ahead of us." He lifted his gaze to the black man. "Could you hand me a water bottle from the back?"

The Iranian gazed at Romero in silence. Finally the Mexican shut his eyes. Ali returned, stepped over the prone body and handed Stalin the liter-sized water bottle.

He accepted it from Ali without remark, grimaced as

he forced open the cap, tilted his head and glugged about half of it down. He then let out a sigh of satisfaction as he wiped his mouth with a bare arm. He moved forward a couple of steps so that the toes of his boots were in proximity to Romero's inert body. He lifted the water bottle and tipped it. The water poured through the air and splashed over the Mexican's head and face.

"*Pinche cabron*! *Baboso pendejo*!" Romero burbled as he struggled to escape the shower of water, but he was too securely tied to affect much movement.

"It's time to get up, Senyor Romero. We have things to do and a place to go. Are you ready to take this airplane into the air?"

"It is difficult to fly an airplane from this position," the fellow wryly quipped.

"Are you suggesting that I untie you?"

"I don't give a fuck. I'm not flying this plane for you. You are going to kill me in any event. It might as well be now!" He stared up with hostility in his face and continued an unwavering gaze at the Iranian. "Go ahead, shoot me," he finally challenged, "and then we'll see to how many places you go."

"As you wish," Stalin sighed as he extracted his pistol and pointed it at the man. Ali watched with his mouth slightly agape. "Well, perhaps not exactly as you wish," he then added.

He shifted his gaze to the black man. "Senyor Romero is in a bad mood, Ali. I believe it is because he hasn't had breakfast. We need to prepare him something to eat.

Could you take out your knife and slice him a cut of meat?"

Ali pulled the knife from his scabbard. It was as big as a Bowie, and looked every bit as mean. "What meat?" he inquired in a hesitant voice, sensing that Moustache was making a show to intimidate their prisoner.

"The piece of pork we have on board." He pointed his finger at Romero. "See, that piece of pork lying there. I would suggest you slice a breakfast ear from this pig so that we can offer Senyor Romero his breakfast. And then if the Senyor's appetite is still unsatisfied, we can offer him the pig's scrotum."

"I'm not frightened," Romero protested. "Without me you can go nowhere!"

Stalin gave Ali a curt nod. "Please serve our esteemed guest his breakfast."

The black man hesitated as he gaped at Stalin, attempting to discern if the man was really serious about this. The stern expression on the face of the Iranian quickly convinced him that the man was in dead earnest. Ali placed a boot on Romero's cheek, forcing his face to tilt to the side. And then the black man bent down on one knee with a grunt while he awkwardly continued to leverage the man's head. Romero was grunting a protest. Finally he yielded in a strained voice.

"Alright, alright!" he screamed. "I'll fly the *pinche* airplane! I'll fly! I'll fly!"

Ali looked up at Stalin to receive a final affirmation as to whether or not he should continue. The man again gave him a curt nod of approval as he proclaimed, "Breakfast time!"

Ali placed the knife to the top of Romero's ear as the victim began to scream. Blood appeared as he deftly employed several sawing strokes before the ear broke free. The Mexican howled with pain and panic.

"Now feed him his breakfast," Stalin coolly instructed.

Ali stood up and drew back his boot. Romero's screams subsided into gurgling invective. The Black Muslim held an ear in his left hand as he gripped the knife with his right hand and swiped both sides of the blade against his trousers. He cast a quick survey of the steel surface and then returned the knife to its scabbard. Next, he kneeled down again on one knee, reached for Romero's nose and pulled it so that the man's head faced straight up.

"*Pinche cabron*," the Mexican spat.

The black man then attempted to shove the ear into Romero's mouth, but in the process, the fellow bit him. Ali immediately withdrew his hand with a grimace of pain. The ear slipped out of his hand and landed on the Mexican's chest.

"Sonovabitch muddafukker!" the Sultan yelped and shook the fingers of his hand. There was a clear set of bite marks turning purple at the base of his thumb.

Stalin sighed with impatience. He extracted his pistol and knelt down beside the wriggling body of his captive. Next, he raised his pistol over Romero's face threateningly. "Open your mouth!"

The response by the Mexican was not cooperative. He attempted to spit into the Iranian's face, but the meager launch fell far short of its mark. Down came the butt of Stalin's pistol smashing into Romero's front teeth. The sound of them breaking was accompanied by a spurt of blood and a shriek from the assaulted man. Stalin then deftly snatched the ear off the man's chest, and fearlessly pushed it into his bloody mouth. He quickly cupped that same hand over Romero's mouth to muffle the screams of agony and to prevent the Mexican from spitting out his own ear.

"Now chew and swallow," the Iranian calmly instructed. "It's not polite to disparage your host's cuisine."

Stalin had been too involved with the task at hand to notice the clamor outside the airplane, but Ali's attention was diverted. He raced forward to the cockpit to get a view of the outside, stood there for a moment and then hustled back. He nudged Stalin on the shoulder.

"Moustache, we all've got company, and it don't look none too friendly!"

Tucson, Arizona, Border Patrol Offices

The Patrolman began to regret that he'd ever filed the verbal report to his supervisor in the field concerning the "Black Muslim" incident. After all, the violence occurred on the other side of the border. It suggested all the appearances of two rival drug gangs settling accounts with one another.

Of course, he knew better than to even presume that such a report was optional, which was why he'd officially offered the account. One of the groups was American, purportedly Black Muslims on a religious retreat. The Americans had won that skirmish with the Mexicans. However, the massacre had occurred entirely on the Mexican side of the border; so, technically, no U.S. or state law was broken.

Moreover, he wasn't entirely convinced that they were drug traffickers, although he had to admit that it was certainly a reasonable presumption. Still, there remained a federal violation which the Border Patrol by rights needed to address. It happened when the American group illegally crossed back over the border through an unauthorized port of entry. That's why he'd been required to make an official statement.

Anyway, it wasn't the Border Patrol conducting this investigation for which he'd been summoned to Tucson. Nope, it was the DEA who now wanted the particulars… detail by detail. Two DEA guys were in the room, along with a Border Patrol Supervisor. But it became clear to him early on that even though they were meeting in the Patrol Headquarters building here in Tucson, it was the DEA conducting this investigation. It was one of the Drug Enforcement Agents who informed him that they were recording the session. They didn't bother to ask if he objected.

"What're the names of those two other witnesses?" one of the DEA guys asked.

The Patrolman shrugged his shoulders. "Bob and Charley is all I know. They're a couple of them Minutemen. They said they were witnessing a potential drug crossing, and I was dispatched to investigate their claim."

"You don't know their full names?"

He paused several moments before responding. "Nope, I guess I don't."

The two Drug Enforcement Agents looked at each other with a hint of disparagement, which did nothing to endear them to the Patrolman. He resented their uppity attitude. He resented being interrogated this way.

Never volunteer nothing you don't need to, and cover your ass! That was the operating procedure to which Patrolmen increasingly subscribed. He glanced over at the Patrol Supervisor, seeking a little support against the chafing attitudes of the two Agents. The Supervisor blinked and turned away his eyes.

The press, the judiciary, and even the other enforcement agencies all seemed to be coming down on the Border Patrol these past few years. But why this was so remained a mystery to him. It was as if they perceived Patrolmen to be a bunch of bullies picking on the little guy. He'd thought more'n once about getting out; but the benefits of government employment kept him from following those inclinations. A lot of the younger fellows were moving on.

He didn't understand the attitudes he heard on TV or sometimes read in the newspaper. Everybody he talked to in his neighborhood and church all were against illegal immigration and against any sort of amnesty for the illegals. Moreover it would be the same TV talk shows and front page news stories accusing the Patrol of brutality which would come out the next day criticizing the organization for allowing so many illegal aliens into the country, and for so much hard drugs slipping over the border. You couldn't win for losing!

Like a lot of his colleagues, he put up with it so's not to lose his retirement benefits. But his heart was no longer with the cause. What was the cause? It had become a garbled message and a blurred vision.

Now he would have to endure derisive comments and haughty innuendo from these DEA jerks. Well, during the entire incident under investigation he hadn't pulled a pistol from his holster, so they couldn't indict him. There were a bunch of Patrolmen doing time in jail for having misunderstood their mission, and then having aggressively pursued it… like firing on a Mexican who'd just smuggled almost one ton of marijuana across the border into the U.S. and who fled the scene as he was apprehended by the Patrol. One Patrolman fired at him. The Mexican alleged that he'd been gravely wounded. He couldn't have been wounded very seriously because he kept on running and made it across the border.

The Mexican government protested, because the smuggler claimed that the wound was incurred after he'd crossed the border. The Patrolman was indicted by a Federal Prosecutor, and found guilty of the alleged violations. It was the opinion of the Judge that firing a lethal weapon with intent to do injury at a man for having crossed some *cannabis* into the U.S. was an unwarranted abuse of his authority. The hapless Patrolman received a sentence of nine years imprisonment. Evidently the judge was sending the Border Patrol a message. The Patrolmen were hearing the message loud and clear.

There had been scores of convictions for similar allegations like the one that had ended in a nine year sentencing for the aforementioned Patrolman. They were also put behind bars. Yup, the Border Patrol was getting the message. What was the point of trying to do your job? So, many of them did little more than go through the motions. And that's what this Patrolman now sitting in Tucson HQ intended to do… go through the motions.

As he'd expected, it didn't take long for the DEA interrogator to get to the subject matter which he'd all along supposed would dominate the purpose of this interview. The Agent unfolded a large map which covered almost half the conference table. It was a 1:10,000 "topo" of the area he had encountered in his controversial observations yesterday evening.

"Where's the tunnel?" the Agent asked him as he swooped an inviting hand towards the map.

Puerto Penyasco, Mexico

To look at this town, one's impression would probably be that it was much more a modern American creation than a scion of colonial Spain or a consequence of Mexican culture. However Puerto Penyasco was definitely south of the border, and specifically located in northwestern Sonora. Forty years ago it had been a sleepy fishing village.

Now this specific stretch of beach along the Sea of Cortez shoreline was put upon by lovely chalets with modern kitchens inside them, air-conditioners groaning outside, and satellite dishes on the roof. The vehicular license plates were preponderantly from the various states north of the border, and these resident visitors did not abandon their language or customs. Puerto Penyasco offered either the best or the worst of both worlds, depending on one's specific perspectives.

There were several RV parks in the immediate area as well. They looked like a still-shot of grazing elephant herds. And at the port, able Sea Captains stood ready and eager to take the American tourists fishing. Anchored in the harbor were of fleet of various boats, a few of which could accommodate parties numbering as many as twelve and some of them offered reasonable amenities.

For a more budget-friendly excursion, visiting fishermen could find water conveyance using oars or outboard propulsion. In short, it was a consummate example of a sea-side Mexican tourist village, and the magnet attracting visitors was fishing, peaceful repose, fishing, fun at the beach and fishing. During summer months the water felt as warm as a tepid bath. The sand would burn all but the most calloused feet. The sea-floor was too shallow for aggressive surf, thus the only real attraction for the younger generation was being able to order a beer or a mixed drink without getting "carded".

Northwest of Puerto Penyasco lay Chola Bay. The *gringos* were "discovering" that area as well. They'd built an RV park nearby. Overlooking Chola Bay was a large property.... actually it appeared to be a compound which most Americans who noticed it assumed the place belonged to the government. It was walled. Out beyond the walls was a cyclone fence with barbed wire above. It surrounded the entire estate. Immediately to the east, just outside the cyclone fence was an airstrip, an air-sock, a conspicuous radio antenna and a small hangar. Moreover, there were signs discouraging any visitor on foot, horseback or vehicle to proceed further.

But it did not belong to the government. It belonged to Sammy Sanchez. This property at Chola Bay was one of his "vacation homes". He was a rich man. In Sonora, he was a very important man, and perhaps even more powerful than the Governor. He was a successful *narco-traficante*. His operations-center resided in Hermosillo, capitol of Sonora.

When Romero---then hostage in his own airplane---had suggested to Stalin the transit airstrip at Benjamin Hill for their gas-up, it had not been a random choice. Sammy Sanchez was a cooperating associate of Romero, and Sammy Sanchez owned the transit airstrip.

His people would immediately recognize the unique BT-67 flown by "Gomero" as he was endearingly known to them. They would become suspicious when he remained in the airplane, and did not show his face. They would contact one of Sammy's lieutenants who in turn would inform the boss concerning this report from Benjamin Hill.

For Romero, this was more than just a desperate hope, it was a predictable outcome. The *narco-traficantes* were a distrusting bunch. They guardedly suspected each other, but they were absolutely paranoid about strangers who dared to tread upon their turf. Moreover, Sammy and "Gomero" had an additional close bond at this moment. Sanchez had arranged for a very large shipment of "blanco" to pass through Romero's tunnel. It was in fact that very consignment which Romero had designs to steal, employing Moustache and his band of Black Muslims as the perpetrators.

Sammy Sachez had listened to his lieutenant, Jesus Calderon as the man explained this disturbing situation, and the boss immediately order him to investigate why "Gomero's" BT-67 was parked on his strip, but the *pendejo* had refused to show his face. It made no sense. Sammy had an overarching concern about the crossing of his upcoming shipment. He was depending upon Romero's tunnel as his method of conveyance. Anything out of the ordinary concerning this fellow was therefore amplified in his mind.

Having learned this disquieting information concerning "Gomero", Sammy allowed his paranoia free rein. He cursed under his breathe. The smuggling plans for his "blanco" must be aborted!

Still, there were many unanswered question. Sammy was a curious man. In his business, one dared not overlook inconsistent details. It was a part of the constant vigil which a *narco-traficante* must maintain if he is to survive.

He, of course, had not gone to Benjamin Hill. He'd relied upon Jesus Calderon to investigate the call which had come from his air-strip operations supervisor. The man suspected that a foreigner---who was not a gringo--- had stolen "Gomero's" BT-67. Sammy had instructed Jesus to insist that the operator somehow disable the airplane until they could get there. Evidently the operator had succeeded in doing so, because Jesus now had "Gomero" plus two foreigners in custody. Jesus had explained on the telephone that he'd found "Gomero" battered and apparently being held prisoner by two foreigners.

"One of them is a *negrito*," he added.

"Why do you want to bring these two foreigners to Chola Bay, Jesus?" Sammy acidly protested over the telephone. "There is plenty of desert around Benjamin Hill where they can be buried."

"I suggest that you meet them, *jefe*, because these two foreigners have an interesting story to tell you. It's all a question of whether or not you choose to believe them."

"And you say that you're taking "Gomero" to the hospital? Which hospital?"

"Pardon me, *jefe*, but what I said is that he *should* go to the hospital, given his condition. However, in light of the story these two foreigners have told me, you might not want to waste my efforts on taking "Gomero" to the hospital. Anyway, he will live without hospital attention. He's lost some teeth and he's missing an ear... oh yeah, and a finger!"

"You did this?"

"No the foreigners did it to him. Do you want to meet with them or not?"

"Who are these foreigners?"

"One is a black man… a gringo. And one says he is from Iran."

"Iran?"

"That's what he claims, *jefe*. And he looks like he could be from there."

"What's their story which you say that I should hear?"

"It's better if you hear it from their lips, don't you think? They claim that "Gomero" intended to betray you."

"How would they know that?"

"Well, during my questions to them, the black man mentioned a large shipment scheduled to go through the tunnel, and that "Gomero" had hired him to seize it. So I immediately wondered how this man could know about our shipment unless "Gomero" told him. And why would that *pinche cabron* tell him?"

"Yes, what you say has logic. But it is not strong evidence. I must have incontestable evidence if I am to castigate Senyor Romero, understand? We need good relations with our associates in Culiacan. I must have an irrefutable case against him. Tell these two foreigners that if they wish to live, they must come up with stronger evidence than just a story. Bring all three of them to my villa at Chola Bay. Can you fly the BT-67?"

"I think so; but "Gomero" is not so damaged that he cannot give me guidance. The control panel doesn't look very complicated, but anyway, I will put "Gomero" in the right seat. I will let him think that we are bringing the two foreigners to Chola Bay in order to punish them."

"Fine, it's no more than a one hour flight. See you soon."

"*Si jefe*, but there is one more important thing."

"I'm listening."

"If what these foreigners say is true, you better hold off crossing the shipment of *blanco* through "Gomero's" tunnel."

"Yes, I concluded that for myself; but why *do you* think that I should not?"

"Because they made a lot of noise and probably attracted some attention."

"Who?"

"The foreigners… they claim that they had twenty men. They killed all of "Gomero's" people at his airstrip near the tunnel. There are dead bodies lying all over the place. Even "Gomero" admits that this is true."

"Who in the devil are these foreigners? Who do they work for?"

"Well, it's only a guess, *jefe*; but I think "Gomero" hired them to steal your shipment for him."

"We've been over that already. Tell those two foreigners that if they wish to live, they must provide me clear proof to back up their story! Anyway, why would they betray the man who hired them? You see, your presumption really isn't entirely logical, Jesus. What does "Gomero" say to you?"

"Not much, it is difficult for him to talk. His lips are swollen as big as green chiles. And they knocked out some of his teeth, like I told you."

"He says nothing?"

"Well, he says they are *pendejos*. He thinks maybe they are terrorists. The black man is a Muslim and the Iranian, y'know, I guess they're Muslims too, aren't they?"

"So, why is "Gomero" involved with them?"

"He didn't say."

"What do *they* say? Did you ask them?"

"I told you. They say he hired them to knock off your shipment."

"Why them?"

"They needed a carpet transported from Quintana Roo and then smuggled through his tunnel, but they didn't have money to pay him, so they agreed to exchange services."

"A carpet, did I hear you right? What is it a *magic* carpet? Why is it in Quintana Roo? How can you argue that what they say is logical? To me it sounds absurd!"

"I'm just telling you what they said, *jefe*."

"How do they know that you are involved with me? And how do they know that it is *my* shipment?"

"Because "Gomero" said so. It was one of the first things "Gomero" said to me. He warned me when I came on board. He screamed to me that these guys were planning to knock off your shipment, and that it was now unsafe to use the tunnel. He said that I should immediately call you and warn you. They heard him say these things. And that's when they argued that it was "Gomero" who had hired them to do this."

Jesus Calderon endured an uncomfortable silence. He felt the need to fill this vacuum, but experience had taught him to hold his tongue. Finally he heard his boss reply, "Yes, Jesus, bring all of them here to Chola Bay. And come in "Gomero's" airplane. It's worth a lot of money."

"*Si*, but what about the airplane on which we flew here, *jefe?*"

He sighed impatiently. "Stow it in the hangar at Benjamin Hill or tie it down outside."

He did not await any further response from Jesus Calderon. He'd issued his final orders. Sammy Sanchez pressed the disconnect button on his telephone.

FBI Offices, Phoenix

Leslie Nellis's supervisor read the report a second time. He couldn't come up with any plausible connection to the Moustafa Rajai case, yet the scenario presented in this report dogged at the edges of his mind. Maybe it was his frustration with the dead end he faced in his investigation of the Rajai case that compelled him to grasp at straws. The Palo Verde Security had raised their alert level and felt that was as far as their concern should take them.

Nope, there was nothing in this report that could be plausibly argued as having a substantive connection to Moustafa Rajai. But nevertheless the FBI supervisor read it again. And then he read it yet again.

The tribal police had investigated the site of a compound leased to a Black Muslim cult. The land was part of their reservation. Sounds of profuse gunfire had been reported by a tribal member coming from across the border in the vicinity of this compound. When the tribal police investigated the following morning, they found the compound chained, padlocked and abandoned.

They searched the area and came upon two mounds that looked suspiciously like shallow graves outside the compound. They dug them up and discovered two bodies. That's when they called Tucson and got the FBI involved. The bodies were not tribal members. The corpses exhibited bullet wounds which clearly indicated that they had been executed. That evidence coupled with the mysterious abandonment of the cult from their leased compound had prompted the tribal police to call in the Federal authorities.

The agent reporting had investigated the crime scene. One of the victims had been given what appeared to be a proper Muslim burial. The victim was laid out with his head pointing east. He was naked save for having been wrapped in a white sheet, which the agent called a *kafan*. Evidently the reporter had some passing knowledge of Muslim ritual. The deceased was not black. He had straight hair, but his remains were already fairly decomposed, and his head had been partially blown away from the impact of a bullet.

`The second victim had not received ritual treatment. She was dumped into her grave, her head pointing west, in street clothes. She appeared to be Mexican from her hair and dress.

At the crime scene, the tribal police had apprehended two elderly gentlemen who claimed to be Minutemen. They were extremely evasive about their reasons for being there. Finally one of them broke down and admitted their observations of the previous evening.

The police held them for further questioning by the FBI. The reporting Agent had interrogated these two witnesses and noted what they allegedly had observed that previous evening. They were obsessed with the notion of a tunnel. So the Agent followed them as they led him to where this supposed tunnel surfaced. Sure enough, it was there.

The two Minutemen mentioned the Border patrolman that had accompanied them on their second observation, and he was named in the report, but had not been contacted by the Agent. The Minutemen were released. They had continued to insist their opinion that a drug-smuggling event had occurred through the tunnel sometime during the previous night.

Leslie's supervisor found it hard to believe that if this Muslim cult was engaged in the use of this tunnel that the purpose was for drug-smuggling. Why would the *narco-traficantes* want to connect with these Black Muslims? They didn't trust their own people much less a band of black gringos.

It was the fact that the cult was Muslim that dogged Leslie's supervisor. Sure, there were known cases of terrorists resorting to drug trafficking as a means of subsistence.

The Balkan terrorists were particularly inclined to this mode of fund-raising. But that didn't necessarily mean that this was what these Black Muslims had in mind. He was thinking something along the line of high-density explosives… something like C-4 which he supposed could inflict enough damage to the Palo Verde retaining walls to make it the next Three Mile Island disaster, or worse. This Rajai case haunted him.

He picked up the telephone and called the Tucson office, identified himself and asked to speak with the reporting Agent. "Have you run the prints on those corpses you found in the desert?"

The Agent assured him that it was in process.

"I want you to call me the minute you get the results. If there's a match in our files; that information would be very helpful."

The Agent agreed to update him, but inquired concerning the nature of this investigation by the Phoenix office.

Leslie's Supervisor ignored the question. "What about the Black Muslims? Any leads on where they might have gone?"

The Agent from Tucson had no clue.

"You say in your report that these Papago Indians leased them the land. They must have some notion of where those Black Muslims came from, huh?"

"The person to whom they leased the land was named Lewis Reddy. We have 209 *Lewis Reddy's* in our file. And for all we know it was an alias. He paid the Indians cash. This has all the earmarks of a drug-smuggling ring, sir."

"What about the prospect of terrorism. They're Muslims."

"I'm an anti-terrorist specialist, sir. That's why they initially sent me to the site. Like you observed, those fellows at the compound were Muslims. But I think it's a simple case of drug-smuggling. Homicides go hand in hand with that M.O., as I'm sure you know. Given the information of those two Minutemen, it really appears that there was an altercation between two rival drug gangs, and it got very ugly."

"So where does this leave the investigation?"

"Out of my neighborhood. Sounds like something for the DEA to take over, but that's not my decision."

It became increasingly clear to the supervisor that Tucson's FBI office was relegating this event to the dead file. "Well," he stipulated to himself after hanging up the phone, "we're gonna resurrect it!"

What in the hell were a bunch of Black Muslims who'd come out of nowhere doing camped out in the Sonora Desert. Mustafa Rajai confessed that the Iranians had an untoward interest in PVNGS. He further insinuated that in his opinion they intended to blow it up. As far as Leslie's Supervisor was concerned, that made any suspicious activity by Muslims in the area a cause for alarm.

Chola Bay

A stable for horses lay behind the villa of Sammy Sanchez. He'd recently built it with the intention of having a quartet of Andalusians, but as yet he'd not gotten around to buying them. It required a lot of red tape. He'd intended to import them from Jerez de la Frontera in Spain. He'd seen a program devoted to this breed of horse on Mexican television. They were very expensive horses, but money was of small concern to him. He could afford to indulge himself.

Anyway, it wasn't the busy job of paperwork which had dissuaded him from completing the project. He had clerks for that. But what bothered him were the blanks on the forms which the authorities required to be filled in. To import animals from abroad was not so simple. He was a very private man, most of all when it involved exchanges with the government. They asked all sorts of personal questions. There was a penalty for imparting false information on these forms. He was unwilling to expose himself to such risk. So, the procurement of these animals remained a work in progress which he'd largely set aside.

There were several small rooms invested at the stable in addition to stalls for the animals and the large open area under roof where bales of hay could be stored. The purpose of these rooms had been proposed as a place for equipment storage; and two of these spaces would be provided as quarters for the grooms. Whatever their original purpose, without horses the stable had little use… except for occasions like the one now in progress.

These relatively small spaces had never been plumbed, floored, painted or furnished. But each had a sturdy door with lock installed. The three prisoners had been split up and then summarily thrown into separate empty rooms inside the stable. These quarters were windowless and the earthen floor was bare. The prisoners had been provided neither food nor water. Not even a pot to piss in.

The cunning *narco-traficante* had ordered the prisoners isolated so that they could not contrive a common theme. He deprived them of sustenance in order to break their will and fill them with fear. Evening was the best time to interrogate these men who would be fatigued by the heat of their cells during the day, and from thirst. Sammy had perfected his breaking of wills to an art-form. Moreover, he enjoyed the exercise.

He would have left them there much longer than the eight hours which had transpired since their arrival. Thirty sleepless hours was optimal. To extend it any longer would risk over-fatigue which could numb a man's sense of pain. It could induce a sense of hopelessness that blunted his fear. An interrogator does not want his subject resigned to death. One must always dangle hope within grasp of the subject if only he would satisfy the interrogator.

However, Sammy was in a hurry. He was concerned about the shipment of *blanco*. It was a large shipment. He'd already cancelled any notion of transporting it through Romero's tunnel; however he needed to ascertain how badly compromised was the information concerning his load. What involvement did this *negrito* have in the deceit, and where did this Iranian fit in?

He was quite certain that "Gomero" had betrayed him. Nevertheless, he needed to be positively convinced…

beyond a reasonable doubt, so to speak. The Culiacan connection was an important link in his business. "Gomero" Romero had friends and influence in Culiacan. He was a reliable and respected smuggler. The case against this man needed to be iron-clad.

So far Sammy's perceptions were largely formed through information given to him by Jesus Calderon. Now he would ascertain this notion of "Gomero's" betrayal for himself. If confirmed, he would then broadcast these finding to the *narco-traficante* community at large. He needed to demonstrate clear justification for his execution of Romero.

Jesus held a pistol at the ready as two men dragged the big black *gringo* out of his cell. The victim struggled and finally gained his legs in order to awkwardly shuffle as they continued to drag him into the open stable area. It was sheltered by a roof, but the walls were staggered wooden planks allowing fresh air to breeze through this space for comfort of the anticipated horses. They had put a chair and a small table right in the middle of this open area originally designed to store the bales of hay.

Sammy stood leaning against the planks, resting his elbows between the gaps as he clenched a burning cigar between his teeth. One eye was almost shut to avoid the smoke curling from his cigar. His mouth was distorted by the cigar, but he nonetheless appeared to sneer as he observed them deliver the man. His hands were free. His pistol remained holstered. He continued to watch with that implacable sneer as the two men shoved Ali into the chair while Jesus hovered behind with his drawn pistol aimed at the fellow's head.

"Put your arms behind the chair with your hands together," growled Jesus.

There was a pile of Teflon ties on the table. They looked like the kind that an aircraft electrician would use to bind cables together or secure wire harnesses to the airframe. One of the men grabbed a tie and moved in between Jesus and the chair, kneeling down as he did so. He slipped the loop over Ali's hands and then secured his wrists together. Ali winced but made no sound.

Sammy pulled his arms free of their perch on the planks. He sauntered up to Jesus as the man who'd bound Ali's wrist recovered to his feet and took several short steps back in order to give the big boss a berth. With one hand Sammy pushed Jesus to the side, and with the other he reached out and grabbed the back of the chair. With a grunt he pulled it.

The chair toppled backwards as Ali's legs flailed in a hopeless effort to regain his balance. It crashed to the bare ground with a thud so that the black man was now facing straight up. His head had hit directly on the ground, but nonetheless he uttered no sound. He defiantly stared up at Sammy as his feet explored how to touch the ground. He twisted his torso so that one foot was able to gain a modicum of contact while the other leg just hung there uselessly. He'd lost all possibilities of practical leverage.

Like Jesus, Sammy spoke good English. "So, I am very curious about something, negrito," he stated in calm voice. "Why did you cut off the ear and the finger of my good friend, "Gomero"? Why did you knock out his teeth? In what way did my good friend offend you?"

The black man offered no response. Sammy raised his boot and dangled it menacingly above Ali's face. Finally he set his foot back on the ground. "Are you able to understand my English, Senyor Negrito? Shake your head yes or no."

"My name is Ali Ul-Faqr. My rank is Sultan. And if'n I gots a serial number, only Allah and his Prophet know it!"

Sammy chuckled as he slowly nodded his head in disbelief and then looked over at Jesus with an expression of mirth clearly radiating from his face. The deferential lieutenant immediately responded with forced laughter, although he wasn't sure what exactly his boss found funny. The other two henchmen also laughed in a rejoinder to Jesus. Ali stared straight up looking at no one in particular.

"Jesus," Sammy exclaimed, "have I heard this *puto* correctly? He calls himself *Sultan Fucker*?

"*Si, jefe*" the lieutenant affirmed now with a genuinely mirthful transition, "I believe you have heard correctly."

Sammy continued to gaze at Jesus, and then he discreetly pulled on his right ear. "Perhaps you should put a bullet through Sultan Fucker's balls and see if that loosens his tongue."

Jesus understood his boss's signal of a pulled ear. He'd been through this drill several times before when they interrogated. "*Jefe*, let's give him one more chance. I think he has things to tell you which you should hear." He then knelt down and whispered to Ali in a soft pleading voice.

"Tell him what you and the man you call Moustache explained to me at Benjamin Hill. You must tell him now, or I must follow his orders!"

Ali drew his legs back together. They still dangled over the chair but now shielded his balls safely between them. He glanced over at Jesus. The man's face was close enough that Ali could smell his breath."

"Last chance," the Mexican warned.

The Iranian Embassy, Ottawa, Canada

Although he was the Ambassador, he spoke to the MOIS Agent attached to the Embassy with a careful deference. He answered the knock, opened the door and invited him into his office. With a light touch he then closed the door, and immediately offered tea, but the man waved off the amenity. With agility the MOIS Agent plunged into a sofa chair closest to the Ambassador's desk. He gazed with a poker face as he watched the man take his position behind the desk in a western style high-backed leather chair.

These Embassy stooges have a soft life, the Agent silently mulled… maybe too soft! Most of them don't even pray. He counted the Ambassador in that group. More than once, he'd suggested to the Ambassador that praying should be a mandatory component of staff duties here at the Embassy.

"We are an Islamic Republic," the Agent had reminded this man more than once before. "It's the duty of our staff to pray."

"That is a duty each man owes to Allah," the Ambassador had calmly rejoined, "not to the Republic."

The Agent now impatiently scratched with the nail of his index finger against the fabric covering the arm of the sofa chair in which he sat. "So," he finally offered when the Ambassador having seated himself behind the desk did not immediately speak, "have you brought me here to discuss this woman from the American FBI?"

"Ah, so you are aware that she has officially appealed to the Canadians on behalf of the Jewess and her two monkeys who we are holding here?"

"Of course I am aware of such things. It is my business to be aware!"

"I think it's dangerous to continue to hold them here. There is no longer any purpose. Moustafa Rajai is dead. What do you intend to do with them?"

"Dangerous? That is an interesting word coming from a man who has sovereign jurisdiction over this Iranian Embassy. Please explain to me what danger you perceive."

"Well, let me say that at the very least it could become embarrassing."

"I see, so what would you suggest, Ambassador? Turn her over to the American as the Canadians have requested? Thus, we will avoid embarrassment?"

"What harm can it do? She knows nothing."

"Well, let us think through your proposition. If we let her and the monkeys go, than it is an admission that we have them here. If we have them here, then it ties us to Moustafa Rajai. If we are tied to Moustafa Rajai, then the project I am undertaking will have a direct link back to the Embassy here. You are unaware of the scope of this project. It is a very bold and aggressive project. It is something which Usama Bin Ladin will turn his face away with awe and jealousy when he receives the news. It is an appropriate response to the American belligerence towards our nuclear program. But, nevertheless, it must remain a deed without Iranian fingerprints. So, I believe your proposition is flawed."

"I'm not privy to the particulars of your project. It leaves me at a disadvantage for making an appropriate decision."

"Quite so. Therefore I suggest you leave the decision making to me."

"And what then should be my response to the Canadian request on behalf of this American FBI agent?"

"Deny that we have any knowledge of the Jewess."

"But that would be a transparent lie. They wouldn't have made the request to us if they weren't certain that she was here. It will only raise their suspicions and clearly tie us to… uhh… your project."

"How did they learn?"

"That is a question I must ask you. Even the cooks in our kitchen must have some inkling for whom they prepare the food. So, I can not rule out leaks from the staff. We must always operate under the premise that we have spies inside this Embassy. Nevertheless, is it not possible that before he was killed, Rajai went to the FBI?"

The MOIS Agent didn't answer. He was aware that the Ambassador already knew that this was so. He stared into empty space rather than gazing at the fellow behind the desk and muttered in a low voice sounding almost as if he was speaking to himself.

"What is the reason these Americans give for requesting the Jewess?"

It took a moment for the Ambassador to realize that the question was addressed to him. "They claim that she may have information valuable to their anti-terror effort. Does she or either of the children, in fact, have such information?"

"No, of course not!"

"Then what is the harm in turning her over to them?"

"The two monkeys each have a missing thumb. They will certainly bawl to the Americans how that occurred. Wouldn't you consider that embarrassing as well?"

The Ambassador's face blushed as he took in a deep breath. "Well, we will deny that allegation, of course. Certainly, it should not affect your project. The fact that we have released them will argue in our favor. Uhh… we can stipulate that her husband was a brutal fiend who did this to the poor children, and she is simply making up a story in order to acquire political asylum from the Americans."

He did not respond. He clearly was in deep thought,

and so the Ambassador leaned back in his chair and gave the man his space in which to think. Finally the Agent reacted in a quiet voice.

"Tell them that we will release her. But the paperwork will take several days. My project will be completed soon. Once it's over, there is little damage that the Jewess and her monkeys can do. She can add very little to what the Americans apparently already know."

"Yes, that seems like an appropriate response. I'll take care of it."

"There is something else that you should take care of, Ambassador."

"What?"

"Prayer."

"We've been through this before."

"Those on staff who refuse to pray or who are caught shirking their duties to Allah should be immediately expelled. You could create a great deal more security in the Embassy if you would follow my suggestion!"

El Paraiso, Quintana Roo, Mexico

They were docked in the harbor of El Paraiso. The sun had gone down more than an hour ago. Flecks of light from the shore and from a few of the ships played off the calm ripples of water. The MOIS Agent and the Ukrainian stood on the deck of the trawler, both leaning their arms on the railing as they gazed over the bay. The Agent suddenly realized that his view of the bay was unduly obscured by his sunglasses.

He quickly removed them and stuffed the folded glasses into his shirt pocket. The picture brightened, but his mood remained dark. The sea breeze blew gentle tepid air. It felt fresh against his lightly perspiring face. The slosh of water against the ship's hull created a pleasant white noise; but the pungent aroma of diesel fuel spoiled this otherwise tropical dream-scene. The two men stood together, but their frames of mind were cast in quite different contexts.

The Agent now wished that he'd lied to the Ukrainian. It would have been easy, and all this tension could then have been avoided. Perhaps he might have said that an unforeseen event had delayed Stalin for twenty-four hours. Of course, at the time he'd had no reason to believe his counterpart would not show up as scheduled. And if so, he would certainly receive a communication either from the man himself or from the Embassy. He refused to blame himself for the clumsy situation he'd created with the Ukrainin. If Stalin had made a timely appearance, then nothing now would need to be remedied.

The man standing next to him had questioned the Agent concerning Stalin's tardiness. And the longer time passed, the more this man pressed him. Yes, he wished that he'd made up some cover story when he'd returned to the trawler at sundown alone. Instead the Agent had shared his concern with the Ukrainian. Now it was too late to revise his story. Stalin was supposed to have landed sometime this afternoon. Not only had he not shown up, but he'd not even communicated a revised schedule.

This outcome was inexplicable which is what made it so maddening. The Ukrainian was clearly exploiting Stalin's failed timeliness as an excuse to complain. He taunted the Agent with hypothetical situations that might explain Stalin's unexplained delinquency as well as what this tardiness might portend. At last the Agent had a nose-full.

"Enough! Enough!" he exclaimed. "He will be here. It's not like he's riding on a Japanese train. He's coming on an unscheduled twin-engine aircraft. There's been a delay, and he will explain it when he gets here. Not that it really matters, anyway! Your concern is with fusing the bomb. I'm the one who gets paid to worry, remember?"

"But why wouldn't he have advised you of the delay?" the Ukrainian insisted.

The Agent could smell his foul breath. The man had a habit of leaning his face towards whomever he addressed. Perhaps it was due to myopia, which was suggested by those thick spectacles which magnified the Ukrainian's eyes as he stared through them.

"He is a professional. He has his reasons. There is no point for us to speculate and worry ourselves unduly."

"But you told me that it is your job to worry. Now you have something concrete to worry about, and suddenly you stop worrying? What if something has gone wrong? What do you intend to do with the bomb?"

"Nothing has gone wrong!"

"Clearly, something has gone wrong. We just don't know yet how serious it is. But I pose the suggestion that if something very serious has gone wrong---if your martyr does not show up---then we should be discussing what's to be done.

"There's nothing to discuss! He's coming."

"Alright!" The Ukrainian drew back a step as if to gesture his acquiescence. "Then why don't I fuse the bomb tonight? It's a very calm sea. The crew has gone ashore. Now would be a good time."

"How will we move it?"

"There's no need. We can open the crate. You hold the torch and I'll work on it right there." He pointed to the large piece of cargo substantially longer than a coffin and twice as high which was wrapped in a tarpaulin.

"That will be dangerous."

"No danger at all!"

"I don't mean the prospect of doing it now. I mean *later*! The bomb must be smuggled all the way across Mexico, through a tunnel and then taken to a secret camp in Arizona. It will be extremely dangerous to carry this fused bomb through that distance."

"You know nothing about bombs!"

"I'm applying common sense," the Agent spat.

"Do you have any notion of what forces act on a ballistic warhead during launch acceleration? Do you even understand the concept of g-forces, or the vibration generated? There's much more to it then common sense, my friend. It's a matter of engineering science. I am an engineer. I know what I'm saying, and I tell you that there is absolutely no danger in moving a fused bomb, even if you were to accidentally drop it! I'm not going to arm it with an impact actuator."

"What then?"

"It will be a timing device which can be set by anyone. No technical skill required."

"How much time will it give us?" the Agent inquired warily.

"Us? You mean him! He can set it for as long as 99 hours and 59 minutes, or for a duration as short as six seconds. I will teach him how to set the timer and how to activate it. Assuming he comes, of course."

"He'll come!"

"But first I must install it. There's more to fusing a bomb than hanging a wall clock, you know? It requires some wiring. I'll need to do some soldering. I think we should get started."

"But then you'll need a source of electricity!"

"No, my equipment is all battery operated."

Chola Bay

Andalusian horses were just one of the fascinations Sammy Sanchez held for southern Spain. His favorite adult sipping beverage was *Granduque de Alba Brandy*. However, his choice of cigars was certainly not Spanish.

He eschewed Canary Island cigars in favor of Habanas or Domincanas. Honduran cigars were also pretty good in his opinion.

It was midnight as he sat in the veranda at the back of his villa. He faced in the direction of the swimming pool, due east. It was a perfect spot from which to watch the sun rise. Beyond it laid the stable. Of course there was no prospect of a sunrise at this moment. Night had fallen some two hours ago.

He continued deep in thought as he chewed on the stub of his *La Flor Domicana*, which had gone out. He casually took the final sip from his brandy snifter. As Sammy swallowed, he began to run over in his mind those preceding interrogations of the *negrito*, of "Gomero", and of the Iranian who they called "Moustache".

From these interrogations he'd concluded that "Gomero" had intended to fuck him. This much he believed, but the rest of the story related by both the *negrito* and Moustache he did not believe. They spoke of a magic carpet being smuggled from Iran to Mexico, and then across Mexico and into the United States. He remained profoundly incredulous. But he also found the mystery of their true purpose fascinating.

His curiosity would not rest. It was not idle nosiness. Sammy sensed that the package which "Gomero" had been hired to deliver by the foreigner must have a great deal of value for this fellow. Why else would he go forward incurring such expense of time, money and trouble? But both the *negrito* and Moustache had refused to relent concerning their proposition that what they intended to smuggle was merely a magic carpet.

It of course wasn't, they maintained, a carpet which flew like in fairy tales. It had a spiritual magic which would summon the Twelfth Imam when he returned to Earth, and this would occur very soon. Moustache insinuated a sense of extreme urgency. This holy apparition could appear at any moment, and they must be prepared to welcome him.

Sammy considered this to be transparently bullshit, but he didn't let on. You never use brute force to reel in the sailfish. No, he finally decided, I have a second way of discovering the truth to this mystery! Thus, he had resolved the question concerning his disposition of these two foreigners. He would play them like a fighting sailfish on the hook... patiently. Do not force the catch. Time is always on your side in these matters. Just maintain control.

Sammy enjoyed playing chess. He was pretty good. Only Ramon in Hermosillo could regularly beat him. Well, Ramon was Sonora State champion. And Ramon would not pander. Sammy had played him to a draw once, but had never prevailed against this young University student. Those were the kind of opponents he relished. Moustache now represented just such an opponent in this new game of chess upon which Sammy now intended to embark.

As the *narco-traficante* chewed on his cigar stub and stared mindlessly at his empty brandy snifter, he contemplated his next few moves in this chess game. There is a limit to the moves which the imagination can advance before the permutation of possibilities based upon the unknown responses of your opponent create a horizon over which nothing more is distinguishable. So, one must create a strategic concept rather than a tactical order of battle. You must react to your opponent's moves with a response that defends your position while still advancing your agenda. It was called the *gestalt* approach. It required patience, and even restraint. You spin your web carefully until at last your opponent has no choices left but to make a flawed or fatal move. Ramon had taught him this concept.

There also remained for Sammy the dilemma of what to do with "Gomero" Romero. Fortunately, the *pendejo* had obstinately refused to admit his conspiracy to usurp the shipment of *blanco*. It was fortunate because this allowed Sammy to exercise clemency. There was no upside other than the sweet sense of vengeance in executing "Gomero". The downside could result in fatally alienating his connection with the Culiacan "family".

Their reaction would be difficult for Sammy to predict. But it was nevertheless clear that executing Romero certainly would not be particularly good for business. He needed to preserve that connection, if it were still possible. That would largely depend upon how he perceived "Gomero's" attitude towards him materialized over this matter. He would guide his moves depending upon this colleague's reactions. He would defend his position while continuing to advance his agenda.

For this reason, Sammy had dispatched Jesus Calderon to retrieve "Gomero" from the stable. "Let him shower and clean up. He's roughly my size, I will tell Armando to select a clean shirt, a pair of Levi's, a pair of socks and some underwear to bring him."

"And where shall I have him shower, *jefe*?" Jesus asked in a quiet voice, because he'd already guessed the answer, but hoped it wasn't so.

"Why not in your quarters, Jesus? Yes, that way you know where the towels, soap and shampoo are stored without having to ask."

"Jefe, I think he needs medical attention. He can barely walk."

"You'd be amazed at the resuscitating powers of a hot shower. He'll be like a new man. And Jesus... treat the fellow gently and with respect, and then bring him to me here on the veranda. But keep your pistol handy. Take someone with you. That *pendejo* is untrustworthy. He pretends to be more badly injured than he truly is. He has tried to fuck me, and he senses that I understand this. He may feel desperation. I would if I were in his boots."

"After his shower, when we bring him here to the veranda, shall we remain, *jefe*?"

"Would you leave me alone with an untrustworthy *pendejo*?" Sammy admonished.

And so Sammy calculated that by now his houseguest should be arriving at any moment. And finally he did, accompanied by Jesus and one other man. "Senyor Romero is here to join you, *jefe*," his lieutenant announced.

Sammy rose to his feet, discarded the cigar stub into a large standing ashtray nearby filled with sand, and turned to greet the guest. "Come over here and sit down "Gomero". What can I offer you? A brandy perhaps, or tequila. I have home-made *sangrito* I learned to make from the *Tapatios* (natives of Guadalajara). It will bring life back into your body. I'm sure you're tired. You've had a long and rather unpleasant day. I'm pleased that I was able to rescue you. Now we are more than just *amigos*, right? You owe me your life."

Even in the dim light of his veranda, Sammy observed that Romero looked awful. His lips were swollen and purple. He had a wad of gauze covering his ear, and held there by several strips of gauze wrapped around his head, and then fixed with a piece of adhesive tape. His left hand was also wrapped in gauze and taped. No doubt this triage was the handiwork of Armando. He found it hard to believe that Jesus could offer this kind of artful delicacy in such matters.

The man accompanying Jesus supported Romero by an elbow. "Gomero" broke free from him and approached in slow shuffling steps towards the chair which Sammy had indicated with a hand gesture. The invalid didn't say a word. During the interrogation, Sammy had learned that Romero could barely speak, and what he did say was almost impossible to understand. Sammy continued to stand as he watched the man finally reach the chair, and then with a grunt, he turned, hovered as he grabbed the arm of the chair to stabilize his balance, and then descended into it.

"So what would you prefer to drink, "Gomero"?"

The fellow looked over at him, but did not respond. It was hard for Sammy to read his face. The features were far too distorted. "Tequila?" he suggested.

"Gomero" raised one hand with an extended index finger, and slowly waved it back and forth as he burbled what vaguely sounded like "*nada*" (nothing). The host shrugged his shoulders with resignation and sat back down in his chair. "Well, I was hoping we could have a little talk, but I can see that you have great difficulty speaking. So I will talk, and you can nod either "*si o no*"." Shall we try that?" He paused. The man made no response.

"Well?" Sammy pressed.

Romero nodded his head in the affirmative.

"I have your airplane here, your BT-67. Are you able to pilot it?"

Romero looked over at him for a moment. Finally he nodded in the affirmative, and gushed something which Sammy was unable to understand, but it didn't really matter.

"Can you leave tomorrow morning?"

Again Romero nodded in the affirmative.

Sammy knew that the man presumed he would be flying back to Culiacan. That of course would not necessarily be the case. He had not yet finalized his strategy. But one must always dangle hope out for the victim in order to better manipulate him. For the time being he would allow "Gomero" to indulge that notion.

He twisted his torso and motioned at his henchman. "Jesus, tell Armando to take Senyor Romero to his sleeping quarters. It is understandable that he is very tired and needs to rest. Please, keep someone by the door tonight in case our guest has any needs or requests."

Sammy cast his henchman a wink, and Jesus discretely nodded his understanding of the signal… it meant that guard posted outside that bedroom door should be armed and prepared to deal with any nonsense "Gomero" might initiate, although this battered man did not appear capable of fomenting much meaningful mischief.

"I will personally take care of it, *jefe*."

"No, leave that to one of the men. I have another task for you to perform on my behalf."

"What's that, jefe?"

"I'll explain it to you after you and Armando have seen Senyor Romero to his quarters. You can post Miguel at our guest's door." He cast a smile at the accomplice standing with Jesus. "And arrange to have him relieved at 2:00 AM with someone else."

There was still one more piece of unfinished business which needed urgent attendance. Sammy had a load of *blanco* sitting on a fishing boat in the harbor of Chola bay. He had to get it across the border. As his mind searched for a resolution to this problem, it occurred to him that perhaps the man they called Moustache might be helpful. This Iranian was smuggling a carpet into the United States. Well, whether or not it truly was a carpet didn't matter in the context of Sammy's dilemma. Whatever devices this foreigner intended to employ for his crossing might serve the *narco-traficante's* requirements as well. They needed to talk. He also realized that he'd just acquired a disposable asset from "Gomero" which might prove handy in the smuggling operation… the BT-67.

El Paraiso

The cell phone belonging to Stalin chirped, but nobody answered it. That's because nobody was on board the BT-67 now in the hangar at the Chola Bay airstrip belonging to Sammy Sanchez. In desperation, Stalin had secreted the telephone under the right seat in the cockpit when Ali had warned that the airplane was surrounded by "unfriendlies" back at Benjamin Hill.

He'd presumed that this cordon of men were were the police. He could not allow his telephone to be confiscated by the authorities. He'd been told that it was possible for experts to discern from the chip inside the telephone who'd been called by him. His Control in Ottawa would be among those telephone numbers.

He should have pulled the chip out and swallowed it; but he wasn't certain what level of threat these men outside the airplane represented. Without the telephone, he would be at a disadvantage. He was also concerned that these police would clearly introduce a further delay in reaching his rendezvous. He needed the use of his cell phone to contact his counterpart in El Paraiso and revise his estimated time of arrival. He wasn't even sure that he could find connectivity anywhere along the way. He'd vainly tried here at Benjamin Hill without success.

Stalin's cell phone still under the right hand seat in the BT-67 cockpit finally stopped chirping. On the other end of this futile summons was Stalin's counterpart in El Paraiso. He clicked the disconnect button and glanced again at his watch. It was five minutes past midnight.

The Ukrainian had gone ashore. The ship's Captain had described to them a street just at the outskirts of town that had a line of cabarets with young eager prostitutes. The Ukrainian had urged the MOIS Agent to join him; but the man adamantly declined.

"I don't drink alcohol," he flatly stated. "It's against the teachings of the Prophet."

It wasn't true of course… the part about him not drinking alcohol. But his mind was filled with anxiety. By now the martyr should have arrived. At the very least, he should have communicated. Now, in addition, he couldn't even raise the man on his cell phone. Thus, he saw no choice. He must do it. He'd been warned never to call Ottawa unless it was a genuine emergency. The American NSA might be listening. They had satellites which eavesdropped, so he'd been cautioned. Well, he perceived his present situation as a genuine emergency.

The Ukrainian had installed the fuse. It was a timer, which after a brief period of instruction even the Agent clearly understood how to set it. There were three LED numeric display-sets, the first double set indicated hours; the second double set indicated minutes; and the third single display indicated seconds in tenths of a minute. The fuse could be set from 99:59:9 down to 00:00:1, although the latter was not recommended since it would initiate a nuclear holocaust in six seconds.

"What happens," he asked the Ukrainian, "if you set it, and then for some reason you must stop its progress."

"There is no means of stopping it, other than to cut

the wires. And you must know in which sequence to cut them… or *poof*!"

"So there is no room for miscalculation?"

"That is true in such an operation as we now participate, is it not?" he stated as he leaned forward into the Agent's face. "If your martyr were to suddenly have second thoughts about his short-cut to paradise, it will not afford him any reconsideration. You see, we engineers think of everything. That's why we don't have to worry."

The Agent stared at him with a poker face to camouflage his thoughts. 'You stupid infidel,' he silently mocked in his mind's voice. 'Enjoy your round of drinks and your whore. It will be your last. We in MOIS also think of everything. That is because we worry.' The Ukrainian would draw his last breath prior to this fishing trawler launching back to Cuba.

He dialed the number to MOIS in Ottawa, and braced himself for a very unpleasant exchange. He needed to choose his words with extreme care in case the NSA was listening. But he also needed to make perfectly clear to Ottawa the urgency of this matter at hand, and that they must give him further instructions.

Chola Bay

Stalin accepted the invitation to a brandy. Although he sat an easy meter and a half away from Sammy, the host could smell the stench of this Iranian's perspiration. He ignored it. There were bigger issues at stake than body odor which he now engaged. The *narco-traficante* nodded at Jesus who watched attentively every movement made by the foreigner sitting near his *jefe*.

"Have Armando prepare our guest a snifter of *Granduque de Alba* and tell him to bring me a fresh one as well."

Jesus cast him an uneasy expression. His concern at leaving Sammy unattended was patent. The boss gave him one more nod to re-enforce his instructions and narrowed his eyes just enough that his henchman had no doubt about the boss's conviction.

"*Si,*" Jesus dutifully mumbled and turned to go.

Sammy drew a cigar from his shirt and reached across the table offering it to his guest. "Do you smoke? These Domincanas I have recently discovered are absolutely the best. Before I would only smoke Habanas, but these cigars from the Domincan are their equal. Here, try one."

Stalin gently raised his hand, extending his palm forward in a gesture of refusal. "I don't smoke, but thank you."

"Is that part of your religion, to not smoke? Does it offend you if I am smoking?"

"I am not a strictly religious man. As you can see, I have accepted your invitation for an alcoholic drink, and that is also forbidden. No, you do not offend me by smoking."

Nonetheless, Sammy returned the cigar into his shirt pocket. "So, Senyor Moustache… uh, is that what you wish me to call you? It seems that is how the others refer to you. Perhaps you would prefer that I address you with a proper name?"

"My friends call me Moustache. Do you object to being my friend?"

Sammy considered his answer several moments before responding. "I have very few friends, Moustache. I take the concept of friendship very seriously. It is like an oath. It is like the sacrament of marriage. But you are a Muslim, no? How do Muslims approach the notion of friendship?"

Stalin smiled. "We approach it with reservation. It takes a great deal of trust to form a friendship. And it is dangerous. Only a friend can betray you. To be done in by anyone else shows careless oversight, and you must blame yourself."

"Yes, it appears that perhaps I was a bit careless with Romero, doesn't it? And he was clearly careless concerning you."

Again Stalin smiled. "Well, I was not his friend." After a momentary pause his face melted back into a serious demeanor. "Is he your friend? Back in the stable you referred to him as your *amigo*. That means friend in Spanish, doesn't it?"

"Literally, yes that is the translation. But depending on how it is used and the speaker's intentions, it can have a variety of meanings."

"Well, is he your friend… in the sense that we were both previously referring?"

"No, he is a business acquaintance."

"I see. That too requires a certain amount of trust, does it not?"

It was Sammy who now smiled. "I would prefer to say that it requires a certain amount of care."

"Yes, but how can someone exercise care to such a degree that leaves no latitude for mischief. It seems to me that in the end you must fall back on trust."

"I have a different approach, Moustache."

"I would find it fascinating if you care to share this approach with me."

Sammy was warming up to the Iranian. He suddenly wondered if the man played chess. "It's very simple. A bargain is only viable if both party's have something to gain. I never attempt to deprive my business partner of an advantage in the deal. Otherwise it is predictable that he will resort to all sorts of mischief."

"Is that what happened in the case of your shipment through Romero's tunnel?"

Sammy sighed, and rotated both raised hands as a sheepish look overtook his facial expression. "No, it was a careless oversight on my part, and I have only myself to blame. One must never underestimate the component which greed plays in any bargain."

The Iranian was surprised to hear this *jefe* make such an admission. It also gave him heart. The fellow clearly needed him for something, else Stalin would probably be laying in a shallow desert grave by now. He guessed that it had to do with the *blanco*. Sammy needed to get it crossed. But how does he calculate that I can help him, the MOIS Agent wondered? He is a *narco-traficante*, surely with many connections. What makes him think that I can be of help?

Stalin's train of thought was interrupted by the feel of Armando brushing the back of his chair as he leaned forward and placed the brandy snifter on the table in front of the guest. He then moved forward and laid a second libation in front of his boss. Sammy immediately grasped his snifter and raised it in an apparent toast as he gazed at Stalin.

"To a business relationship between us," he proposed. "Let it be one that will offer each of us an adequate advantage." He slugged down a generous gulp and then placed his snifter back on the table. However, Stalin had not joined him in the toast.

Sammy gazed at the man with a puzzled stare. "You do not wish to drink to our mutual enterprise?" he finally inquired.

"I can not respond to a toast in which I have no knowledge of the consequences. I presume that in your culture it is a gesture which is binding, like a handshake. How can I make such a promise when I have no idea of what it is that you have in mind?"

"Yes," whispered Sammy more to himself than to his guest. "Yes, you're quite right. So just have a drink of my brandy as a sign of accepting my hospitality, and then I will explain to you what I have in mind."

He watched as the foreigner slowly raised the snifter to his lips, gave it a swirl, a sniff and then imbibed a liberal swig. He smiled approvingly at Sammy as he set the snifter back down. "It's very fine. The flavor reminds me of the brandy they produce in Armenia. It has a similar quality."

"It seems you are an honest and educated man," Sammy stated pleasantly. "But I am confused in one point, if you don't mind my asking?"

"Please, by all means."

"Moments ago you said that you were not a... uhh... strictly religious man, I think is how you put it."

"Yes, that is what I said."

Sammy cocked his head and offered in a quiet voice, "But your mission is to smuggle a religious carpet into the United States. So, if you are not doing this out of religious conviction, then I must presume that you were hired as a professional smuggler."

This question came as no surprise to Stalin. It was almost predictable that the conversation between them would finally turn on this very point. Yet, it represented for the Iranian a dilemma. He'd not resolved it. If he continued to characterize his mission as a courier of this mystical carpet, he would lose the *narco-traficante's* trust. Without that trust, there would be no further interest by the Mexican to entertain a bargain. That would lead to a dead-end for Stalin, quite literally. The truth would of course be compelling, but he dared not risk such a disclosure, so how should he respond to this man? How could he dispose of this patently absurd mystical carpet story without divulging the true nature of his mission?

Stalin drew in a deep breath, and slowly exhaled his reply, "It is not a carpet."

Sammy smiled. "I didn't think so." After several moments of silence, he reached for his snifter and took another gulp, set it back down and returned his gaze to the Iranian.

"So, what is it?"

"Why do you need to know?"

Sammy chuckled. "It is not a *need*, it is a *right*."

"In what manner?"

"Your life is in my hands, Moustache. It gives me an absolute right!"

"I guess I was mistaken. I thought we were here to bargain."

"Bargain? I offer you your life. What do you offer me in return?"

"A means by which to cross your *blanco*."

Standing vigilantly behind him, even Jesus reacted to that proposition with visible alacrity.

"I'm listening," Sammy urged.

"My plan requires the cooperation of the Black Muslims. I need Ali, the black man in your stable, to participate. He is their leader."

"What is your plan," Sammy pressed impatiently, as he wondered if this wily Iranian intended to sacrifice his queen in order to surprise the Mexican with a checkmate.

Stalin ignored the demand as he added with a touch of sarcasm, "I will also need your *amigo*, Senyor Romero, to pilot his aircraft. I can fly the plane. I think I can even take-off, but I've never attempted a landing and I don't know where to go for gas-ups or the protocol for landing in El Paraiso."

"El Paraiso?" Sammy gulped. "In Quintana Roo?"

"Yes, El Paraiso! That is where I have my shipment of shoulder-launched missiles. We are engaged in jihad against Satan America. I'm Iranian, so it should not surprise you. Do you have an objection to our jihad?"

Jesus leaned forward so as not to miss a word, fascinated by this unfolding scenario.

"How does this have anything to do with my *blanco*?" Sammy complained.

"We will cross my weapons and your shipment together. The Black Muslims will recover them on the Indian reservation, unless you want to place your own men there as well."

"How?"

"We will fly across, land and abandon the plane, unless Senyor Romero wishes to fly it back across, if it is still flyable. There is no landing strip… just a dirt road. If we cross the border below four hundred feet we will avoid the American radar.

"What about the Indians? They have tribal police!"

"They'll be no match against the Black Muslims armed with automatic weapons."

Sammy considered the proposition for several moments before continuing. "What makes you think the American radar can't spot you below four hundred feet?"

"We Iranians have studied their defenses carefully. It is something our Intelligence has determined."

"You're certain of this?"

"I would not risk my arsenal of weapons and the success of my jihad against this Satan if I were not certain."

"So, you are a terrorist, no? Like the Zapatistas we have in the south of Mexico. I've never met a terrorist before. Do you do this for money?"

Stalin calculated his answer. "No," he finally replied. "I do it for honor."

"Honor? That's it?"

"Isn't that enough?"

Sammy shrugged his shoulders and smiled weakly. "It is… uhh… unusual. So, please tell me more about these weapons. How big are they? What exactly do they do?"

"The Russians call them Strela-3. They are fired from the shoulder."

"Russian," the *narco-traficante* muttered.

Stalin sensed he was creating suction, and so he continued intrepidly. "They can be used against any target you choose. The missile carries roughly one kilo of high explosive. It can bring down an airplane. It has a practical range of up to 4 or 5 kilometers, but the target must be at least 600 meters away to give the fusing time to engage."

"Like you see in the movies? Is that how it works?" Sammy asked breathlessly.

"Yes, like in the movies."

"And how big… how heavy?"

"The Strela-3 when it is loaded with a missile weighs about 15 kilos, and it is 1.5 meters long."

"That's not so bad. We could carry back a lot in the airplane, no? How many you got?"

Stalin carefully considered his answer. He needed to play on this man's greed. "Enough to fill your airplane."

"Are they reliable?"

"They've been using them in Africa and Asia since 1978. They are as reliable as a Kalishnikov."

Jesus straightened up as Sammy twisted his torso and looked over at him. His *jefe* cast him an inquiring look. "You've heard his plan?"

"Si, jefe."

"What do you think?"

The henchman gave his boss a non-committal shrug. "I do not think, *jefe*. I follow your orders."

"If we do this, I will want you on the other side of the border to meet the airplane. And you must make arrangements with our connection in Casa Grande." He turned back to Stalin.

"Where exactly shall we land?"

Stalin felt exhilaration. He sensed that the man was buying into it. "You pick the spot, Senyor Sanchez. I'm sure you and your people are more familiar with the terrain than I am. Ali will instruct his people to be on station with your group. But there is one more issue."

"What's that?"

"We must leave as soon as possible."

"Why?"

"Because my weapons are in port, and the one's delivering them will become very nervous. They were expecting me this evening. Is there any means here by which I can contact them?"

Sammy gazed at the Iranian without immediately responding. Finally he stated, "In port? They are on a ship?"

"Yes, a fishing trawler."

"Ah yes," he chuckled, "I am familiar with that means of storage." It brought to mind his *blanco* stowed on board a fishing vessel docked in Chola Bay. "We can leave early tomorrow morning, assuming I accept your proposal. If I do, you can make your contact then. I would like to… uhh… consider your proposition over a good night's sleep."

"And Ali? It is not very comfortable in his empty room."

"He's a *negrito*. They are like animals. They can sleep anywhere." He turned back to Jesus. "See that this *negrito* is given some food and water."

"Thank you," Stalin responded in a somewhat pandering voice. "And where may I sleep?"

Again he addressed Jesus. "Have them bring a pillow and blanket for our guest. He will be spending the night in our stable as well." He stood up.

"Well Moustache, have a restful sleep. We'll talk again in the morning."

As Sammy walked away he began to think through this proposition offered by Moustache. It might provide a solution to his problem, but he hadn't decided whether or not to trust this Iranian. There was something bizarre about this foreigner which still confounded the Mexican. Moustache genuinely appeared to be absorbed with his war against the United States, not in absconding with the *blanco*, he granted. But the narco-trafficker had long ago learned to distrust appearances without credible verification.

Anyway, Sammy still needed to work out with Jesus where they could land the load before any plan could go forward. The closer to Casa Grande, the better, he calculated. His buyers operated out of Casa Grande, Arizona. What was new in his calculus was the BT-67. If it had to be abandoned, it would auger a financial loss for Romero, not for himself.

Aircraft represented a financial investment, even stolen ones. In the case of this particular operation, they needed a twin engine turbo-jet in order to haul the load speedily to its destination. That's why Romero's BT-67 had made this new plan possible. Losing the value of this aircraft would have sucked out most of Sammy's profit in his *blanco* transaction if he would need to sustain such a loss. But now the loss would be Romero's

Landing on a dirt road held risks of damage to the plane; but most risky would be attempting a return trip back towards Mexico. The American radar surveillance might easily have alerted the DEA on the flight through Arizona. They would scramble to intercept the aircraft. By the time they found it, the plane would be abandoned. The safest measure would be to forsake the BT-67 and have Jesus and his entourage returned by surface. Jesus would be carrying a lot of money. Sammy did not intend to place it in jeopardy.

On the other hand, who would he then send to supervise this Iranian and the harvest of shoulder-fired missiles? Sammy himself never personally participated in smuggling operations. It was a cardinal rule of his. He'd come too far and gained too much to lose it all over one slip-up. Sooner or later a mistake would be made. He had no intention of paying for these consequences with his life or even with incarceration.

His methodology required that he embrace an *ersatz* representative totally trustworthy. There were few such persons one touched in an entire life-time. That's why a man like Jesus was so valuable to him, and so necessary. But Sammy couldn't have this loyal lieutenant simultaneously in different places... guarding his *blanco* as it flew to Arizona and then guarding his money on the return trip, and as well baby-sit the Iranian and collect a plane-load of shoulder-fired missiles. The challenging complexity of this enterprise aroused him. He loved to crack tough-nut conundrums.

Sammy needed Jesus with the load of *blanco* at all times. And in a pinch, Jesus could even land the BT-67, although he would not be as skillful in handling the plane as would Romero, but it remained open to question whether that injured man was still able to perform. He'd have a better idea of that in the morning.

One thing had become clear to Sammy. There was absolutely no linkage between flying his *blanco* into

Arizona, and flying to Quintana Roo to pick-up shoulder-fired missiles as proposed by Moustache. The BT-67 must be used to fly his *blanco* to Arizona. If they had to abandon it, the problem and loss would be "Gomero" Romero's. It would be his penalty for having become too greedy.

Jesus could go to Arizona and return with Julio in the SUVs. Sammy had a specific reason for wanting "Gomero" to pilot the plane which went beyond a consideration of aviator skill-sets. The reason was political. It would leave his Culiacan connection undisturbed. It would allow Romero to perform a propitiation for his sin, and thus allow Sammy to forgive him for the indiscretion. The man would probably pay the painful price of his precious BT-67.

Yes, that is what he would do! And he would give "Gomero" a little bonus for his pain and courage. More importantly, he would magnanimously forgive "Gomero" for his transgression, and the Culiacan connection would remain in tact. It was a business decision which trumped his natural inclination for revenge. Most importantly, he could save the relationship without appearing weak.

So then what to do about Moustache and the *negrito*? The Iranian insinuated having an arsenal of shoulder-launched missiles waiting in El Paraiso. That could be worth a small fortune. It would be a shame to see them wasted on the so-called jihad this terrorist intended. He wondered exactly how many of these weapons were in the Iranian shipment. It might represent an even greater treasure-trove than his *blanco*. Sammy immediately brought to his thoughts several likely buyers, and he wouldn't mind having a few for himself.

Sammy further calculated that he could have his Beech King-Air pilot fly to El Paraiso. It had the range to reach there from here without a gas-up. It was a twin engine turbo-prop, and based upon what Moustache described as the size of these launchers and missiles, he could probably load 10 of the launchers and one hundred missiles in his aircraft. He had little idea of the market price for that load, but guessed that it might be as much as a million dollars. Not a bad harvest, he silently applauded.

He would need the Iranian along for the ride down there in order to convince the ship's crew to unload some of their stash. He also must offer the Iranian a plausible cover story for this change of plans, and propose a reason why he was willing to carry the man clear across Mexico. Moustache was a clever fellow. Sammy mustn't underestimate this foreigner. Well, his mind was in a muddle. He needed to sleep on these notions. He'd have his answers in the morning.

As he passed Armando, he turned to him. "I want to be awakened at six tomorrow morning. And wake up Jesus, as well."

"Si, jefe," the man immediately responded.

Sammy's pilot for the Beech King-Air lived in Puerto Penyasco. "And call my *pinche* pilot, Paco, at five-thirty and tell him to come here by six… six sharp!"

There was one more party who Sammy intended to call in the morning… Guillermo Ray. They'd worked together on a few deals. Sammy would need some muscle to back up the operation he contemplated in order to acquire these shoulder-launched missiles the Iranian claimed to have. He'd send a couple of his own men just to make sure his interests were served, but it would be impractical to send a whole squad down there. Besides, Guillermo Ray was connected with the local authorities down there, and Sammy was not. He needed to cut Ray into the deal.

His King-Air was configured to carry no more than eight passengers. He'd installed the deluxe option which offered maximum seating comfort but restricted the number of positions. Anyway, how would he carry a large group of men back if it were loaded with weapons? He would probably need the space and would max out the load before his men even got on board. Besides, there was no getting round cutting Ray into the deal. He had the political clout. So why not use his muscle as well?

Sammy felt relief at the prospects of his evolving scheme. He didn't really trust Moustache. Hell, he didn't trust anyone outside of Jesus and to a lesser degree Julio and Armando. He didn't trust Guillermo Ray either. He just had to make sure that in the end this king-pin of Quintana Roo would feel satisfied with the deal.

Anyway, in their initial conversation he mustn't tell Guillermo what the reason for this "party" would be all about. Just meet his plane in the little airport at El Paraiso with a gang and some automatic weapons. His men would explain the mission when they arrived, and Sammy would promise to make the effort worth Guillermo's while.

That's when it occurred to him. If he could get the name of that fishing vessel out of Moustache, then he wouldn't even need the Iranian to come along. Moustache said it was a fishing trawler docked in the port of El Paraiso. Guillermo's gang and Sammy's pair of men could take over the vessel and help themselves to the weapons. Certainly Ray had the muscle to pull this off. There would be enough for everyone to have a generous portion, and there would be no need to bring the Iranian.

That would be a much better plan, Sammy conceded. The trick was how to get the name of that fishing trawler out of Moustache, or at least enough information to identify it. Yes, this chess game was getting him all excited.

Sammy had a lot to sleep on and not a whole lot of time in which to churn all these considerations through his subconscious mind. Moreover, he was beguiled by the complexities of this challenge. It filled him with the same thrill and resolve as when he faced Ramon over a chessboard. Sleep would come with difficulty because there was so much to calculate. He was wide awake with enthusiasm.

Sammy Sanchez smuggled foremost to enrich himself. He was devoted to his self-indulging life-style. But there was a second important component to his motivation. He was also an adrenalin addict. However, he was a cerebral one, not a dare-devil willing to gamble with his life. He was like a poker player. He loved his game. The money he accrued also served as a way of keeping score.

El Paraiso

The Ukrainian had "befriended" one of the Cuban crew members on board the fishing trawler. The trawler made irregular deliveries on behalf of Cuban drug and contraband weapons smugglers---a group of Castro's military officers who operated these franchises---to the Quintana Roo organization in Mexico. This particular crew member who the Ukrainian took into his confidence had been to El Paraiso several times before. Although it was just a small town primarily dependent upon tourism and fishing, it was safer here for transacting "business" than in Merida, the State capitol. The American DEA was very active in Merida where Columbian and Peruvian connections conducted their commerce.

Here in El Paraiso there was little meddling by the American Agents. The Cuban component of drug-trafficking was small by comparison to those channels coming directly from producers into Mexico. Anyway, the crewman knew a few of the girls and one of the bouncers at a cabaret on the outskirts of town. So, the Ukrainian's "friend" made arrangements on behalf of the foreigner.

He'd offered the fellow five hundred dollars to connect him with a car and driver who would transport him tonight to Cancun. If they left immediately, he could reach Cancun by morning. For this "taxi" service he offered one thousand dollars. It was a generous tender, but he needed to arrive there with certainty.

At Cancun Airport there were three flights a week to Havana. The next one left at 1:00pm tomorrow. He would be at the boarding gate before the MOIS Agent finally concluded that he was missing. The Ukrainian didn't trust these Iranians. They were notorious for leaving no loose ends in their operations, and he would clearly be viewed as a loose end. He'd done what he was hired to do. It was time to go... quietly.

Over the years, the Ukrainian had accumulated a comfortable sum of money in his Credit Suisse account. Then, he'd made a bad investment and lost a significant portion of his treasury. But now with this last deposit for the job he'd just completed, he was whole again.

He wished to continue existing in order to enjoy a well-deserved retirement. In Cuba, he could easily live in style off the interest earned from his Swiss account. Moreover the Castro regime was friendly to his kind. He knew other parties from the old days who might wish him harm, but these accounts were now old and hopefully forgotten. MOIS was really the only group whom he needed to fear. However the Ukrainian calculated that he would remain safe from them in Cuba.

He had another issue over which he could chuckle. The digital timer he'd installed was bogus. His principals who'd put him in contact with the Iranians, and who'd paid for his services, made it clear that the weapon must be destroyed. They were the ones who'd sold the weapon to MOIS. His engineering services and instruction on how to use the bomb had comprised a part of the deal. However the overarching mission was to ensure that the bomb was exploded.

The principals were very concerned over the final disposition of their product. It must be detonated, they insisted to him. Otherwise, the bomb could be traced. And that would prove very problematical for them. The bomb must be exploded, they repeated, or he would be held accountable. The Ukrainian knew he would not be safe from their grasp hiding in Cuba.

So, the digital box he'd instructed the MOIS Agent to use was not connected to the fuse. It was a dummy. Instead, he'd hard-wired a detonation timer to the fuse and set it for 36 hours. By then he would be comfortably ensconced in Havana. Where the bomb would be at that point in time was MOIS's problem, and the problem of those in the vicinity of a ten kilometer radius around the bomb.

As he stood at the port entryway thinking all these thoughts, he was suddenly distracted by an oncoming set of headlights. The car stopped at the curb beside him. It was a pick-up truck. A guy leaned from the driver's side to the open passenger window.

"You the one who needs a ride to Cancun?"

"Yup."

"You got the money?"

"Yup."

"One thousand dollars?"

"Five hundred now and five hundred when we get there."

"Put your luggage in the bed and hop in."

He didn't have any luggage. If the Iranian had

spotted him carrying anything off-board, it would have immediately raised his paranoid MOIS suspicions. As he opened the door, the Ukrainian glanced at his watch now illuminated by the overhead cab light. The man was on time.

"My name is Javier," the driver cheerfully announced and extended his hand for a shake.

"How do you do," the Ukrainian responded as he tentatively accepted the man's hand for a shake. He gave the gesture a single pump and then quickly released his grip from the driver.

The Mexican withdrew to an erect position in order to give him berth to enter and asked nonchalantly, "You got a name?

The Ukrainian ducked his head inside the cab and gazed at the fellow. "I'm the gentleman with one thousand dollars. I think that's as much as you need to know, right?"

"Whatever," the fellow sourly replied. "Can I have my first five hundred?"

Bob and Charley's Hill

At the request of the DEA, the FBI Agent from the Tucson Office who'd been dispatched to investigate the two corpses on the Indian Reservation had arranged with the tribal police chief to post a twenty-four hour watch on the tunnel and report immediately if they observed any activity. Bob and Charley had climbed the hill undaunted by threats from the authorities to keep their noses out of this business. They were surprised as they came upon the stranger. In fact, all three were mutually startled by the encounter.

"We're the ones who discovered the tunnel," Bob stipulated in response to the stranger demanding who in the hell they were and what were they doing here.

"Don't point that thing at me. It might go off!" Charley added sourly.

The stranger holstered his weapon. These two old coots appeared harmless enough, and furthermore he'd been told about them during his briefing. "You're not supposed to be up here. Who sent you?"

"We don't work for nobody," Bob stated resolutely. "We sent ourselves! We're volunteers. There ain't no pay, nor are we provided with beer or women folk in appreciation of our services. So the way I see it; they got no authority to say where I go, when I git there, or what I do. Now, jest who are you?"

It was dark, being the wee hours of the morning. They hadn't noticed any vehicle parked at the base of this elevation, which is why Bob and Charley had been shocked when they came upon this stranger here at the crest of their hill. Nonetheless, they could distinguish from the moonlight and starlight enough of this guy's features to realize he was probably either a tribesman or a Mexican. And the pistol he'd drawn suggested either he worked in an official capacity or that they were in deep shit. He was dressed in ordinary denims and a dark tee-shirt. And he wore a baseball cap, but darkness obscured to their vision what the emblem on the front of that cap represented.

"I'm with the tribal police," he grunted. "You're off limits. Get on back down this hill and get off our reservation. This is none of your business. Otherwise I'll have to arrest you."

"We've done been arrested once," Charley grumbled, "and we survived it!"

The Indian seemed immobilized by their refusal to obey his order. He wasn't precisely sure of his authority in this matter. "This is official business. There's been a double homicide we're investigating."

"Well," Bob sarcastically offered, "I don't see no yellow tape strung out around this here hill, so it don't look particularly official to me. We was there when you people dug up those two bodies. You wouldn't have found nothing without our help."

The policeman sighed. "I don't need your help to watch that tunnel down there. Why don't you two go back to wherever it is you came from and get some shut-eye?"

"Did you guys round up all them nigg… uhh… black folks who was camping down there?"

"They're off our Reservation. That'll be up to the FBI."

"Well it's pretty obvious, ain't it, that them's the homiciders?"

Charley held up a two-quart thermos he was lugging. "How's about a cup of coffee?"

The tribal policeman stared at the two of them for several moments and again let out a sigh. "Sure, why not."

Charley immediately began cranking off the top of the thermos which also served as a cup. He twisted of the stopper and began pouring as Bob quietly moved around the Indian having advanced towards them in order to accept his coffee. Bob stealthily inched his way to a position at the crest of the hill. As the policeman approached Charley he unfolded the cotton shirt sleeve and retrieved soft pack of cigarettes. He gave the pack a flicking motion and then pulled out a cigarette.

"Either of you guys care for a smoke?"

Bob ignored the offer as he continued his progress towards where the policeman had originally been hunched down. Charley nodded his head in the negative. "I smoked for almost thirty years before I gave up them coffin nails. You'll do the same when them doctors start throwing scary numbers at you all predicting your imminent demise, if'n you're lucky enough to get that far in life."

Charley handed the young policeman the cup off coffee. "We sort of all share this cup. That coffee's hot enough to kill the polio virus, so don't pay it no nevermind."

The policeman glanced over his shoulder and noted with annoyance that Bob had taken over his watch position when he'd come down a few steps to accept the cup of coffee. Once more he sighed and squatted down, took a careful sip from the cup, and muttered, "Ain't half bad."

He used his free hand to flick a disposal gas lighter, took in a deep draw from his cigarette and slowly exhaled. "So what's your theory on this here development?"

"Drug smugglers," Charley opined, and then with several grunts he collapsed his posterior portions on a flat rock nearby.

"Yeah, yeah, but why did they kill those two, and what about them blacks? They're supposedly Muslims. You think they're into the smuggling?"

"Well, it seems to me like an awful out of the way place to come and pray. What's your ideas?"

"Maybe they're terrorists. Did'ja ever think of that?"

"Who they gonna terrorize out here?" Charley laughed. "Maybe put on some cowboy clothes and come after you guys?"

The policeman turned his head towards Bob and called out, "If you see anything, anything at all, you let me know, hear?"

"I see a lot of desert," Bob responded in a smart-alecky tone of voice.

"Very funny! You guys are a pair of real comedians. I wouldn't quit my day job though, if I were you two." The policeman turned back to Charley. "The DEA is coordinating with the Border Patrol to destroy that tunnel. Meantime they want us to watch it. I don't think them smugglers are stupid enough to use it anymore. They got spies everywhere. They probably know we're up here right now."

"Well, they didn't know me'n Bob was up here when

we watched em maneuver," Charley boasted. "They might not be half as smart as you think!"

The Iranian Embassy, Ottawa

The Embassy MOIS Agent hung up the satellite telephone located in the communications room. He didn't like using it for confidential exchanges. Everybody knew that the American NSA was eves-dropping on these satellite communications. They even said so in the *New York Times*.

But that was not the overarching issue now gripping his mind. His man in El Paraiso was worried, and for good reason. Stalin had not showed up. He was due to arrive in the early afternoon. It was now in the very wee hours of the next morning, and the man had heard nothing at all from his counterpart.

"You're sure he meant today, not perhaps tomorrow?" the Embassy MOIS Agent sputtered. He was fully aware of course that the rendezvous was scheduled for the previous afternoon, but he was trying to buy time as he wrestled in his mind with this dilemma. He needed to instruct this man on the other end of the phone, but he was conflicted by the notion that they should abort this mission as his colleague was now suggesting. Failure would not bode well for his future.

"Yes, I'm sure," the man responded with irritation. "But can you rule out the possibility that maybe your martyr has lost his zeal for Paradise?"

"Nothing can be ruled out," the Embassy Agent admitted.

He allowed his thoughts to flit through all options available to him. It didn't take long. There weren't many. He had to assume the worst, he counseled to himself. The worst would be that somehow the operation had been compromised. Thus, he concluded what the proper instructions would be to his man in El Paraiso.

"If you don't hear from Stalin and he doesn't show up by noon your time today, then tell the captain of your trawler to cast off immediately and get into international waters."

"And then to where?" the man asked.

"Await further instructions," he answered. "Call me when you're out of Mexican jurisdiction. I'll advise you at that time."

In fact, there was no *other* place to send the trawler. It had a nuclear bomb on board. But until this matter with Stalin could be clarified, he wanted the vessel to be free of the Mexican constabulary and maritime authority. The Mexican Federales cooperated with the Americans. Under no conditions could he allow the bomb to be compromised.

Of course, it was not unusual for the Americans to interdict shipping in the Caribbean without regard to the internationality of waters. But how could these infidels have gotten wind of his operation? Moustafa Rajai had no inkling of the Mexican operation. There is nothing he could have told the FBI that would have been compromising.

His thoughts turned for an instant to the Jewess and

her two monkeys. In a fit of spleen he resolved that he would execute them rather than turn them loose! Could it have been someone here at the Embassy? Perhaps the Ambassador himself? Or was it the Ukrainians? His mind was in a muddle.

He calmed himself and attempted to think dispassionately and analytically. If the Americans were responsible for Stalin not having shown up, then he should send the fishing trawler back to Havana with all due haste. At the moment, however, nothing was clear. The Embassy Agent glanced at his watch. Stalin had ten hours to meet the deadline which he'd had just imposed.

There was another possibility. He could send the fishing trawler to Corpus Christi under a Mexican flag. The Agent in El Paraiso would probably not martyr himself, but he could set the bomb. He could then make an excuse to leave and explain that another representative would meet the Captain of the trawler in Texas. But that would require the vessel having to port in the U.S., and doing so would not be easy. The Americans would probably seize the ship. The Captain would never agree, he sighed.

Besides, there was no symmetry to simply detonating a nuclear device somewhere in the distance from an American city. The statement to be made must occur at one of their nuclear generating stations. There was a hidden message intended by the Iranian regime: *You bomb our nuclear plants and we'll bomb yours. See, we can do it!* That was the concept which had finally wrested approval from the regime and the lavish funding for this project. That was the only acceptable end-state with which the regime would be satisfied.

There was no one left for him to avail. It crossed his mind that he should immediately fly to El Paraiso, and should prepare himself for martyrdom in the now likely event that Stalin did not show. This flash was momentary in duration. He had no plan, no connections, no clear idea of Stalin's intended tactics; but most of all, he had no inclination to martyrdom. On the other hand, if this project failed then he might consider martyrdom as a benevolent alternative to what could await him in Teheran. Well, he had ten hours before that hard decision needed to be made.

His thoughts turned again to the Jewess and her two monkeys locked up here in the Embassy. Could she possibly serve as a usable asset? In what manner, he challenged his own question? His brain began to hum. If he released her, but held the children, then he would have a vital leverage on her actions. He could control exactly how she moved and what she said to whom. It was an interesting calculation, he complimented, but what could he implement through her?

Perhaps she could act as a widow bringing the corpse of her husband to Peoria, Arizona in order to bury him nearby to where she would settle with her sister. But he immediately realized that even if he could manage to procure an oversize casket in which to secrete the bomb, it was unlikely to get past port inspection. Besides, she would not find a burial plot close enough to the nuclear generating plant which would allow the steel enclosures to be ruptured by the blast.

He groped and grasped for concepts. He needed to come up with a remedy. He breathed in and out in a deep measured lungful of air, desperately attempting to avert the panic beginning to immobilize his mind.

'Allah,' he mumbled in his mind's voice, 'give me light!'

Chola Bay

By the time Armando rapped on the door to wake him, Sammy was already shaved, showered and dressed. He'd just patted his face with cologne and was enjoying the scent when he heard the summons. He aggressively crossed the room and opened the door.

"It's six o'clock, *jefe*," his man muttered.

"Did you call Paco, my pilot?"

"Si *jefe*, I called him last night. He just arrived and is waiting on the veranda. Julia is mixing him a Bloody Mary. And Senyor Romero waits there as well."

"Does Senyor Romero look like he's in a condition to fly?"

"He's drinking a Pacifico beer, *jefe*... through a straw."

Sammy silently mused; one of the requirements for a pilot's license must be that you are a bona fide alcoholic. "Can he speak?"

Armando shrugged his narrow shoulders. "He was able to ask for a beer and a straw."

"And Jesus?"

"Shall I fetch him, *jefe?*"

"Immediately! On the veranda. And have Julia fix me a Bloody Mary, too… lots of Tabasco, but have her go easy on the pepper. Last time she put in too much pepper."

Julia was an on-the-premises celebrity kitchen matron known for her knack at mixing drinks, especially Bloody Mary and Margarita concoctions. Down in Penya Penasco at the morning fish market she was also famous for her relentless bargaining and an eye for a fresh catch. No one dared even try passing to this portly middle-aged lady a fish from yesterday's stragglers. They were all familiar with her sharp tongue, earthy expletives, and most of all, the household she represented. Sammy Sanchez was the "Don" in this hinterland.

Sammy joined his pilot and "Gomero" on the veranda. "Gomero" looked a bit recovered, but his lips were still swollen and his nose remained distorted. The guaze bandage wrapped around his head to cover the ear looked slept-in, and clearly had not been changed. But his eyes flashed with life. Sammy didn't like the face.

A poker player relies on "tells" to read the cards of his adversaries at the table. A habitual twitch, hand movement, posture change, or fingering the chips all betrayed that proverbial poker face, and disclosed whether or not the bet was a bluff. In much the same way Sammy practiced this art of studying "tells" to determine the sincerity and veracity of what his associates were telling him. The injured face of "Gomero" made these "tells" far less discernable.

The broken faced man from Culiacan called out for a second beer. It was difficult to understand the words, but easy enough to determine his request as he held the empty bottle up in the air with the one hand that was not bandaged. One of the first questions Sammy had asked him was whether or not he felt fit to fly.

"I can fly drunk, blind and with my *pinche* pecker up a pussy," he burbled angrily. Again, Sammy hadn't understood all the words, but he got the gist of the message. However, "Gomero" then continued.

"I want that Muslim and that *negrito*," he growled, speaking slowly to ensure that his words were understood, and repeating the message again when he realized he'd slurred badly. He wiped the drool on his chin with his sleeve several times as he spoke.

"I will fly your fucking *blanco* across the border. I owe you. But you owe me those two. I want to put a bullet through their heads and then I will fly for you. I want to do it now, before we talk further."

Sammy had not yet disclosed to these two men gathered on the veranda concerning his second enterprise... the one involving the cache of weapons held by the Iranian in El Paraiso. He might need Moustache, but this was one of the men "Gomero" now wanted to shoot. So Sammy had to suddenly consider if he might have to disclose this second enterprise in order to rationalize to "Gomero" why the execution of Moustache must be forestalled.

Well, naturally he would need to confide in his pilot, Paco, who would be in charge of this second operation, in cooperation of course with Guillermo Ray. He finally decided on what to say to "Gomero". He would offer a compromise.

"I will allow you to shoot the *negrito*. You may do it just as soon as Jesus joins us. But not the Iranian. I need Moustache alive for a little while longer. He has some important information I must get out of him."

"Gomero" narrowed his eyes as he gazed at Sammy. "Then let me get it out of him. I'll cut off his fingers one at a time. And when he has talked I will cut off his cock and watch him bleed to death."

"I will allow you to have your way with the *negrito*. Cut off his cock if you wish. And we'll let Moustache watch. A little intimidation never hurts in a negotiation, no?"

"Gomero" just stared back at him without either assenting or protesting. Then he was momentarily distracted as Armando delivered him his second bottle of beer and a fresh straw. Paco availed himself of the lull to speak. "If Senyor Romero is going to pilot the plane, then what do you need me for, *jefe*?"

Sammy had considered the situation. "Gomero" would be occupied in Arizona so it would be impossible for him to compromise the operation in El Paraiso. "Gomero" would fly out this evening at sunset. Jesus would fly with him accompanying the *blanco*. By that time Paco would have his Beech in El Paraiso loaded with weapons and would have already departed.

He ignored his pilot's question. "Gomero", is there any problem landing at night?"

"To deliver your *blanco*?"

"Yes, and you must fly over the desert at four hundred feet, to avoid detection by the gringo radar."

"Four hundred feet," Romero burbled incredulously.

"*Si*, to delver my load."

The pilot carefully sucked up some beer through his straw, then wiped his chin with his sleeve and gazed over at the man. Again he spoke with deliberation, "You want me to fly at four hundred feet, land on a dirt road, and do this in darkness?"

Romero glanced over at Paco and pointed a finger at him as he carefully enunciated his words. "You tell him. He's your *jefe*. If you think that is possible, then you fly my *pinche* plane!"

Sammy gazed inquiringly at his pilot. The man shrunk in his chair and avoided his boss's eyes. "Well?" he challenged Paco.

"It would not be advisable, *jefe*. We could lose the load. He will need daylight to do this. Landing on a dirt road cannot be done blindfolded. Neither can flying at four hundred feet above a ground full of hills."

The boss raised his hands defensively, "I thought we might have better chances of avoiding detection if we flew at night."

"It would be very dangerous, *jefe*. I wouldn't advise it."

Just then Jesus entered the veranda. He lingered close

to the entrance as he nodded a salutation towards his boss. Sammy was sitting in a position that easily spotted him. "We are discussing the *blanco* delivery, Jesus. These two pilots believe it is not a good idea to wait until tonight. Have you talked to Casa Grande yet?"

"No, *jefe*."

Sammy sighed. "Gomero" needs your assistance, Jesus."

"How can I help?"

"He wants to shoot the *negrito*."

"I want to cut off his cock and watch him bleed to death," Romero burbled with consternation.

Sammy understood the man's garbled speech because he had context from the previous conversation, but the blank expression on the face of Jesus informed him that his henchman had not understood. So he repeated the words.

"He wants to cut off the *negrito*'s cock and watch him bleed to death."

The blank stare continued to occlude the Mexican's face as his boss turned and faced Romero. Actually, Sammy was not keen on putting a gun in the hand of this *narco-traficante*. There was no telling what this man half out of his head might suddenly decide to do. Armed with only a knife he would be no match for Jesus and another one of the boys. Besides, the psychological affect on Moustache watching his comrade slowly bleed to deeath would have a far more powerful effect. Sammy rotated his attention back to Jesus.

"Take someone with you, and stay vigilant, you hear? I want Moustache to observe the execution. Don't give "Gomero" a knife until you get to the stable, and I repeat, it is important that Moustache witness this. Make sure the *negrito* is securely tied up before you let "Gomero" have his way."

"*Jefe*, I don't think the *negrito* is going to be as cooperative as a tethered *chivo* about to be slaughtered. Maybe it would be better if I just shoot him."

Sammy understood that it was not the *negrito* which provoked his lieutenant's concern so much as a knife in the hand of "Gomero" at close range. "You are a resourceful *pendejo*, Jesus. That is why I honor you with my trust. You will figure out a way."

Jesus offered a pained look, but said nothing. As "Gomero" struggled to his feet, he warily eyed the *narco-traficante*. Sammy stood up as well, and breathed out a sigh.

"When you gentlemen have finished your chores in the stable, we will have breakfast. I will have Julia prepare us her delicious *juevos rancheros. Esta bien?*

They didn't respond because the tone of his question clearly did not offer an option for them to disagree. As they filed out, Paco rose from his chair. He waited until they were out of earshot before addressing his boss in an elevated whisper .

"*Jefe*, if Senyor Romero is flying your load into Arizona, what is my purpose here?"

"Do you think he is able to fly?"

"I know he is a good pilot, but I am not a doctor."

"I asked for your opinion." Sammy growled.

"*Si, jefe*, I think he can fly. But I could familiarize myself with his BT-67. It's not a problem."

"No, I have a different destination for you, Paco. You will fly the Beech."

"To where, *jefe*?"

"To Quintana Roo… to El Paraiso, you know where that is?"

"*Si*. On the gulf, but that is a long way."

"Can you get back from there to here without stopping for gas?"

"I will have to check the charts. It will depend on the load. What's the load?"

"A full load coming back. But going down there will be only you and two others. Anyway, on the way down there I don't care if you stop for gas. However, it is important coming back that you can reach here without stopping. Go check your charts and then let me know."

"It would be closer if we could come back to Hermosillo," he cautiously suggested. Sammy had a dirt strip and hangar at his villa on the outskirts of Hermosillo. That is from where they conducted most of their operations, not here at Chola Bay. But Chola Bay would be far more discrete. These sophisticated weapons would be an entirely new enterprise for Sammy Sanchez. The prospect intrigued him; but it also caused him to proceed with extreme caution. He could store them below deck of his yacht anchored in the bay.

"Go check your charts. I prefer to bring the load here. Otherwise, we can consider Hermosillo."

Sammy had a chore of his own to do. He needed to call Guillermo Ray and determine if the man would be amicable to partnering with him on the weapons cache deal. He was quite certain that this *narco-traficante* would want participation. But they needed to agree on terms. Frankly, it would be risky for Sammy to pull this project off in Ray's territory without cutting him in for a piece of the action. Disrespecting your colleagues in the Mexican drug underworld could lead to serious consequences somewhere down the road.

El Paraiso

The MOIS agent on board the fishing trawler had slept restlessly for less than three hours. He'd not even bothered to undress. Day would be breaking above deck. He needed to ascertain if the Captain and his crew had come back aboard ship. They must prepare for the possibility of launching at noon, or even sooner if suddenly conditions called for such emergency. He hadn't heard any commotion, which left him to suspect that they had not yet returned.

He splashed some cold saline water on his face and climbed the stairs leading to the deck. He determined conclusively as he passed through the below deck berths that the Captain and his crew had not yet returned. Neither had the Ukrainian come back. The Agent presumed the Ukrainian was with them. The early morning air was cool and the waters were calm. He leaned against the railing as his tortured mind continued to roil over this dilemma concerning Stalin's no-show.

His suspicions were aroused by the lack of even a communication from the man, and from the utter dismay he detected when speaking to his counterpart in Ottawa. He began to brood over a possibility that his mind wished to deny, but this prospect became more and more difficult to suppress. What if Stalin had been picked up by the authorities? It would explain his sudden disappearance. And if that were so, might he possibly compromise this operation. But how would the authorities have gotten wind of the operative? It would have to be leaked by one of a handful of persons cognizant of what was underway.

Could it have been someone at the Canadian Embassy? Someone in Tehran or possibly even Cuba? And what about this organization for which the Ukrainian worked? They were the one's who'd sold the bomb to MOIS. They'd be the most likely traitor, he hastily concluded. However, he was hard put to formulate a reason for why they would commit the betrayal. Well, it was still merely hypothetical that Stalin had been apprehended. Nevertheless, paranoia was beginning to grip his mind.

All at once his thoughts were interrupted by the sound of boisterous voices. Heading towards the trawler was the captain and his crew of three men. It was obvious from their elevated mood that they'd spent the night drinking and carousing. Then it suddenly struck him that the Ukrainian was not with them. He'd understood the man to have stated that he would be joining this group at one of the cabarets. The Captain waved at him.

As the Captain, leading the group, walked up the gangway, the Agent moved to intercept him so as to inquire about the Ukrainian. But the Captain beat him to the punch. He broke away from the others and moved directly towards the Agent.

"What's going on with your colleague?" he shouted as he approached.

The question took the Agent completely by surprise. "Has something happened to him?" he responded frantically.

The Captain halted directly in front of him, close enough that his booze-breath accosted the Iranian as he demanded, "Look, I want to know how long we must remain tied up here?"

The Agent took an aggressive step towards him placing them now toe to toe and causing the Captain to reflexively retreat a step. The Iranian thumped him on the chest with a stiff index finger, "I am paying you $1000 a day for this piece of shit boat. As long as I pay, you will do as I say. Now what are you squealing about? What has happened to my associate?"

"You don't know?"

"Know what?" the Agent fulminated as he clenched his fists.

The Captain exhaled a long breath and then inhaled another. "He's gone to Cancun. I thought you knew."

"What?" the Agent exclaimed. "How do you know this?"

"Jose knows. Your *amigo* paid him five hundred dollars. We all got drunk with the money and had a good time, *ai Maria*, such a very good time. But I tell you this because it must mean that you intend to stay here for a while. I would like to know for how long."

The MOIS Agent's mind went in a spin. He grabbed the railing and squeezed it so tightly that his knuckles went white. Finally he growled in a voice scarcely louder than a whisper, "Why did my associate pay Jose five hundred dollars?"

The Captain gazed at him with an expression of incomprehension. "Don't you know?"

"Would I ask you if I knew," the Agent spat.

"Jose arranged for the driver. You really didn't know that he was going to Cancun? What does this mean?"

The MOIS Agent stared out over the water trying to organize his churning mind. Finally he turned back to the Captain. "Prepare to take this vessel out of here!"

"Is there trouble?"

"Just do as I say."

"But where are we going."

"I'll let you know once we're in international waters."

"But there is a question of fuel, Senyor. We need to refuel if you want to go back to Havana."

"Why haven't you already taken care of that?"

"You didn't authorize me to refuel."

"Must I also authorize you to pull down your pants before you take a shit?"

The Captain looked away without answering. The Agent had balled up his fists again as he stood there in a burn. "How long will it take to refuel?"

The Cuban returned his attention, but avoided the Iranian's eyes. "Maybe an hour or so."

"Do it!"

"I'll need money! You agreed to pay for any re-fuels, remember? That is why I needed your authorization."

The Agent was sorely tempted to reach for his pistol and put a bullet through this imbecile's head. Two conditions prevented him from doing that. First, he needed the Captain to launch this ship. And secondly, he'd left his pistol below deck.

Now he had a clue which might explain why Stalin never showed up here. The Ukrainian's organization had betrayed them. MOIS should have never put their trust in Infidels!

He needed to get away from Mexico as soon as possible. He would contact the Ottawa Embassy once he arrived in Cuba. It would not be safe to transmit while they were underway. The Americans might be listening for his transmission, and then they could pin-point his location.

No, the MOIS Agent revised. He would call them just before launching. Ottawa must be informed! If the Americans knew anything, then they probably knew that he was in El Paraiso. He would call from here and then abate all further transmissions until he reached Cuba.

Bob and Charley's Hill

The Tribal Policeman's replacement showed up at a little before seven that morning. The one on duty immediately complained upon seeing him trudge up the hill and approach, "Where in the Hell have you been? I was supposed to get relieved at six."

"Hey, I had to have some breakfast, man," the other young fellow countered. But then he added in an apologetic tone of voice, "Actually, we got a young baby, if you want to know the truth. She kept us up half the night. I overslept... sorry."

Bob yawned as Charley gazed at the replacement with bleary eyes. The short night's sleep was affecting both men. The Indian stared at them and then glanced over at his colleague with a clear facial expression of inquiry. His counterpart gave an *I-dunno* shrug of his shoulders in response.

"Who are you?" the newcomer asked in none too friendly a delivery. "You don't look like Border Patrol to me."

"We ain't," Charley retorted with an equal measure of orneriness in his voice.

"They're Minutemen," the guy on duty intervened. "They make a damn good thermos of coffee. That's Bob, and this here's Charley."

The replacement nodded a salutation but stood there without offering a handshake. Bob grappled to his feet. "C'mon Charley, I need to go grab me some vittles and shut-eye. We're jest wasting our time. Nothing's gonna happen now thet the sun's come up."

Charley grunted as he moved to his knees and then pushed himself upright leveraging an arm against the rock on which he'd been sitting. He glanced over at the Indian with whom they'd spent the night, "You coming back on station this evening?"

"Not if I can help it."

The replacement policeman interrupted, "Well what's happening. Did you see anything?"

His colleague finally struggled to his feet. "Yeah, the moon, the stars and lots of desert. And these two guys moving their mouths for the last hour or so." He winked at the pair to signal he meant them no disrespect, and then added, "Kind-a short stay, ain't it fellas? Anyways, thanks for the coffee."

Bob responded. "I don't 'spect nothing to go down during the day. Too damn hot even for drug-smugglers. We'll come back this afternoon." He glanced over at Charley for affirmation.

Charley nodded. "Nothing to watch lessing that plane lands again over yonder."

"I'll walk on down with you fellers," the Indian on duty remarked. "I just bin relieved!"

The replacement gave his colleague the middle finger and then croaked in a complaining voice, "Man, it's supposed to get up to 110 degrees today. This watch sucks! There ain't no contraband or illegals gonna be moving in this heat! Who the hell's put a feather up the Chief's ass to do this?"

"The DEA."

"Yeah, that's what I heard. That's because we're cheap labor. Fuck 'em! I have half a mind to resign."

"Well," the other Indian chortled, "half a mind is more'n you got else you wouldn't be a tribal policeman."

Bob butted in, "We'll be on are way, gentleman." He nodded at the replacement. "Keep your feet covered and your head cool and you'll be just fine."

However, the replacement reacted with clear resentment to that off-handed advice which Bob had just proffered. "You're talking to a Tohonah O'odham Indian, man. My people have been walking this desert for three thousand years. You wouldn't last a day in this desert you old fart if'n we left you here with nothing but your empty thermos."

"C'mon Charley," Bob urged, ignoring the Indian's gruff retort. He began trudging down the hill.

"You better hurry on down, old man" the Indian yelled out. "I've a mind to scalp you!"

The other Indian laughed out loud, but then whispered, "Hey, those two guys are okay. Just a couple of harmless old coots." He then called out to them. "Hold up, I'm coming too."

Charley called over his shoulder to the pair of policemen. "We'll be back here this afternoon. I'll bring you guys some beads to play with."

The replacement ameliorated his tone of voice. "If you're really gonna bring something for us, how's about a six pack of cool ones!"

Chola Bay

They were seated at a large round table. Sammy Sanchez modestly referred to it as the "breakfast nook". Truly, this room situated next to the kitchen was far too spacious to be called a nook and the table was far too large. However, the formal dining room lay on the other side from the kitchen, so the term "breakfast nook" was certainly a way to distinguish it from that room on the other side. It table at which they now sat was meant to accommodate eight if you abided by the number of chairs around it. But there were only four places occupied… Sammy, Jesus, Paco and Moustache.

However, Julia had served her plates of *juevos rancheros* and warm flour tortillas wrapped in a napkin to only three of them. Moustache sat before a space devoid of plate, tableware or even a napkin. And behind him hovered one of the henchmen with a drawn pistol.

Romero was not present. Sammy had sent him with Armando to have his wounds bathed and then re-bandaged. Anyway, he needed Julia to prepare him sustenance which could be taken through a straw. She had suggested serving the injured man some chicken broth, and Armando had agreed that it would be an appropriate meal. Romero had grunted a response which lacked the enthusiasm of approval, but clearly had not constituted a protest either.

Jesus now indulging Julia's Mexican cuisine clearly demonstrated an appetite unaffected by what he'd witnessed less than half an hour ago; the bleeding death of

Ali Ul-Faqr. Paco of course had remained on the veranda having eschewed any part in this spectacle. Moustache recalled Ali tied to a chair as the naked Sultan struggled against the knife Romero wielded which finally found its mark on the shriveled penis of the screaming man. His stoic behavior had finally been disrupted by the prospect of castration. Sammy had joined them just in time to witness this *coup de grace.*

The subject of most interest for Sammy was watching Moustache's reaction. If he'd expected any wailing or gnashing of teeth, any last minute appeals for clemency on behalf of his black colleague, then the *jefe* was sorely disappointed. The Iranian stood there observing the event dispassionately. At last Sammy tired of seeing Moustache stand coolly detached as he watch the castrated man who refused to expire in spite of the large pool of blood puddled at his feet and around the legs of the chair.

"Cut his throat," he directed Romero, "and let's be done with it! "I'm hungry. Julia's breakfast will get cold! C'mon, Romero, get it over with!"

Now, here at the breakfast table, Moustache still dominated Sammy's attention. Even as the *jefe* chewed a mouthful of *juevos rancheros* mixed with a bite of flour tortilla, and finally swallowed, his eye remained fixed on the man. The Iranian showed no emotion.

'They're a tough breed,' he silently acknowledged. Maybe in the end he would have to resort to torture. Nevertheless he decided to probe the fellow.

"It's a shame you lost your appetite seeing your friend

die, Moustache. These *juevos rancheros* are really very good. If you've changed your mind, I can call Julia to bring you a plateful."

The Iranian responded in an almost robotic voice without directing his gaze at Sammy. "There is pork in the sausage. I can smell it. That is forbidden for me to eat. Anyway, he was not my friend. I have very few friends, Senyor Sanchez. I think we already spoke concerning that subject last night."

"Do you have *any* friends?" Sammy asked mockingly.

"Once you fully embrace Allah, there is no room for other serious relationships. And I might add, neither is there anymore a fear of death."

Sammy stared coolly at the man. Finally he replied, "I get your point. But I believe we made a deal. I will fly you to El Paraiso, and for this you will give me a share of the weapons on board your fishing trawler. Tell me, from where did these weapons come? Are they American-made? Russian?"

The clever *narco-traficante* knew that by determining the flag flown on this ship he could greatly narrow if not outright identify which vessel held the treasure-trove of weapons. El Paraiso was not a busy port. There was mostly local fisherman and tourist fishing yachts. A foreign trawler would immediately stand out. It had been one of the first questions asked by Guillermo Ray. Of course Sammy had no answer for him, nor would he have supplied it if he had one. He didn't even disclose that the trawler was necessarily from afar. Sammy had to protect his interests from Guillermo Ray.

Moustache ignored his question. Instead he posed one of his own. "May I make that telephone call I requested last night?"

"To whom must you speak?"

"If I don't report in immediately, the ship will leave port and then our deal will no longer be possible."

"To where will it go?"

"Somewhere away from Mexico, Senyor Sanchez, and the deal will no longer be possible."

Paco continued eating without paying particular attention to the conversation going on between his boss and this foreigner. But Jesus had left his fork on the plate and was alertly paying heed to every word exchanged between them. The henchman standing behind Moustache continued to vigilantly attend the man at whose head he pointed the muzzle of his pistol.

"So, you must make a call to El Paraiso?"

"No, to Canada."

"Canada!" Sammy protested. "Why would you need to call Canada?"

"Because that is where my principal resides. He must instruct the vessel to release a portion of the weapons on board to us. They belong to him. Otherwise you'll be opposed by the crew. They are armed as you might well expect."

"So, the ship is from Canada?"

"I didn't say that. I stated that my principal at the moment is in Canada."

"I see." Sammy looked over at Jesus. It was not really an inquiring look. He gave him a discrete nod, and then turned his gaze back to Moustache. "Write down the telephone number you wish to reach, and Jesus will connect you."

The henchman with the pistol retreated a step as Moustache pushed back his chair and stood up. "Just show me from where I can call. I know how to dial a telephone."

Sammy laid down the empty fork he'd been holding. "Sit down, Moustache. In my house we will do things my way. Jesus will bring you a pen and paper. You will right down the number with whom you wish to speak. When the connection has been made you will hold your conversation here at the table where we can all indulge it."

What the host did not disclose to Moustache is that he intended to put the Iranian's anticipated conversation on speaker phone.

The Iranian Embassy, Ottawa

The MOIS Agent in Canada who'd master-minded the PVNGS attack plans had just received a frantic call from his counterpart in El Paraiso, Mexico. The man was clearly in a panic. It concerned the Ukrainian engineer. The Agent on Ottawa was aware that this man had been provided by the source who'd sold them the nuclear weapon. This engineer's job was to fuse the bomb and ensure that the mechanism was in solid working order. Now the Agent in El Paraiso had informed him that suddenly the engineer had fled to Cancun, evidently during the wee hours of the morning.

He listened to the man in El Paraiso spill over in Farsi, "He's there by now… in Cancun. I can only conclude that this operation has been compromised. First, Stalin has disappeared, and now the Ukrainian engineer. I have instructed the Captain to refuel, and then we'll head out to sea. Where do you want me to go from there? Back to Guane, Cuba?"

"You've heard nothing from Stalin?"

"No, of course not or I would have said so!" Panic had not abated from his tone of voice.

The MOIS Agent knew that this was a correct course of action for his counterpart in El Paraiso to take, given the compelling circumstances. But it also spelled failure for the project, and that would have consequences for him personally… very grave consequences. "How long before you are ready to cast off?"

"Not more than an hour."

"I want you to call me before you launch. Is that clear?"

"What for?"

"If we are to abort this operation, then I want clearance to do so from Tehran. Do not leave until you've called me back and I have given you the authority."

The Agent in Mexico heard the other end disconnect before he'd even been given the opportunity to protest his colleague's demand. This was nonsense, he groused. There was too much risk in staying. And there was risk in making a second telephone call. In fact, there wasn't a moment which he could afford to waste. All the circumstances pointed to a compromise of their mission. If the authorities seized this boat, there would evolve extremely serious consequences.

Meanwhile the Agent in Canada prepared in his mind the communication he would present to Tehran. He was already in the communications room and felt a burn in his stomach as he steeled himself to make the call. So, it came as something of a jolt when suddenly the com-technician hailed him over.

"There's a call for you… in English. But it's from Mexico!" The com-tech knew it was for the MOIS Agent standing nearby because the call had been received on a distinct telephone number within the cluster of numbers which rang into the Embassy. This number was reserved exclusively for MOIS communications.

The Agent grabbed the telephone transceiver and rushed it to his ear as he placed his rump over the edge of the desk instead of sitting in the available chair. "Hello?"

"There is someone who has given me this number, and wishes to speak with you. Could you please identify yourself?"

"Who wishes to speak with me?"

"Please identify yourself," the voice repeated without compromise.

"You've called the Iranian Embassy. Are you sure you've dialed the correct number?"

There was a pause and he could hear a muffled whisper,

as if the man on the other end had cupped his hand over the receiver. Then there was a click. Finally, the voice addressed him once again. The quality of the transmission had changed. It sounded suspiciously to the Agent that the other end was now on speaker phone.

"Hold on," the voice from the Mexican side instructed. "He'll be with you shortly."

The Agent felt a sense of urgency tax his tolerance. He needed to make that call to Tehran. He was tempted to hang up on this mysterious call from Mexico; but the fact that it came from Mexico held his impatience in check. It might be Stalin. When the voice sounded from the other end, it spoke in Farsi. My God his fevered mind jubilated, it was Stalin!

Stalin continued in Farsi, "I'm being held by drug-traffickers. I want to bring them to the trawler where the crew can overpower them. Then I will force the pilot to fly me and our carpet to Arizona. Can that be arranged?"

The Embassy MOIS Agent sat there with the phone to his ear, but his mind had become frozen in gridlock. He slowly absorbed what the man on the other end had said. "What exactly is your plan?" he finally demanded and then added, "The crew is a bunch of fishermen, not gangsters. They will be no match for drug-traffickers!"

Stalin pleaded. "It's our only chance. What about the agent on board. Can he set the bomb? When I get there, I will tell them that we have the bomb. We will show them the bomb. And then we will threaten to detonate it immediately if they do not cooperate."

Suddenly the Embassy Agent heard a crackle. "A different voice sounding from a distance demanded, "Speak in English or I will hang up your phone."

He heard another crackle, and then disconnect.

FBI Offices, Phoenix

Leslie's supervisor was going through a necessary drill to cover his ass. The Moustafa Rajai case had hit a brick wall. There was no imminent threat or even compelling evidence of a plot to damage the PVNGS. But nonetheless, he'd been in this business long enough to know that you never leave any loose ends which could come back to tickle your butt.

He called the Agent in Tucson. By now the Bureau office there should have run fingerprints through the system on those two corpses found by the Tohono O'odham Indian Reservation police. He also needed to inquire whether the Tucson Bureau office had initiated any follow-up investigation on the Black Muslim cult which might have shed more light on the incident.

"Nothing positive to report on the corpses," the Tucson Agent responded apologetically. "We ran the fingerprints, but came up empty. They're not in the system."

"And the Black Muslims?"

"They're building a mosque on the west side of town… a small one, and they intend to start a school, according to our informant. But apparently they're recent arrivals, we don't have anything hard on them yet. Their leader, Sultan Ali Ul-Faqr is ex-military. He's also an ex-con…

involuntary manslaughter. He was involved in a bar-room brawl down in Atlanta. We could have him picked up on a probation violation; but I'd prefer to hold off and see where he might take us. Anyway, according to my informant, he ain't with the group who returned to Tucson."

"Where is he?"

"Don't know."

"Sounds like par for the course."

"However," the Tucson Agent added with renewed enthusiasm, "There is one other piece in the puzzle which we've discovered."

"I'm listening."

"We got a report back from the authorities in Sonora via our cousins in the DEA. There was a major fire-fight at that dirt airstrip not far from the tunnel. A bunch of known drug-traffickers were killed. They're part of the Culiacan organization. A witness claims that they were wiped out by the Black Muslims."

"Is he credible."

"According to the DEA, he's one of the Culiacan gang."

"What's their conclusions?"

"They didn't say."

"It must have been for drugs. You just said those Black Muslims are back in Tucson. It seems to me you have grounds for probable cause. Why don't you get a search warrant and check out that mosque for contraband drugs? You should bring in that band of Muslims and sweat them out? One of them's liable to break."

"That's DEA turf, sir. I've been advised to butt out."

"What?"

"You heard me. Anyway, according to DEA, the witness maintains there were no drugs or anything like that. They stole the Culiacan boss's airplane. His name is Romero. He's the same guy who perates the tunnel."

"*Who* stole the aircraft?" Leslie's Supervisor interrupted in a tone expressing abject incredulity.

"The Black Muslims, sir!"

"Did the cult fly it back to Tucson?"

"Nope, the plane headed into Mexico. They kidnapped Romero and some guy named Moustache, a foreigner, and took the plane. We figure the Sultan must have been on board since he hasn't shown up with the rest of his gang. The Black Muslims apparently closed up their camp and came back to Tucson on wheels."

"What in the hell would be their reason for stealing the airplane, and for setting up that camp in the first place? It's gotta be drugs… unless they were paid by someone to go there and snuff that drug-lord. That's a possibility, isn't it?"

"Well, with all due respect sir, it's not FBI business."

"What do you mean?" he huffed.

"It happened in Mexico, sir. And it seems to be about drug-smuggling. That makes it DEA turf, right sir?"

After a moments pause, the supervisor muttered with resignation, "Thanks, if anything new turns up on this case, I want to know immediately."

"Roger that, sir!"

The supervisor hung up the phone and stared into the ether. Yup, he'd hit a brick wall all right! Suddenly, his phone rang. He picked it up. "There's a call from Ottawa, Canada," the receptionist informed, "Agent Leslie Nellis."

"Put her through."

"Hello," he heard her exclaim.

"I'm listening," he sighed.

"Chief, like I've got some great news."

"Well that's nice. I haven't had any yet this morning, Agent Nellis. Please cheer me up with your good news."

The Iranian Embassy here in Ottawa has responded to the Canadian request for the release of Moustafa Rajai's sister-in-law."

"They're going to release her?"

"Yes, sir."

"When?"

"In a few days."

"I'm thrilled to hear this, Agent Nellis," he responded sarcastically.

"Like, you don't sound particularly thrilled, sir. What's wrong?"

"Lot's of things. And they're all above your pay-grade. Anyway, good work. Congratulations. Make arrangements to fly her and the kids down to Phoenix once they've been released."

"Like, there's also some bad news, sir."

The supervisor moaned. "Of course there is. How else could it be! What's the bad news, Agent Nellis?"

"There's no indication that they will release the two children."

He paused as his brain began to fever. "Deal with it! Right now I've got a head full of problems." He pushed the disconnect button and slammed the transceiver back into its cradle.

The FBI supervisor could not shake a gut-feel that the threat to Palo Verde was real. Partly, it was the Iranian connection. What better way for them to retaliate against American obstinacy over their nuclear ambitions than to create a nuclear incident here in the homeland. He was always a sucker for symmetry.

El Paraiso

Guillermo Ray had contacted the Mexican Federal Officer in charge of Port Authority. The Officer held the rank of Lieutenant. He was also becoming a very affluent man thanks to the generous indulgence of this *narco-traficante*. The Lieutenant was totally in Guillermo's pocket.

"Si, Senyor Ray, I will look into the matter immediately and call you right back," he'd promised.

Guillermo had inquired how many foreign fishing trawlers were berthed in the port. He needed to know quickly, he urged. It was a delicate matter. He warned the man not to raise suspicions.

Now the Lieutenant returned his call. "Senyor Ray, I have made my investigation."

"Well?" he urged.

"At the moment there is only one foreign fishing

trawler docked here. It's from Cuba. There also is an American yacht. But you said fishing trawler. The one from Cuba is the only fishing trawler. Usually they are full of fish. Foreign trawlers seldom stop here. The fish will get bad. And we are not a market for them."

"Cuba," he muttered. "That's it? Only this one?"

"Si, Senyor... but..."

"But what?"

"They have refueled and are preparing to cast off."

This information confused him. Certainly the plane bringing the crew of Sammy Sanchez would not arrive until this afternoon. Well, it had sounded to him like Sammy had a fix on the shipment. But, as he further considered the proposition he concluded that maybe this was not the case. Maybe Sammy simply had gotten inside information that there was a load of weapons on board. That's why he needed Guillermo's help. They would need to board the trawler and take possession of it by force.

"Are you there, Senyor?" the Lieutenant meekly tested.

"Si, si, I'm thinking. Let me think!"

He resumed the silent monologue in his mind. So, this is my territory. Therefore the booty is rightly mine. There is no need to wait for the Sanchez people, he deftly concluded.

"Lieutenant, do not let that trawler leave port!"

"On what grounds, Senyor?"

"It must be inspected for contraband. But not officially, you understand. My men will be there in half an hour and conduct the inspection. I want you to arrest the Captain and hold him in custody until we've completed our… uhh… unofficial inspection. Do you understand?"

After a moment's pause, he responded, "I do not want to understand, Senyor Ray. I will arrest the man, as you request, and hold him until you've completed your inspection, and then I will release him. They are Cubans. I hope there will be no bloodshed. If their Consulate lodges a complaint, I could get in big trouble with the Federal District."

"I pay you very handsomely for your trouble, Lieutenant. Just do as I say! Hurry up! Don't let that Cuban trawler leave port! And I need you to do one more thing."

"Si, Senyor Ray?"

"When you board the vessel and detain the Captain, find out how many men he has on board, and report this information back to me."

After hanging up the telephone, he decided that he must offer a courtesy call to his Sonoran amigo, Sammy Sanchez. He needed to manage this in such a way that it did not sour future relations with those boys up north. It wouldn't be good for business. The imminent departure of this Cuban vessel would serve as a credible pretext for him taking matters into his own hands.

He had to dial three times before he finally got through. *"Pinche Telofonos de Mexico,"* he cursed under his breath.

The voice who answered was not Sammy, so he politely

asked to speak with the *jefe*. "Who is calling?" the voice gruffly inquired.

"Guillermo Ray."

"*Momento!*"

The next voice he recognized to be Sammy. "Hello Guillermo, *mi amigo*! How can I be of service?"

"It is I who serve you, *mi amigo*, Sammy. Pardon me, but I must immediately get to the point. I have good news concerning your mysterious foreign fishing trawler. I've determined which one it is."

"You have?" the Sonoran responded suspiciously.

"Yes, it is Cuban, no?"

Sammy didn't want to appear uninformed, so he bluffed. "Yes, of course, you are absolutely right! How in the hell were you able to determine this?"

"I easily determined it because I own this port. It is where I do business. I know everything which goes on here!" he bragged. "But there is a small problem."

"What?"

"The trawler is departing."

"Can't you stop it?"

"Is that what you want me to do?"

"Of course."

"Good. Then I will board it and relieve the Captain of his cargo." He laughed out loud, "But I will allow him to keep his fish. So there is no need for you to come. By the time you get here, the fun will be over. I have buyers for such weapons as you have described. I promise to cut you in for your fair share."

Sammy knew he was between a rock and a hard place. He'd told his partner down south too much. But he'd done so in order to whet his appetite. Sammy had needed his cooperation. Anyway, there was no way he could stop Guillermo Ray from going it alone. Now that the man had determined which trawler was loaded with weapons, Sammy became inconsequential. There is never room for excess baggage in the narco-world. He understood Sammy's position because in his shoes, he'd have reacted in precisely the same manner. Whether or not his story that the vessel now prepared to cast away had reflected fact or fiction was at this time a moot point.

"What constitutes my fair share?" he challenged.

"Haven't I always been fair with you, Sammy? I need you to remain my amigo. I wouldn't cheat you. It would be bad for our long-term business relationship."

"Hang on one minute. I'll be right back!" He carefully laid down the phone. He'd taken this call in a room adjoined to where they'd taken their breakfast. He burst through the closed door, clearly startling everyone around the table as he rushed like a mad bull toward Moustache. The henchman holding a pistol to the Iranian's head stumbled back a step to give his boss a berth.

Sammy grabbed the prisoner by his hair and gruffly pulled back the man's head so strenuously that it caused the chair to tilt. "It's a Cuban trawler, isn't it?"

Suddenly, he pushed the man's head forward, amplifying his own force by the energy Moustache had exerted in resisting Sammy's previous backward thrust. The Iranian's nose smashed against the table with a loud thud causing a seismic tremor that rattled the plates and moved the tableware. When the *narco-traficante* pulled his victim's head upright again, blood profusely drained from his nostrils and puddled on the tablecloth.

"It's a Cuban trawler, isn't it?" he repeated.

Moustache made no response.

"Fuck you! You no longer are of any use to me!" He looked at Jesus. "Feed this piece of shit to Romero. But have him do it in the stable!"

He paced in long determined strides back to the door which led into the room where his telephone call still abided. He picked up the transceiver and immediately realized from the tone that Guillermo had disconnected.

Cancun Airport

The Ukrainian arrived with time to spare. He thanked the driver, but ignored the Mexican's cheeky request for an additional gesture of appreciation. He was amazed at the size of this airport. It was his first time here.

He could see the hotel skyline way off in the distance that offered amenities for tourists from around the world coming to the *Riviera Maya* in order to enjoy the blue Caribbean waters and soft sandy beaches, or to go on tours of *Chichen Itza* where one learns how the Mayan civilization developed astronomy and mathematics in order to precisely predict the corn growing season. It was all about corn, even the human sacrifices. Well, still today this particular grain was the main staple of Mexico, whereas in Cuba it was beans and rice.

Having entered the Main Terminal, he began searching for signs indicating *Aire Cubana*. There were signs galore, and in several languages; but none pointed out the airline in which he was ticketed. He loathed asking for directions; however he finally resigned himself to seek help, and thus sauntered over to the information desk.

He spoke to her in Spanish. "I am ticketed on Aire Cubana," he stated, and then asked, "Where is the boarding gate?"

"Oh," she responded with a smile, "That is considered a charter flight. You must go to the FOB terminal. The main terminal structure was walled with glass, so when she pointed he could follow her direction. She explained to him how to get there.

"Can I get breakfast over there?" he complained.

She responded with serious consideration. "Yes, I think so; but the restaurant here in the main terminal is probably better."

He thanked her and retreated. He ordered breakfast, and ate it mindlessly as he ruminated. This had been his first job with these principals who'd sold the bomb. They also were Ukrainian, which was probably the reason they'd selected him. He had no idea of who they were or if he would have recognized them as colleagues from the old Soviet days.

His intermediary with whom he'd met was brokering the deal. He too was Ukrainian by birth, but practiced law in London. He'd met with this solicitor at his office there. Anyway, he wasn't required to know the principals. They'd paid him in Euros wired to his account, and he'd gotten confirmation of the deposit from Credit Suisse. Thus, he paid scant mind as to who they might be or what nationality for that matter.

Several years ago he'd finally accumulated a nest-egg from his "consulting services" and was able to comfortably retire in Cuba. Like many who'd been involved as a weapons technician in the Soviet Ukraine, he'd ably brokered weapons to the international arms dealers and made enough money to lose himself in some God-forsaken place cheap to live. Cuba was cheap and it was God-forsaken. But one needed to stay on the good side of the authorities.

His passport allowed him to travel to Europe. And so he thought he would be clever. He contrived a relationship with a group of Cuban military officers and plumbed their interest in him serving as a go-between for contraband. They showed immediate interest and dispatched him to the Lada factory in the Czech Republic.

Most of the vehicles still running in Cuba were Volgas and Ladas. The last Chevies were model-year 1959. Of course, few of the American-made cars still functioned after nearly fifty years of the Castro regime. The Russians propped up Communist Cuba with credits against their sugar exports, offering above market prices.

But these credits could only be used to purchase Soviet and Eastern Bloc products. So it was small wonder that Volgas and Ladas dominated the car market in Cuba. However, since the bankruptcy and subsequent dissolution of the Soviet Union, replacement car parts had become so scarce that the black market was the only source for Cubans lucky enough to own a car. For the most part it was officers in the Cuban Military who ran the black markets.

The Ukrainian went to the Czech Republic and procured a load of selected car parts per the list provided to him by these Cubans, but the letter of credit underwritten by the bank in Havana was rejected by the Czech bank. So, he took a chance and secured a letter of credit covered by his account in Credit Suisse. That was of course acceptable. The factory assembled his shipment which he inspected and then the container load of Lada replacement car parts went to port where he accepted a signed bill of lading from the ship's purser and faxed it to Cuba.

However when the shipment arrived and the Cuban military officers took possession of it, they refused to give him the full amount of his investment much less his commission. He received half of his investment back and no commission. They claimed that the Ukrainian had not complied with the list they'd given him, and moreover the shipment was short. They threatened to imprison him for fraud.

Although he suspected that the Cubans had given him a fast shuffle, he could not rule out the possibility that the Lada factory or the ship's crew had not dealt him a sleight of hand. Anyway, he was powerless to protest. He quietly accepted what they gave him. But now his retirement fund had been severely diminished. Thus he went back into the weapons market. He no longer had sources, but he had contacts on the demand side, and therefore was able to broker small deals for a commission. He worked bit by bit at repairing his retirement fund.

That is why he'd accepted this job with these Ukrainian principals selling the bomb. Their offer had been extremely generous and they'd wired the money to his account in advance. They warned him of one thing, however. If the bomb was not detonated and it fell into unfriendly hands, they would hunt him down and kill him. He knew their warning was no idle threat.

It was for this reason that he'd hard-wired a 36 hour timer to the fuse. He glanced at his watch. In approximately 24 hours the news networks around the world would be chattering about a mysterious nuclear explosion, no doubt the work of terrorists. Whether it would reach America or blow up somewhere in Mexico was not his problem.

The Iranians would conclude that their operator screwed up. He certainly wouldn't come forward to contradict that theme, nor would any of the witnesses for that matter. In all likelihood, they would be vaporized.

Anyway, the bomb would not fall into unfriendly hands un-detonated. And the Ukrainian could again enjoy a comfortable retirement. With a sigh of satisfaction, he swore that this was his last project, and he felt relief as he basked in the notion. He would take pleasure in a quiet and comfortable old age in Havana.

He would take a stroll along the beach in the morning, and then enjoy a *corto* (espresso coffee with a bit of milk), indulge a siesta after lunch and carouse cabarets in the evening. He could even afford a maid to cook and clean and wash his clothes. Perhaps a young one, dark-skinned and ambitious, who wouldn't mind providing him with other services as well. It would be a retirement in Paradise.

El Paraiso

The Lieutenant informed the Captain that he must stay in port until his fishing trawler had been inspected. "It is only a routine inspection," the officer assured. "It won't take long, and then you can be on your way."

The Captain eyed him suspiciously, "But as you can see, we are already prepared to cast off. What is your reason for this?"

The Lieutenant deftly improvised, "It is a new regulation from the Federal District. We must ensure that you have no fish which are on the endangered species list. Mexico has signed a treaty, and all of the Port Authorities in the Republic must enforce this new regulation.

The crew was preparing to embark from the fueling pier, and so all hands were on deck. The three of them quietly gathered in a semi-circle behind the Captain who raised his hands palms open at the Lieutenant to express his frustration, "But we have no fish on board. Do you smell any fish?"

The Lieutenant had two men standing behind him. They were armed with pistols but had not drawn them. "That makes no sense, *Capitan*. You are a fishing trawler.

Why have you come all the way from Cuba and have caught no fish?"

The MOIS Agent remained below deck. He'd scurried down there as he spotted the uniformed Lieutenant and his pair of men stepping onto the pier. He hurried to his berth and extracted a pistol from his bag. Next, he pulled the shirt out of his trousers so that he could lodge his pistol in the small of his back at the belt-line and then draped his shirt-tails over it.

He remained below deck because as a foreigner he might only draw out suspicion. But what if they pulled away the canvass which covered his "carpet"? What if they insisted that the Captain must open this crate containing the bomb? Beads of sweat accumulated on his hairline and in his armpits as he contemplated what measures he must take in that event.

Guillermo Ray had of course been the force behind stopping the embarkation process of this vessel; additionally, he'd instructed the Lieutenant to get a body count of the hands on board this Cuban trawler. "*Capitan*, first I must see your identification papers, and those of all your crew. Please assemble your men on deck."

"You are looking at them." The Captain gestured with his hand to the three men standing behind him.

"Is this everyone? Are you sure?"

The Captain lost his nerve. "Well, there is one other. But he is not part of my crew. He is a passenger."

"A passenger... on a fishing trawler? I find that a bit curious, *Capitan*!"

"Is that also against your Mexican regulations?"

"Please, I am trying to be civil with you. There's no need for sarcasm. Where is your passenger?"

"Below deck, he feels ill. That is why we came to port. We thought he might need a doctor. But now he is better. And so we must return to Cuba."

The Lieutenant was in a hurry to get back to Guillermo Ray with information concerning his request to report the number of men on board this vessel. "The inspection party will check your papers. I will leave my two men here until I return with the inspectors. It won't take long, and then you can be on your way."

"But you can have a look now. I have no fish!"

"I am not an expert in such matters, *Capitan*. The inspectors must make these determinations."

"But we have no fish!" he pleaded. "You can easily determine that for yourself!"

"If you continue to resist, *Capitan*, I will have no choice but to take you into custody!"

The Captain took a step backwards, colliding with the man directly behind him. "No, no, that will not be necessary. I will wait for your inspectors!"

The Lieutenant turned to his two men. "Wait here. This vessel is to remain docked until I release it, do you understand?"

Both men saluted, and watched their officer disembark from the trawler and hurry down the fueling pier. Once the Lieutenant had turned his back and strode away, the Captain addressed the two Port Authority men left to mind the ship. "I have matters to attend to. You don't mind if I go about my business, do you?"

He did not wait for them to respond. He pushed his way through the gaggle of crew and whispered, "Stay here and keep these two occupied."

The trio grunted their accord. One of the crewmen stepped forward as he withdrew a pack of cigarettes from his shirt pocket. "Have a smoke?" he offered.

The soldier immediately in front of him waved an index finger in the negative. "Smoking at the fueling pier is prohibited!"

Meanwhile the Captain skipped hurriedly down the steps below deck and made a beeline for the Iranian. "They're holding us here," he exclaimed. "It sounds very suspicious to me. They want to inspect the ship."

"That's not advisable. Let's get the hell out of here!"

"But then they will come after us. To run will be even more dangerous than to wait. They are inspecting for fish! Besides, there are two Port Authority soldiers up there, and they are armed."

"What do you mean? Inspecting for fish, you say? We have no fish!"

"That's what I told the *pendejo*, but he says that he is just following orders. All fishing trawlers must be inspected for endangered species fish. Anyway, what is there to fear? We have no contraband… do we? What is in that container you have above deck? Is it something which might cause us trouble?"

The MOIS Agent glared at the Captain, causing the

man to take a step back. Finally he grunted, "Yes, it carries something which could get us in a great deal of trouble."

"What is it?" the Captain gasped.

"It's none of your business. What do you think; I hired you for a pleasure cruise?"

"But now it is very much my business. I am the one they will throw in prison. I am the Captain. I am responsible!"

The Agent leered at him with a mocking grin, "Then it is in your interest that we leave immediately, no?"

"What is in your container on deck?" he insisted.

The Agent grabbed the cell phone holstered on his belt. "See this?" he growled and waved it in front of the man's face."

"It is a telephone," the Captain dully responded.

The MOIS Agent intended to bluff this seaman in order to provoke him into action. "Yes, but it has a second purpose. It serves as a detonator as well. I have put my telephone into detonation mode. There is a very powerful bomb on board your ship sitting under that tarpaulin. It will destroy your ship and kill us all. I am prepared to die… are you?"

The Captain's face turned pale and his lower lip quivered. Clearly the man had bought this bluff. "A bomb?" he whispered.

"Yes, a very powerful bomb!"

"Why do you have a bomb?" he stammered.

"To deliver it to my colleague… the one who never showed up. So, you must make a decision, Captain!"

The seaman's eyes widened as he waffled momentarily, but then suddenly clenched his fists and looked at the Agent with resolve. "What exactly must I do?"

"You get the engines started and have your crew cast off. Is that clear? I'm going on deck, and I will get rid of those two soldiers."

The Captain made no audible response, but he nodded in affirmation.

Chola Bay

Sammy had retrieved Jesus at the last moment before he headed off with Moustache, and instead sent two of his henchman to accompany Romero and to secure the discredited Iranian prisoner as they marched him to the stable for his summary execution. He ordered Jesus to take an SUV, and three armed guards, and off-load the *blanco* from his fishing boat berthed in the harbor.

"Take it to the BT-67. Romero looks like he can fly. I will call Casa Grande and let them know you are leaving at four this afternoon."

"We need to know where they want us to rendezvous," Jesus reminded.

"Good point," Sammy sheepishly admitted. "I'll call them as soon as Romero has finished his business in the stable, and they can explain to him exactly where to land."

As he waited for Romero's return, Sammy went to his humidor and selected a cigar. Even so close to the bay, the air here was very dry. A cigar left in the open for no more than four or five days would dehydrate. The leaf wrapper would become brittle and separate as one tried to smoke it. He poured himself a brandy and retired to the veranda where he lit his cigar and was about to relax into his favorite chair when Armando came rushing towards him.

"The telephone, *jefe*, it is a call from Guillermo Ray!"

Sammy nodded an acknowledgement. He had an extension here in the veranda. He hurried over to it, picked the transceiver out of its cradle and placed it to his ear.

"Guillermo, did you find our treasure?"

There was a long pause.

"Hello," Sammy exclaimed; not sure if he remained connected to the other end, although he thought that he heard breathing.

"They got away," he heard Guillermo finally mutter.

"Huh?"

"It's a long story. I'm not in the mood at the moment to go into it!"

"But what do you mean that they got away? The boat left?"

"Yes."

"You're sure it's the right boat?"

"I'm not retarded, Sammy," he sneered.

"Why don't you go after them? It's just a fishing trawler. How fast can it go?"

"The Port Authority Officer inspected the vessel. He says the trawler was empty. Nothing in the hold, not even fish. They had a foreigner on board. He pulled a gun on the two soldiers who were holding the ship and forced them to jump into the water. I believe the weapons were already off-loaded, Sammy. The only contraband they still had on board was that foreigner. Your source has tricked you… and has made me look very foolish. I don't like to appear foolish. It's bad for my business image." Guillermo ended his tirade with a click of disconnect.

The first thing to cross Sammy's mind as he pulled the transceiver from his ear and placed it back in the cradle was that Guillermo was double-crossing him. He'd off-loaded the weapons cache and now intended to keep it all for himself. That would be a secret difficult to keep, he further reasoned. But he knew better than to challenge Guillermo on those grounds at this point in time. He was in no position to make that accusation, especially since the man had hung up on him. Anyway, he had no proof. And frankly he'd grown tired of this entire endeavor… the *pinche* foreigner and his *pinche* weapons!

Now he hoped that at Romero's hands, Moustache would suffer a very slow and painful death! But he was in no mood to watch. He still had his *blanco* to deliver, and he must clear his mind of all these other distractions. He picked up his cigar out of the ashtray. He thrust it into his mouth and drew on it to check if the cigar was still lit. He savored the nutty taste, and blew out a mouthful of smoke. He then deposited himself into the chair and reached for the brandy snifter.

Well, he silently mused, I have the blood of a *negrito*

and an Iranian on my hands. It would provide an imaginative theme for a *corrido*. Unfortunately, no *corrido* composer would learn of this event. He chuckled and took a generous slug from his snifter. To bad, he lamented with a touch of jocularity, *corridos* about a *narco-traficante's* exploits enhanced his image. And that was good for business.

Bob and Charley's Hill

"Hey, you're late," the Tohono O'odham Resevation policeman fretted as he saw the two Minutemen slowly trudge up the incline towards the crest where he sat.

Bob glanced at his watch on the wrist of his free arm. He and Charley were toting a small ice chest, each of them hanging on to it by a handle. "Twenty-five minutes," Bob protested. "It's only twenty-five minutes past four."

"Close enough for gub'ment work," Charley added in a voice clearly winded.

"Man, like twenty-five minutes is forever when you've been sitting in this sun for nine hours with nothing on your mind but that beer you been promised by the two Great White Fathers."

"Who says we got beer?" Charley teased.

"Well, man, I don't figure you two old coots are lugging Viagra in that chest."

The two men both grunted as they laid their ice chest to the ground. The Indian gathered to his feet, also with a grunt leaving his binoculars where he'd sat, and sauntered over to the two Minutemen. "Let's see what you brung."

Bob gazed at him for a moment before responding. "You sure comport yourself more friendlier than you was this morning," he stated sarcastically.

"How come they ain't relieved you yet, youngster?" Charley intervened.

"My relief comes at six. C'mon, man, open up that ice chest, and let's see what you brung."

Bob was tempted to prolong the Indian's agony. But his ornery streak was trumped by the thirst he'd incurred during the trek up here. He knelt down and snapped open the two latches that secured the top, and then lifted up the cover, swinging it as far at it would go. At that relaxed angle, the cover remained upright on its own.

The Indian stared down into the container as alacrity beamed out of his face. "Oh man, you brung the one thing White Men gave to the land that has definitely made it better. The six-pack!"

The container was a third full of ice. Resting on top was a six pack of beer. Loosely surrounding this crown jewel rested eight 12 oz bottles of natural spring-water, leastwise that's what claim was made on the label.

"Call it a peace offering," Charley announced. "We didn't get off all too friendly this morning."

"Offering accepted, man!" He pointed into the ice chest. "May I?"

"Help yourself," Bob encouraged. "Charley and I are drinking water. We're on duty."

The Indian looked at him for a moment quizzically. "You follow your rules, white man, I'll follow mine!"

He bent down and thrust both hands into the ice. "Man, that feels good!" He then rubbed the cold moisture on both hands over his face and neck.

"How's about you grab your beer before all thet ice melts," Bob groused.

"And toss us each a bottle of water while you're down there," Charley added.

The Indian secured a bottle of water in each hand and rose up his arms without looking at either man. The pair each relieved him of his load, muttering thanks and immediately cranked on the bottle caps. The Indian meanwhile grabbed a can from the cluster, pulled the ice chest cover down into the closed position, and with this free hand he then latched it. He straightened up. With a big smile he popped the beer and immediately thrust it to his mouth as he cocked back his head and chug-a-lugged.

The two Minutemen paused in their thirst as they watched him down the entire can. He breathed out a loud sigh of satisfaction followed by a raucous belch. With one hand he then crushed the can and tossed it down beside the ice chest. The two Minutemen gazed at each other for a couple moments, and then went about the task of slaking their own thirst.

Bob wiped his mouth with the back of his bare arm and screwed the cap on his bottle. He looked over at Charley. "I thought Indians were environmentally responsible. Leastwise, thets the word they spread on the TV."

The Reservation policeman folded his arms across

his chest. "Now, man, what's that comment supposed to represent?"

"You just littered the environment with that empty beer can."

"Why, did you also bring along a litter bag," he expressed in a theatrically sweet voice.

"Just toss it back in the ice chest," Charley clarified, not wanting their playful banter to cross the line.

From the Indian's side, he quickly calculated that a tactical retreat was the only maneuver that ensured his getting another beer. "Sorry. I intended to clean up the area before I left. But if you don't mind me stowing it in the ice chest, hey, no problem, man."

He bent down and picked up his crushed can, duck-walked a step sideways, unlatched the ice chest top and opened it up. He tossed in the can and then looked up at Charley. "Being as I got this thing open, you mind if a grab another?"

Charley looked at Bob, but the other Minuteman quickly diverted his eyes from the inquiring glance. The Reservation policeman quickly interpreted their non-response as acquiescence. He reached in and twisted another can out of the cluster and then closed the ice chest. He got up, clutching the beer in one hand, and stretched out the arm of the other to counter his balance.

"I reckon I better get back to my look-out," he stated and turned away from them as he walked back to where his binoculars lay. ""Hey, man, thanks for the beer," he called out over his shoulder.

"Anything happen while we was gone?" Charley asked.

"The biggest event passing through my life this whole day is when I went behind them rocks yonder and took a shit."

the Indian nursed his second beer over the next twenty minutes as he stared out over the desert from his post at the crest. Bob and Charley mostly just stared into the ether of their minds, immersed in their own private world. The two Minutemen were summoned back to reality by a sudden loud crunch. The Indian had collapsed his beer can in one fist, just like the first time. He got up and walked over to the cooler, opened the top and tossed in the can, and then he grabbed a handful of ice. He closed the cooler, and began rubbing the back of his head and neck with ice, making sounds akin to a purring cat as he did so.

"I gotta go take a leak," he announced to no one in particular and strode off in the direction of those big rocks, evidently his self-appointed latrine.

Bob got up and went over to where the man had again left his binoculars. This perch had the best view of the desert below. He was still standing when suddenly he called out to Charley.

"Hey, you hear that?"

"Hear what?"

"Shh!"

"Hear what?" Charley repeated and got to his feet.

"Sounds like an airplane."

As Charley approached he suddenly stopped and cocked his head. "Yeah, I hear it now. Ya see anything?"

"Not yet." Bob had left his binoculars in his backpack so he leaned over and grabbed the Indian's pair. He put it to his eyes, and then pulled it back to figure out where the adjustment wheels were. He fiddled with it for several seconds before gazing through them for a while.

Charley had to cup his hands over his eyes as he stared in a southwesterly direction where he could now see the figure of an airplane with his naked eye. "Can you read the tail number? Is it Mexican?"

"Charley, it looks to me a whole lot like that same airplane we saw on the dirt strip over yonder."

"He's flying mighty low. You figure he's getting' ready to land?"

"Looks that way to me. By God, we may get us a drug bust yet!" Bob jubilated.

The Reservation policeman returned. "Sounds like an airplane headed this way," he announced as he walked up to where the two Minutemen stood. "Jesus, he's flying kind of low, man! Is he getting ready to land? Here, gimme my binoculars!"

He grabbed the binoculars out of Bob's hand and pressed it to his eyes. "Jeezuz, you fucked with my settings!" He fiddled with the adjustments, and finally stared through them at the approaching airplane. "Shit, he's heading straight for us!"

The Indian finally pulled the binoculars from his eyes as the approaching aircraft zoomed towards them flying no more'n a hundred feet higher than where they stood. The whining roar of those twin turbo-prop engines drowned out their exclamations as they watched it zoom past them having passed directly over the Black Muslim compound.

Bob cupped his hand to Charley's ear, "It's that same DC-3 as we seen on the dirt strip. Only it ain't exactly a DC-3. Them's turbo-props you hear!"

They all watched in silence as the airplane continued north but maintained an extremely low altitude. Bob turned to the Indian now that his voice could carry freely. "He's flying low to avoid the radar. You can bet they've got a load of drugs."

"Bob, we gotta radio a report to home base!"

"Well don't just stand there flapping your jaw. Go do it!"

Charley scampered back towards the ice chest where he'd left his back-pack. He fished out their hand-held radio and called in, while Bob and the Indian watched from afar. What Bob discerned was more from Charley's face than hearing the words he spoke. Finally, Charley unceremoniously dropped the radio on his back-pack and watched it roll off onto the ground. He didn't bother to bend down and retrieve it. Slowly he trudged back to the other two.

"What's wrong, Charley?"

"They're all pissed off at us for coming back up here. We've been fired. If'n we don't get our asses outta here, the Border Patrol is gonna arrest us for… hell I dunno, fer something. I've had enough of this horseshit! I'm heading back to Prescott. You coming?"

"Hey," the Indian pressed, "cudya leave me one more beer?"

Caribbean Sea

The Captain assured him that they were definitely in international waters. They all felt relief because there was no sign that they had been pursued. But the MOIS Agent nevertheless was filled with disquiet.

He was convinced that this operation had been compromised. How and by whom was a matter of pure speculation; even to whom it had been divulged remained unclear. But he was certain that the project had been leaked. First, Stalin failed to show up. Then the Ukrainian deserted. Finally the Mexican authorities attempted to detain them.

He suspected that Ukrainian weasel was the party who sold them out. However, the Agent didn't rule out anyone, including the Captain. For this reason he dared not use the shipboard communications. He would report to Ottawa once he'd landed in Cuba.

He made one other decision based on his paranoia. He would not go to Guane. No, he would bring the bomb directly to Havana where it would be far easier for them to retrieve. Once there, he would seek new operational instructions. They couldn't possibly hold him responsible for aborting the project. Of course, he realized that the view from Tehran was not always a particularly rational one.

The Captain was disconcerted by this decision. His home port was Guane. "I am paying you by the day. You will go where I instruct you to go!" the MOIS Agent insisted. "I must take my bomb to Havana. You go to Guane and I'll blow up your ship!"

The Captain informed him that they would reach Havana harbor in time for lunch. "When will you offload that bomb so I can go back to Guane?" he asked.

The MOIS Agent paused before answering. "I will know after we've landed and I've received my instructions. I will pay you for your days in Havana harbor, that's as much as I can tell you at this moment."

Epilog

As the Ukrainian had thoughtfully predicted yesterday while munching his late breakfast at the Cancun Airport, his nuclear explosion would cause the world's news media to wag their collective tongues in all sorts of peculiar ways. However, he would be the only one who truly knew the entire inside story. Needless to say, he had no intention of offering this insight to news media outlets. Having grown up under a totalitarian regime, he had no respect for these mendacious portals. Well, regardless of his motivation and impervious to his intent, circumstances would ensure that his secrecy was maintained. Moreover, he would have scant time to mull the irony of his position.

He understood that the news media of the world at large would each tailor an analysis of this coming fateful event to fit whatever agenda they marketed. The facts were of little consequence to them. After all, *they* were the authors of truth. They were the self-anointed oracles, and those who subscribed to their wisdom demanded strict adherence to that particular catechism. These media pundits were not hoodwinking their masses. No, their relationship was clearly symbiotic. When the media choir sang a hymn, the congregation would immediately detect any out of place word or dissonance, and they would cringe uncomfortably.

But for what little it might matter he alone knew the real truth. At least, that is what the Ukrainian believed. After all he occupied the very epicenter of this event. Of course, when he'd silently expressed this thought in those last moments of his life, he'd meant it in quite a different context than what prevailed. Not in his wildest imagination could he have predicted correctly that this explosion would occur where it did, and that he would occupy a ringside seat.

The apartment which he rented was near the beach on a hillside three kilometers from Havana harbor. He was among the immediate casualties of the nuclear explosion. But he did live long enough to consider the irony, although how it had come to pass absolutely baffled him. His last bubble of thought still did not fully recognize that it was his own bomb that had created the holocaust in which he suddenly found himself. But at the edges of his mind, perhaps he sensed it.

The whispers in Europe were that the explosion had been arranged by a cabal of the CIA as a last desperate measure of a disillusioned President trying to rally right-wing support for his political party in the coming election, and perhaps secure a legacy for himself. The media voices in Europe clamored for investigation by the U.N. European NGO's called for immediate humanitarian outreach to the Cuban victims and a suspension of the American embargo. They scrambled to assemble the number of European victims caught in this Cuban holocaust.

The American Right speculated that the waning Castro regime in cahoots with the Venezuelan President had procured a nuclear weapon and in playing with this fire had burned their hands. The American Left whined about the catastrophic casualties, and more still unrealized tragedy which would be affected in the coming weeks, months and years, not to mention the poor unborn. Their rally to ban nuclear weapons had found new legs and shrill voices.

In the Middle East and most of the Muslim world moderate voices were drowned out by commentators from Arabic and Farsi language networks which strenuously maintained that it was the Great Satan (USA) who'd employed Little Satan (Israel) to do this piece of dirty work. Some Islamic Internet sites went so far as to show photo-chopped pictures of an Israeli flag-bearing submarine surfaced in Havana harbor. The photos were time-stamped one hour before the explosion. Naturally, the mosques and madrassas were all abuzz with damnation for these Satanic Infidels.

Leslie's supervisor had his hunch about this event;

but he'd learned to keep hunches to himself. He couldn't shake the notion that somehow this nuclear incident in Havana might have been tied to the threat they'd uncovered from Moustafa Rajai who'd admitted passing on vital information about the Palo Verde Nuclear Generating Station to the Iranian Embassy in Ottawa. But her supervisor never would have guessed that the Iranians were colluding with the Cubans. Well, he silently warned, nuclear weapons are definitely on the *menu du jour* for these terrorists. The disaster in Havana proved this premise beyond any reasonable doubt.

He was more convinced now than ever that Palo Verde was at grave risk. Homeland Security has been rolling a lot of sevens and elevens these past few years, he mused. But sooner or later, he continued to fret, any run of luck turns around and bites you on the ass. That's the principle which keeps those gaudy lights burning in Las Vegas and Atlantic City. He couldn't shake the dread grinding through his mind, but he was at an utter loss concerning what to do about it.

He continued to ponder. Yup, that is the dilemma of 4GW (Fourth Generation Warfare). The nations contain myriad hard targets. The terrorist offers only a fleeting mark. The nations have a population of ordinary citizens with ordinary aspirations. The terrorists are made up of fanatical mind-sets.

Armed insurgency is against a government or specific authority. It can be isolated and finally exhausted because the root cause is tied to a specific geographical location.

But Islamo-fascism is a global network. It is mobile. It is made up of discrete components bound by a common ideology without a central command and control. This allows great flexibility as well as local autonomy. Many of these jihadists use the very democratic nations which they attack as their safe haven. They skim resources from the very people whom they target for subjugation or annihilation.

The point being, those methods for destroying the will of armed insurgents will not prevail in the case of a worldwide terrorist movement. Despotic nations have a far easier time grappling with whatever 4GW might occur inside their borders. They are legally and morally unrestrained. On the other hand, democracies are roiled with never-ending dilemmas in dealing with issues of Security vs. Liberty. They further agonize over hypothetical consequences which might result from any proactive policy their various constabularies propose. Thus, it is the democracies against which the efforts of these terrorists appear to concentrate. These Islamo-fascists, like beasts of prey, will pursue the most vulnerable members of the herd.

It's easy to blame poverty, or exploitation by global corporations for this unrest in the world. Easily digestible explanations are always preferable to those which are hard to swallow. A people free to choose will reflexively grasp for quick and painless solutions. And for that reason their choices will almost always be flawed.

The sad fact is that terrorists recruit the *crazies* of the world. These jihadists may be rich or poor, but they are surely brazen and bizarre. They may feel exploited and deprived, but their reaction is outrageous. They may feel religious fervor, but the way in which they express it is bestial. The human race offers a bountiful production of these loons in every generation and will continue to do so. That is what Leslie's supervisor had long ago concluded. He and his counterparts will have a job for as long as humanity exists.

This current struggle against the Islamo-fascists constitutes a contest where no one can really keep score. But the jihadists and their adversaries both have a clear idea of what comprises winning... total capitulation or annihilation of the other side; however, that is a theoretical notion, not a practical outcome. As things currently stand, neither side can realize absolute victory.

The reasons for this are patent. The community of nations is too strong to be vanquished, but on the other hand these terrorists cannot be exterminated because they are in constant replenishment. Thus, this struggle has no end in sight, but the conflict will surely continue to bring misery to the lives of those non-entities euphemistically referred to as *collateral damage* or *innocent victims* who just happened to get caught in the middle of things. And once the jihadists can finally avail themselves of nuclear and biological weapons, the dust is gonna really start kicking up.

Leslie's supervisor slowly shook his head as his mind's voice concluded, 'This situation is a real cluster-fuck!'

Oh well, the one thing to which he still could look forward with optimism was his government pension. But even that sunny prospect suffered dark clouds on the horizon. There were those who said that given the nation's meager replacement birth rate and ever-expanding government welfare benefits, his pension was in future jeopardy.

The End